Deep Waters

NORTHERN SHORES COZY MYSTERY
BOOK ONE

HEIDI HINRICHS

Copyright © 2024 by Heidi Hinrichs

All rights reserved.

heidihinrichs.com

heidi@heidihinrichs.com

Editor: Margaret Dean

Chapter One

The cold hands of the North Sea reached for her. The water was less than sixty degrees Fahrenheit—it felt more like fifty—and it was treacherous. It quickly dragged inexperienced or exhausted swimmers out to sea.

Police inspector Enna Koopmann, however, knew the deep waters of the North Sea off Fleetstedt like no other. She plowed through the water to the drowning man with swift and precise crawl strokes. Her heart was pounding. Her breath came in heavy gasps.

As she felt the temperature of the water change and the pull on her hands lessen, she paused and lifted her head out of the water. She had used the offshore current to help her swim faster. Seconds counted in an open-sea rescue. If the drowning person ran out of strength and went under, deeper currents could catch them and carry them away. If that happened, Enna would not be able to save him.

But he was still struggling. She saw his arms rise out of the water again. But he was no longer screaming. That was a bad sign. Drowning happened in silence.

Enna corrected her course and gave it all she had. Her arms and legs were already burning, even though she trained twice a week at the local lifeguard club. But adrenaline whipped her into action. She crawled toward the drowning man, then switched to breaststroke for the last few feet so she could keep an eye on him.

Despite the urgency, a drowning person was always approached with caution. The person was panicking and often not in their right mind. The danger of them clinging to you, and being pulled underwater to your death, could not be underestimated. Many rescuers gave their lives that way. It was safer to wait for the exact moment when they passed out, then quickly grab hold of them and pull them to safety.

His head reappeared just then. He snorted water, spotted her, and went wide-eyed.

"Calm down," Enna shouted. "Stay calm! Lie down on your back! Lie flat and straight! Use your buoyancy! Can you hear me?"

He heard her but didn't understand. He began to paddle wildly in her direction and sank again.

Enna cursed and swam cautiously towards him. She had to watch carefully and not miss the right opportunity ...

He reappeared in front of her, water splashing in all directions and into Enna's face. The salt stung her eyes. She blinked.

"Calm down!" she shouted. "Stay calm!"

He didn't want to. Or maybe, in his panic, he couldn't. Probably sensing his imminent rescue, he gathered all his strength. As a result, he literally hurled himself at Enna. She tried to back away, but despite her caution, she was surprised by the power of his attack.

Almost immediately, he was on her. His hands reached for her and wrapped around her torso. Enna gasped and tried to raise her arms, but he clung to her with surprising strength. He pinned her arms to her body and pushed her underwater.

Enna's world blurred in the diffuse gray of the North Sea. The water stung her eyes even more. A gulp of water entered her mouth, filling it with salt and seaweed.

She fought the urge to kick her legs and fight the pressure. The one thing a drowning person doesn't want is to be underwater, so Enna dived down and tried to break free of his grip.

But he held on to her, using her as a living buoy.

Enna's heart was now racing. Nevertheless, she remained calm and pushed her stronger right arm upwards. It finally slipped from his grasp, and she slammed it hard into his chin. A jolt went through him as he winced in pain and surprise.

Enna immediately followed up by pulling her other arm out of his grasp and grabbing the crook of his arm. With her other hand, she grabbed his wrist and turned him around, then dove even deeper.

She slid beneath him like a dancer. It was a rescue move she had practiced hundreds of times in lifeguard training. She got his arm behind his back and twisted his wrist.

With a snort, she surfaced and twisted harder—like a motorcycle revving up. But instead of acceleration, there was pain. "Lars!" she yelled. "Cut the crap!"

Lars let out a sound that couldn't decide if it was laughter or a scream. "Let go!" he followed up.

Enna deliberately twisted a little harder, forcing him onto his back. He gasped. "Ouch, Enna!"

"What the hell? Did you have to restrain me?"

"Practice is practice!"

"Then stop resisting now!" She kept up the pressure, grabbed him under the chin with her other hand, and began to pull him down.

Lars struggled for a few seconds before he calmed down. She could feel his chest pumping hard. He was exhausted from the exercise. Typical Lars. The instructor from the local group knew no limits, which was good because it meant they were practicing under near-real conditions. On the other hand, they were taking a big risk. They weren't in an indoor pool.

Fortunately, the others were waiting on the beach and observing the rescue exercise as part of their training. They could still pull them out in an emergency.

But it wouldn't come to that. Enna fell into a pleasant straddle-leg kick and slowly dragged Lars to the beach. Now she took advantage of the waves and avoided the offshore currents of the tidal range.

When she was finally close enough to the beach, with Lars

still in her grip, her feet touched the muddy ground. Her thighs trembled. She sought his gaze.

He grinned. "I'm relaxed now."

Enna just snorted, pushed him under the water for a moment, and then let go of him.

He surfaced with a snort. He started to say something, but suppressed it when he saw her grim expression. Instead, he raised his arms apologetically. "It should be as real as possible."

Enna just nodded and stomped out of the water. The air was chilly for June. A strong wind blew from the east, carrying the cries of seagulls.

Enna immediately got goosebumps all over. Her teeth began to chatter. She wrapped her arms around her body and trudged toward the others, who were waiting for her in fleece sweaters.

"Normally, I would have had to drag him out with the Rautek hold," she explained grumpily, reaching for a towel that someone held out to her.

"But?" asked Julia, one of the participants.

"But I can walk those few feet myself," replied Lars, who was also trudging across the beach towards them. His lips were blue. He massaged his wrist where she had gripped it.

"I hope you saw how dangerous a panicked person can be," he said. "Even though Enna knew I could react like that, she was surprised. But she was able to free herself without any problems. And you can do the same. We've practiced it dry. What's important in the water is to stay calm and dive! That's the most important thing. You have enough air to free yourself."

One of the participants looked skeptical. "But if I didn't understand the currents here, I'd be completely exhausted when I came out."

"That's why you should research the beaches you visit. Or take rescue equipment. The board is the best. It's the fastest way to get out and save a drowning person. We'll practice that next time. For now, you can get in the water and practice rescues. Go, go!" He clapped his hands. "Let's go!"

While Lars dried himself off and the four students ran into the water, Enna slipped into her red DLRG jacket, the distinctive uniform of the German Lifeguard Association, and then pulled a thermos of herbal tea from her backpack. She unscrewed the lid and half-filled it with tea. Spicy steam rose to her nose.

She warmed her hands while the wind played with her hair.

Lars came up beside her while keeping his eyes on the trainees. "Well done." He probably wanted to smooth things over a bit.

Enna didn't look at him but sipped her unsweetened tea. She watched the others' movements, her gaze drifting to the distant horizon. The day was gray and cloudy. A container ship was passing by on the horizon, just a grayish dot.

Otherwise, it was surprisingly quiet for the beginning of the holiday season, but the hustle and bustle would come. She should be happy and enjoy the quiet days. When the crowds of tourists arrived, the beaches and pubs would fill up overnight, and the DLRG's work would really begin.

Enna managed to balance all this with working as a police officer. She loved both jobs, but the tourists were often too much. If you were going to venture out in the open sea, you should at least be able to swim a little. But a lot of people couldn't even do that, and ignored all the safety warnings. There was a reason why bathing times were posted based on high tide, and a reason why there were signs and buoys on the beach marking dangerous spots and currents. As Albert Einstein once said: *"Stress is only caused by dealing with idiots."*

Fortunately, not everyone was like that. Most of them were super nice, and happy that the DLRG had taken over the lifeguarding. Enna often heard a kind word and a thank you for her volunteer work.

Lars said, "I'll go check on them," and trotted over to the others. He halted not far from them in the knee-deep water and began to shout instructions, gesturing wildly.

The tea had finally cooled a bit. Enna drank it in long gulps, screwed the lid back on the thermos, and stowed it in her waterproof backpack. She also quickly checked her cell phone. Fortunately, there were no missed calls or messages.

That was perfect for the last day of her vacation. She had no idea what made the new boss tick. He had only started working in Fleetstedt a few days ago, and it might well be that he would call her into the office at some point, despite her being on vacation, to say hello or something. *Maybe even for cake...*

But he hadn't. She had no idea how to interpret that. Was he not interested, having applied for the job so as to be able to take it easy? She had read in the preliminary email from the directorate that Chief Inspector Pavel Neuhof had previously lived in Kiel and worked at the State Criminal Investigation Department (LKA). Kiel was a very different place than Fleetstedt. Also, the LKA in Schleswig-Holstein was a completely different place than a tiny office on the North Sea in Lower Saxony. Anyone who came to Fleetstedt from the LKA Kiel either had family here (which didn't apply to Neuhof; Enna had checked), wanted some peace and quiet, or had been transferred because they had made a mess of something.

Unfortunately, circumstances favored that last. Moving from one state to another was unusual, and Neuhof could have found peace and quiet in Laboe on the Baltic Sea.

But speculation or not, neither option appealed to Enna. She didn't need a sleepyhead or an idiot as her new boss. In fact, she would have liked to keep her old one, but everyone had to retire sometime.

So now there was Pavel Neuhof. She had googled him and found nothing online. Just great. She would have to wait and be surprised, and Enna Koopmann hated surprises. They were in the same league as stupid tourists, fish poisoning, and sinusitis.

She glanced back at the others, shivering in the water and practicing rescue holds. It looked pretty good. They would probably all get their silver lifeguard badges renewed. Whether any of them would stay active and continue to be lifeguards was another question.

A movement in the sea caught Enna's attention. Something dark was floating in the water about seven or eight hundred feet away.

Enna narrowed her eyes and followed the dark something.

What was it? Flotsam? Garbage? In any case, it was drifting and not moving. On the other hand, it had a very... human shape.

"Shit!" Enna ripped open the squeaky zipper of her jacket and flung it off. While the jacket was still falling to the beach, Enna ran towards the water. The wet sand splashed around her bare feet, leaving dark streaks.

Lars noticed her hurry and looked at her in confusion. "What's going on?"

Enna pointed at the dark something. "Maybe someone in the water! Not practice!" Already in the cold water, she ran further, then threw herself forward into one of the shallow waves.

The cold was a shock and drove the air out of Enna's lungs. She gasped, came to the surface, and, as before, settled into her usual crawl. She had already used up a lot of energy earlier during the exercise with Lars; now she had to be super careful and conserve her reserves. The cold was also a factor not to be underestimated.

Still, she stayed calm, forced herself to breathe steadily, and continued to crawl. She wondered why someone would be floating out there. It was completely stupid. She hadn't seen anyone go into the water, at least not near where they were practicing. Was it a swimmer with a buoy coming from one of the other beaches? They would have had to have drifted quite a distance... Or was it someone who had gone overboard and was floating towards shore?

Enna had no idea and wasn't going to waste any more energy speculating. She concentrated on swimming and pulled through. Clean arm strokes with her thumb up to her thigh. Then lift out without water resistance and dive in gently. Pull through, lift out, and dive in gently. Pull through, lift out, and dive in gently...

Again and again, she stopped and looked around. Fortunately, the swell was not high, just a head-high slosh, but it was enough to make her lose sight of the figure. Enna corrected her course, looked back at the beach, and noticed that Lars was swimming towards her. The others had gotten out of the water and were standing together in a group. Obviously, they were calling for help. That was good. That was what they had been taught. The training had paid off.

The thought spurred Enna on again and she gave it her all until she was within a few feet of the object. Sure enough, someone was floating on their back in the water.

"Hello!" she hissed between two breaths. "Can you hear me?"

No answer.

"Hello, shit!" Enna slowly swam closer. She didn't want to be grabbed and submerged like before. But the figure didn't move at all, even as waves washed gently over it.

"Hello!" she tried again, but there was no response.

She swam right up and approached the figure from the side.

It was a man. A long coat of dark, rainproof fabric ballooned around him. Copper embossed buttons adorned the pockets and lapels. His face was a pale moon in the gray waves. His mouth, surrounded by the shadow of a beard, was open. So were his eyes. He stared up at the cloudy sky while another wave washed over him.

Chapter Two

The loft smelled of hay. Pavel took a deep breath. There was something pungent in the air. Not death—something else he hadn't smelled in a long time. He turned around and saw the room was painted white. Of course! The owner must have smoked his own fish here. The smokehouse didn't look to be still in use. A straw broom leaned against the narrow door.

He'd deal with that later. A crime scene investigator had already searched the place, but better safe than sorry. Pavel looked up at the roof. The house had an unusually steep roof. The rafters were so high that, even at 6'4", he couldn't reach them standing on tiptoe.

He turned to face the direction the dead man had been looking. In his last moments, the old man must have been staring at a skylight, now showing a blue-gray sky with wispy clouds. The incoming light formed an angular tunnel where dust motes danced. Pavel felt a sneeze coming on. He pressed a finger under his nose, and the urge faded. The house was two stories high, high enough to see over the dike. From his position, Pavel could only see the sky, but your perspective changed when you were hanging from the roof beams with a rope around your neck.

Then he remembered what the pathologist had said about the time of death. The old man had died shortly after midnight. Pavel closed his eyes. The sunlight coming through the window vanished. He shook his head. If he ever had to say goodbye like that, he'd want to die during the day. That didn't prove the old man's death had been involuntary, though.

The crime scene investigator hadn't found anything in the attic that could have helped the dead man climb high enough to hang himself. The man had only been 5'7", almost a head shorter than Pavel. He also weighed 243.8 pounds. One person couldn't have lifted him. It would have taken at least two people to commit such a murder.

Too bad the crime scene investigator hadn't found any evidence, at least none that could be tied to this case. The attic was used often; there were sacks of oats in the back, used as animal feed on the farm-turned-horse farm.

Pavel walked under the maligned roof beam. A crime scene investigator had drawn a white circle on the brown-painted boards, marking a liquid that turned out to be urine. The investigator had found a fresh splinter of wood in one of the dead man's fingers. Pavel felt the beam on the right side. It was rough and barely sanded. He was getting closer to solving the mystery, even though he had no idea what it might look like.

The back of the attic was being renovated. The victim's daughter had told him there was a fire there a few weeks ago. No major damage had been done, so there was no investigation. A few pieces of wood lay jumbled on one side. Unlike the floor, there was little dust on them. Pavel lifted one of them—about 44 pounds, he estimated. Even the old man could have lifted it. Pavel leaned the board against the massive beam that ran the length of the room. It slipped back a little but then found support on the attic's outside wall. Pavel placed a second piece of wood next to it, then a third and a fourth.

In this way, he constructed a ramp leading up to the roof beam, which must be a foot thick. The wood was easy to grip, and the angle was shallow enough for him to climb. There was just enough space between the beam and the roof for him to crawl along it. He slowly pushed himself forward on the roof beam until he heard a ripping sound.

Damn it. Why hadn't he taken his shirt off? The outer pocket must have caught on the rough wood. Pavel shook his head and continued to crawl. He wasn't done yet. Soon he reached the point where the beam the victim had used crossed the main beam. The rope that had been wrapped around the dead man's neck was in the crime lab. But as if the old man had wanted to make his death easier to trace, another rope hung over the beam. According to the pathologist, it hadn't been used, probably because it was much thinner.

Pavel reached for it, then thought better of it. Everything had to look the same, so he crawled back a little and pushed the timbers to the floor with his feet. They clattered together as if they hadn't seen each other in a long time. Pavel grinned. He was almost there. From his position, head down, he looked directly at the white circle where the dead man had posthumously emptied his bladder.

He pulled the rope toward himself. The pathologist had confirmed what Pavel had noticed immediately: the rope around the dead man's neck hadn't been tied in a conventional hangman's knot, but a two-strand knot. Probably because the triple overhand knot was easier for the old man to tie than the more complicated hangman's knot.

Pavel passed the end of the rope around the beam, imagining what it would have been like to work with gout-riddled fingers. That was the pathologist's diagnosis. Pavel wasn't exactly sure. The old man had once been a sailor and knew a thing or two about knots. His caretaker, who had found the deceased man and was named in his will, had reported progressive dementia symptoms. The old man had probably wanted to avoid an undignified end. There was only the daughter, but it was hard to judge how much she had cared for her father.

After the third knot, Pavel slipped the noose around his neck so it rested just below his ear. The double knot was self-locking. All it needed was weight, the more the better. He felt his work. It was ... exciting. He didn't feel any different, but his pulse had quickened somewhat.

Maybe what he was about to do was stupid. Fortunately, no

one was watching. At his new office, he had only hinted that he wanted to look into the unexplained death again. His colleague was on vacation and was said to be spending her time swimming. The sun peeked through the gray clouds, but who would voluntarily go into the water when the temperature was below seventy-seven degrees? She probably wasn't interested in getting to know him. He couldn't blame her. After her former boss retired, she had probably hoped to get the job herself. He had specifically asked to avoid such situations in his transfer application!

But there was nothing he could do about it. He would meet her next Monday at the latest. The pathologist thought the world of her, and was almost angry that Pavel wanted to reopen the case Koopmann had closed in favor of new investigations.

At least she wouldn't bother him today.

He slowly let his stomach slide off the roof beam. This must be how the old man had done it. Pavel felt his body trying to swing. That was not good. He had to fall straight down so the resulting broken neck would kill him instantly. He didn't want to strangle. The old man had managed a steep fall, and Pavel managed it now by twisting to the side. This internal twisting of the body, as his dance teacher called it, absorbed some of the excess momentum. Now all he had to do was...

Zip. Pavel plunged down. At the last moment, he managed to grab on to the beam with his arms. The noose hung loosely around his neck. No broken neck, no strangulation. This was a very positive result. Without realizing it, Pavel must have been attached to the beam by his shirt, supported by the cotton fabric. The fabric tearing caught him by surprise.

His position was not very comfortable. His arms already hurt. His toes ached. The tips of his shoes slipped on the beams. Pavel looked out the window. He had been right. You could indeed see the sea, which seemed to be taking a personal interest in his, Pavel Neuhof's, admittedly unpleasant situation. It even sent an emissary to check on him, but the seagull veered away as it neared the house.

He took a deep breath. Air suddenly seemed precious. Should he let go? Did he really have enough strength in his toes to support his own weight? If not, the double knot would strangle him. He was torn. But he wouldn't last long with his arms around the beam anyway. He might as well take the risk and...

Just a moment. No rash decisions. He did the math. If at 6'4", he could touch the beam with the tips of his toes, the underside had to be about 8.9 feet (2.71 meters) from the floor. No, nonsense. He had to subtract the head and neck, making it about eight feet. The noose with the knot was about ten inches in diameter, starting two inches below the beam.

That was it. The two-strand knot would strangle him before his toes touched the ground. Good thing he hadn't given in to his first impulse. He was good at resisting first impulses. "*You never treat yourself,*" his ex-wife had always said. Yet he always treated himself with work. It was great to solve puzzles and get paid for it.

It was just a shame that it would soon be over.

Chapter Three

Lars clapped his hand over his mouth. He bent over the dead man and stared in astonishment as if the body was no longer human. Enna understood his reaction. The dead man didn't look very attractive; he had probably been in the water for some time.

They had pulled him out of the sea together and carried him ashore. Only then had the adrenaline and shock worn off. Now the six of them stood silently in the cold wind around the body, while the grass at the edge of the beach whispered.

Enna raised her hand, and they all looked at her. She no longer felt like she was on vacation. "Please get changed! The life-saving lesson is over."

They nodded and withdrew. Only Lars and Enna stayed with the dead man. Lars swallowed hard and said so quietly that Enna could hardly hear him, "We have to call the police!"

Enna snorted. "I'm already here."

"Oh. Right."

Lars was still staring at the dead man. Then his eyes slowly rose to Enna. "I think I know him."

Enna raised both eyebrows. "Really? Who do you think he is?"

"That's Toni Sattelmacher."

"Toni?"

"Yes, take a good look at him. That's him. Right here ... something..."

"Yes, yes, that's from the water. He was in there for a while."

"Oh. Right." Lars swallowed audibly again. "I think I'm going to be sick."

"Then sit down and have a drink of something. Tea will help."

"Yes. I hope so." Lars tore himself away from Toni and stumbled away, gagging.

Enna watched him go and shook her head before turning her attention back to the dead man. She crouched down beside him. Toni Sattelmacher. Yes, Lars was right. It was Toni from Fleetstedt. But why was he floating dead in the North Sea? He was a few years older than she was, somewhere in his late thirties. And Toni could swim. He had always hung out with the older boys when they were young. They used to lie on one of the wooden rafts on the beach and sunbathe. To get there, you had to swim out a good 985 feet...

Toni Sattelmacher, dead in Fleetstedt.

Enna didn't want to believe it. She vaguely remembered being invited to one of his birthday parties. Or had she only spent a summer with him because their parents knew each other? Enna didn't know. It had been so long ago, and she hadn't thought about Toni in years. Maybe it was because of what he was wearing. It didn't fit at all. It looked like an old fisherman's coat, like the one Enna's uncle Friedhelm had often worn. The older generation all wore such coats, but none of the boys did. So why did Toni?

Was it really Toni?

Enna bent over the dead man again and looked at his face. Then she nodded. Yes, it was definitely Toni. Lars was right. She recognized the swollen features.

So Enna probably had a new case, the first without her former boss. The first with Pavel Neuhof.

She grimaced. Hopefully, Neuhof hadn't come here to take it easy. If he had, his debut with a floater would certainly not be a good one.

Enna sighed loudly. Her teeth chattered with cold. Her vacation was over.

Pressing her lips together, she left the corpse behind to dry off and get dressed. She would then call the office and summon Pavel Neuhof to the beach for his debut.

Hopefully, he wouldn't take offense.

Neuhof did not, because he was not in the office, Berger told her. Nor could he be reached on his cell phone. He had gone off somewhere without saying a word. But he had probably spent the last few days dealing with Dietrichsen's death.

I see. The Dietrichsen case hadn't really been a case as far as Enna was concerned. The old farmer had taken his own life due to the onset of dementia. She had visited the farm before she went on vacation, inspected everything, and put the case aside after receiving the crime scene investigation report and the preliminary report from the pathologist's office. In fact, the only thing still pending was the toxicology report to determine if the old farmer had been under the influence of drugs. The dead man's daughter had insisted on it, so they had ordered it, after a long discussion, to get absolute clarity, but what was the point? There were no motives for murdering the old farmer. Especially not in Fleetstedt.

Enna sighed. Would Neuhof check her work? She didn't like the idea, but it didn't matter. She had done a good job; nothing could change that—unless the pathologist did find evidence of drugs in his system. That would put the death in a different light.

Enna looked down at the dead Toni, still lying on the beach. A seagull approached him curiously, but when the wind ruffled the dark raincoat, it flew away.

She shook her head. What was she doing here? She was on vacation. But instead of leaving the beach, she looked up the number of the pathologist's office on her contacts list and dialed it.

"Police inspector Enna Koopmann," she said. "Hello, I'm

calling about Dietrichsen. Fleetstedt. Yes. It is about the toxicology report. It should be available by now."

The clerk let out an "Ah!" "Yes, a colleague of yours called today. Neudorf or Neuhaus or something."

"Yes, that's my new boss."

"Ah, okay. Well, there are no new findings. The toxicology report—wait a minute—didn't find any toxins. I faxed it to your boss."

The corners of Enna's mouth turned up for a moment. "Thanks, that's all I needed to know."

"All right, then. By the way, your office informed us earlier that there's been a death! Mr. Kettler left to go to the scene immediately."

That was good news. Nils Kettler, the forensic pathologist responsible for Fleetstedt and the region around it, was a good man. He was easy to work with and unpretentious. Enna liked that.

She thanked him, hung up, and thought about Dietrichsen again. As she thought. Definitely suicide. Why was Neuhof still investigating it? This settled everything. He could close the case and let it go. Stamp it and be done with it. He should be at his desk.

He went off somewhere without saying a word...

Actually, the only place he could have gone was to Dietrichsen's farm. There was nowhere else to go in connection with the suicide.

Enna scratched her head, then made a decision: as soon as Kettler got here to pick up the body, she would go to the Dietrichsens'. The farm was on her way home anyway. If Neuhof was there, she would pick him up; if not, he was out of luck.

Yes, that was what she would do. Meanwhile, she had to change. She still had on her wet bathing suit under her towel and jacket.

She looked around. Lars was still busy with his back to her, and the other four had retreated to the parking lot behind the dike. A quick glance at Toni ... it wasn't as if she could expect him to look away.

Enna quickly slipped out of her clothes and got dressed. She already had her t-shirt and jacket on, as well as her trademark shorts, and was just pulling on a pair of colorful socks—today they had bright green avocados on them—when she spotted a figure on the crest of the dike.

Fortunately, it wasn't a passerby, but Nils Kettler.

The man, in his mid-fifties, was a real one-of-a-kind, which might be why Enna liked him so much. No matter what the weather, he always wore a dark blue knit cap, under which his gray temples peeked out. His face was always tanned, which made the gray three-day beard stand out—almost like her socks.

He waved to her from a distance and came down the beach with energetic strides. He carried his metal case in his right hand.

"Moin!" he called over the last few feet. "Nice weather, isn't it?"

Enna smiled and shook her wet hair. "I've been swimming."

"And fished out a body." He stopped beside the dead man and examined him with raised eyebrows. "It's okay."

"What?"

"His condition. I expected worse. He hasn't been in there very long. I estimate twelve to sixteen hours. More details will follow after the autopsy, as you know."

Enna nodded and estimated the time. The deceased must have gone into the water sometime last evening. "Can you tell if he drowned?"

"No. Check his mouth and nose. Do you see anything unusual?"

"No."

"That's the point. The only outward sign of drowning is fine white foam in front of the mouth and/or nose. That's not visible here, but it could have been washed away by the waves."

"I see. So you'll have to cut him open."

"Correct. One indication would be diluted stomach contents, for example. After transferring it to a glass jar, it would show three layers." Kettler raised his thumb. "White foam." He raised his index finger. "Then liquid. And finally, solid food particles." He finished the list with his middle finger. "But there are other signs. The dead man will tell me. Do you have any idea who he is?"

"Toni Sattelmacher. Comes from around here."

"Okay." Kettler sank to his knees and examined the dead man's hands, then his head. He narrowed his eyes. "You see this?" He pointed to a spot on one side of the back of the head.

Enna craned her neck. She recognized a reddish, thickened area under the close-cropped hair. "Looks swollen."

"Yeah. Could be blunt force trauma."

"From..."

"From a fall, for example. Or going off a boat. But could be from a blow. That will also become clear. Have you started looking for abandoned boats?"

"Not yet. But I'll arrange it." She made a note of it.

"That's what I expected." He smiled, then got serious. "I talked to your new boss on the phone today. Strange guy."

Enna took a deep breath. "I haven't met him yet. I'm actually on vacation."

"Really? Oh, I'm sorry you have to deal with dead people on vacation."

"That's okay. At least they don't want much from me."

Kettler laughed, showing the crow's feet around his eyes. "That's why I became a forensic pathologist, Ms. Koopmann. The dead are very peaceful. Although stimulating company like yours is nice." He winked at her, then opened his case and pulled out an SLR camera. Various lenses lay in padded compartments, ready for use.

Enna stood. She knew that Kettler would want to be left alone now. "When will you know something?"

"You'll have a first assessment tomorrow. If all goes well, I'll finish the autopsy in the late morning. That depends on how many secrets Mr. Sattelmacher wants to tell us."

Enna nodded and put her hands in her pockets. "Then I'll see you tomorrow! Can I leave you here?"

"Of course. What could be better than a pathologist's inquest on the beach, with the wind whistling in my ears and the seagulls dancing in the sky?"

Enna could think of a few things, but she kept her comment about his poetically lofty description to herself. She raised her hand in farewell, picked up her backpack, and trudged across the beach to the parking lot.

Neuhof and Dietrichsen crossed her mind again. She sighed. She'd play taxi driver and hope to find Neuhof on the farm.

The Dietrichsens' farm was just beyond the dike. It consisted of several acres of land, mostly fields and meadows, the main house, and a few stables. A few sheep stood stoically along the driveway, chewing grass. Neon pink numbers were spray-painted on their backs, standing out unnaturally from the otherwise quiet surroundings.

Enna stopped in front of the half-open gate, got out, and pushed it all the way open so she could drive through. It squeaked horribly, and left traces of rust on her fingers.

In the courtyard, she spotted a bike that looked familiar. It was the office bike, leaning against the main building. So Neuhof was here.

"Great," Enna grumbled and climbed the worn steps to the front door. She rang the bell, and a moment later young Ms. Dietrichsen opened it.

"Oh, hello, Enna! Your colleague is already here."

"Good. Where is he?"

"In the attic." She shrugged. "He wanted to have another look around. I unlocked the door for him. Any news?"

"Not really. It was definitely suicide."

The younger Dietrichsen had expected that, so she sighed calmly. "Anything else would have surprised me. But I still don't want to believe that he took his own life. Everything was fine."

Except for increasing dementia. Enna pursed her lips apologetically. "Again, I am sorry. But I have to go up there."

"Yes, of course. You know the way?"

"Yes, I know the way."

Enna entered the house. It smelled of old wood and brickwork. It was a unique smell that she only knew from old houses.

A steep staircase led to the attic; first to the upper floor and from there to the top. The wooden banister had been polished smooth by many decades of handling. The original paint had never been renewed; the bare wood shone through.

A groan from above made Enna pause. Something rumbled. Was that wood on wood? What was Neuhof doing up there? Was he still rooting around in the attic?

She rubbed her face, shook her head, and climbed the last few steps.

Something rumbled again. Wood creaked.

Enna stopped in front of the closed door and shut her eyes. She didn't feel like confronting her new boss right now, but there was no turning back. They had a dead man, which meant they might have a case, and she had to inform him.

Her hand reached for the doorknob, pushed down the old wrought-iron handle, and opened the door.

The sight that met Enna's eyes made her grimace.

None other than Chief Inspector Neuhof—she recognized him from the picture in his personnel file—was clinging to one of the ceiling beams at a height of over six feet, visibly struggling with gravity.

When he heard the door creak, he looked at her and said in a strained voice, "Dietrichsen committed suicide!"

Chapter Four

Enna nodded. What a revelation! But why was Neuhof doing pull-ups on the rafters? Was this a new murder investigation strategy he picked up from the Kiel police? Then she noticed the rope around his neck. It looked almost exactly like old Dietrichsen's noose. She shook her head. No way! The housekeeper hadn't been able to get the old man down, so Enna had ended up having to look him in the face, just as she was now looking at her new boss. The only difference was that Dietrichsen's cheeks had been very pale, contrasting with the red spots on his forehead. She wouldn't be able to get that image out of her head anytime soon.

"Would you mind..." Neuhof pressed.

Of course she could. She ran to him, grabbed his legs, and lifted him a little.

Neuhof moaned and his body moved. She hoped he would hurry. She wouldn't be able to hold him up for long... *Rip*. His pants ripped open at the sides, revealing blue, almost knee-length boxers. She noticed the choice of clothing but didn't evaluate it. Why would she? It was enough that people didn't make fun of her style.

"You can ... let go now," Neuhof said. "And ... thank you."

Rescue number three. First the attempt with Lars, then the

failed rescue of Toni, and finally success, with her future boss of all people. Wasn't that the basis for a good working relationship?

"You're welcome," she said. "Rescue is my hobby."

Saying it sounded stranger than thinking it, but she was used to that.

"Technically, you can't really call it a rescue." Neuhof tossed the rope into the corner and straightened his shirt and pants. He touched the tears in the cloth and huffed. It must have reminded him of something. He touched the shirt again and huffed again.

Only now did Enna realize what Neuhof had just said. Wasn't it customary in his world to say thank you? It was in hers. "Come on, you should have seen yourself hanging there with the noose almost tight."

"Well, I still had the possibility of standing on my toes..."

Enna walked back to the door. "You don't know what you're talking about. Why don't you touch the beam you were hanging from?" She bit her tongue. Was it allowed to criticize your boss like that?

"I was hanging on." Neuhof reached up and touched the wood. Then he stood on tiptoe. His fingers did not reach the top of the beam. That must have made him think, because he didn't say anything. Instead, the muscles between his hairline and his ear twitched—the muscles that let her Uncle Friedhelm wiggle his ears so amusingly.

With Neuhof, nothing moved except the muscles. It was as if they were driving a thinking machine in his elongated skull. His high hairline reinforced the impression.

Enna laughed. "Just admit you were in trouble and I won't tell anyone."

That was a lie. Although it was always said that East Frisians were tight-lipped, in their favorite pub in Fleetstedt it was good manners to talk about other people's misfortunes.

"All right," Neuhof grumbled. "I admit I would have run out of options pretty soon."

Men. Like most members of that species, he was apparently incapable of admitting defeat without ifs and buts.

"The pathologist told me to tell you that Dietrichsen was not under the influence of any drugs that could have led to his death. Of course, he took a lot of pills, but everything was within reason."

"Oh, pills? Did we check with the doctor?"

"Of course, I checked with Dr. Sörensen. He didn't know anything about Dietrichsen's death."

"I see. Well, the way he hanged himself seems much clearer to me now, too. It's not a case for us. So let's go back to the police station. Or wait, Enna, aren't you on vacation?"

She shook her head. "I'm not here because of Dietrichsen. We have a dead man!"

"Bye, Enna!" the younger Dietrichsen called after her, and she returned the farewell. Her boss's bicycle was in the back. It smelled of chain oil. It was a good thing she had taken the old Passat. The bike would never have fit in the new BMW.

Enna got out, opened the gate a second time, drove through it, and closed it again. Apparently it didn't occur to Neuhof to help her. He pointed apologetically at the tear in his pants. Oh well. But she wasn't going to let him get away with that forever. Her old boss would have jumped out of the car, despite his sixty-three years. He was old-school.

The new one didn't seem much younger. Maybe it was the round bald spot on the back of his head, or the fact that he sometimes spoke a little stiltedly.

"Would you be so kind as to drive the car a little slower?"

Like now, for example. She took her foot off the accelerator. Okay, the roads out here were narrow, but you could see oncoming traffic for miles. For the locals, fifty on a country road was normal, and Enna Koopmann was one of them, even though her father had immigrated from Bavaria.

"Thank you," her boss said.

She looked over at him, and his face twisted into something that could be interpreted as a smile, but also as an outward symptom of toothache. *Smile*, she decided, and smiled back. Not that she had a choice.

"So, what can you tell me about our new case?"

Toni Sattelmacher. Her smile disappeared. She still couldn't believe that he ... that he ... and so young... Enna swallowed.

"I'm sorry," Neuhof said. He must have noticed her reaction. Good, then he wasn't an insensitive jerk. She had never been able to deal with people like that.

Enna swallowed her emotions and told him how she had found Toni, and that the pathologist hadn't ruled out natural causes during the short examination on the beach, but he didn't want to commit to that either.

"I see. I guess we won't know if we really have a case until tomorrow." Her boss held on to the door handle as she turned the infamous bend behind the Fleeter dike. They had raced mopeds here as teenagers, imagining they were driving through the famous Nordschleife of the Nürburgring. She had always thought it was in Bavaria.

She mentally returned to the present. "Well, if he drowned, there's still the question of whether someone threw him in the water."

Neuhof nodded. "True, I suppose."

He was probably not a man of many words. If his vocabulary weren't so strange, he could be mistaken for a local.

"I had headquarters give me the parents' address," Enna said. "They live in a retirement home. 'Zum Abendrot' or something like that."

"Well, the important thing is we have the address." Her boss leaned his head against the headrest and closed his eyes. Was he nervous? His hands rested loosely in his lap.

"I just remembered, we have to stop by my boarding house first. I need a fresh pair of pants." He pointed to the tear.

"Where is it?"

"Schmale Gasse 23."

"That's right by the marketplace?"

Neuhof nodded.

"That's inconvenient," Enna said. "There's a market there

today. You won't be able to get through. Let's go past my apartment since it's on the way to the retirement home. I'll sew it up for you real quick."

"That's out of the question."

"But it would be much faster that way." What was his problem? Today was her last day of vacation and she didn't want to spend it in the car.

"I'll sew it myself. You're not my caretaker!"

"Very good work." It wasn't a lie. She couldn't have done a better job herself. She started to run her finger over it, but her boss quickly stepped back, sending her crashing into the bathroom door.

"Sorry." Neuhof actually blushed. He turned and shut the door behind him. He had retreated to her bathroom to sew, supposedly because of the better lighting, but then why had he locked the door?

"Can I have a minute?" she asked.

"What?"

What kind of question was that? He was standing right in front of the bathroom door, blocking her way.

"In the bathroom. I need to change."

"Uh, of course." He pushed past her. It was narrow and dark in the hallway of her small apartment. "I'd better wait in the car." Neuhof made a dash for the exit, as if on the run.

"Wait a minute!" she called after him. "The key!"

She grabbed the small bundle from the shelf and tossed it to him. Her boss reached out with precision, and it landed right in the palm of his hand. He had good reflexes. She was looking forward to her first target practice with him. Not that she had fired a gun very often in Fleetstedt, except for the time when she had saved a sheep from an agonizing death after it was hit by a tourist's car. All the other shots had been fired during her six months of training.

"I won't be long!" she called, "I just need to..."

But the door had already slammed shut.

He was a bit strange, her new colleague. Enna pulled down her shorts and sat on the pleasantly cool toilet seat. June had started unusually warm, up to seventy-seven degrees at noon. The poor sheep on the dikes! Her old boss kept a small flock as a hobby and had explained to her that the animals didn't sweat, only panted a little to get rid of excess body heat.

The last few days had been much cooler, but that didn't prevent Enna from wearing her shorts.

She cleaned up and got dressed. As she did so, she thought about her new boss. He was obviously a thoroughgoing investigator. The way he had staged Dietrichsen's death... She thought again of the old farmer's bulging eyes, but instantly decided it was better to think about Neuhof. She turned on the tap and washed her hands. What exactly did she find strange about him? For one thing, there was the way he spoke. He used words that weren't used in everyday speech, and he took everything that was said literally. Then there was his apparent aversion to being touched. Enna loved to hug her friends, regardless of gender. She dried her hands on the small towel next to the sink.

Maybe it was because they hardly knew each other. But that would change, and hopefully soon. If they were going to work well together, they had to get to know each other. She would invite her boss to her favorite pub tonight.

"Those shorts," Neuhof said as she got into the car, but then hesitated.

"Yeah?"

"Forget it. It's inappropriate."

"No, ask away." She knew exactly what he wanted to know, but surely she deserved a fully formed question.

"All right, then. Your shorts are unusual."

"That's not a question."

Her boss squirmed, but she didn't let up. "Why are you wearing them, Enna?"

There you go. It worked after all. "I love shorts, always have. I wore nothing else when I was a little girl. And colored socks are part of it for me."

It was strange that he was asking her that on the first day. The shorts, she felt, defined her life at least as much as her first name or her profession. Few people in the world understood that. Few? She couldn't think of anyone except her father.

"Interesting," said her new boss.

Enna waited for him to say something else, but nothing followed. His expression didn't reveal whether the adjective meant "Oh my God," "For God's sake," "How could she," or "Poor crazy woman."

That was fine with her. Neuhof was probably not one of the people who understood her. He didn't have to. He was just her new boss. And she had to get along with him. Luckily, shorts didn't play a role in that.

Chapter Five

The light turned yellow. Would she...? His colleague stepped on the gas. The force of inertia pushed him into the seat. Pavel checked his seatbelt and grabbed the handle above the window. With a *whoosh*, the car shot through the intersection.

"Do you have to ... like that?" Pavel pressed his lips together. He had already embarrassed Enna earlier with his question about her shorts. Why couldn't he control himself?

"What do I have to do?" she replied.

Now he had to be more specific. He had already learned that she wouldn't let up. He actually liked that in people, even if it could be exhausting. "Drive so fast."

Enna furrowed her brow and looked at him, frightening him. He wasn't afraid of her, of course, since he hardly knew her, but of the fact that she wasn't watching the road.

"Look, the speedometer needle is right on the line," she said, "fifty."

"I don't see a blue sign. If we hit a pedestrian, they hardly stand a chance above thirty."

Enna inhaled and exhaled deeply. She clearly wanted to increase the oxygen supply to her cells. Pavel imitated her. People feel better when another person mirrors them. He had learned that in a dating class.

"What am I doing wrong now?"

The question surprised him because he hadn't criticized her again, even though they were still driving through Fleetstedt at a completely unnecessary fifty miles per hour. The dead man's parents would not benefit from receiving the news any quicker. On the contrary, in his experience, the situation of those affected often deteriorated dramatically as a result of the information.

"Well?" Koopmann asked, activating the turn signal. Pavel loved the rhythmic clicking sound. It tickled his spine, but he couldn't concentrate on it fully because his colleague was waiting for his answer. Enna Koopmann had emphasized "wrong", so it must have a special meaning for her too, consciously or not. Then there was the adverb "now", which positioned a process in time. Was Enna trying to signal a contrast between expectation and reality? Did she want to suggest a negative answer? Did the word serve to create a certain emphasis? Did she consider the fact that she had made mistakes to be unchangeable?

Pavel nodded. At least that was a true statement. People made mistakes. He didn't exclude himself from that.

"So?" Enna insisted.

"Yes, of course, we all make mistakes," Pavel explained. Hopefully, she would leave it at that. Couldn't she ask him what he knew about the dead man's parents instead?

"Huh? What kind of answer is that?"

"That's an exculpatory answer. Knowing that we all make mistakes all the time allows us to practice tolerance toward each other."

At least that's what the psychologist he visited regularly in Kiel had told him. It didn't apply to him. When he realized how high the risk of making a mistake was, he lost the ability to act. But other people felt strangely relieved.

"Dear Mr. Neuhof, you're talking nonsense."

Enna Koopmann obviously didn't belong to that group. Maybe she was more like him than he thought.

"We're here," Enna announced, which was obvious as the car approached a colonnaded archway along a gravel path.

Pavel waited for the car to stop, then unbuckled his seatbelt and got out. The gravel under his feet was crisp. The house, painted a fresh yellow, looked like a Tuscan villa. Just looking at the columns gave him a headache. They alternated between Doric and Ionic styles, and had no base or plinth.

"Nice place," Enna said, walking up the three steps to the entrance. Pavel didn't point out the architect's obvious mistakes. There were ramps to the left and right of the entrance, but wasn't gravel extremely impractical for people in wheelchairs?

A young woman approached them. Her uniform consisted of a white polo shirt and white pants. Pavel was still trying to decipher her name tag when Enna pulled out her badge.

"Police Inspector Enna Koopmann," she introduced herself. "And this is my colleague, Chief Inspector Pavel Neuhof."

"I'm Jenny Kring, assistant to the director of Haus Abendruh." The woman held out her hand, surprising Pavel, who had forgotten his gloves. Surely there would be somewhere to wash his hands.

"We'd like to speak to Mr. and Mrs. Sattelmacher," he said.

"Sattelmacher?" The young woman closed her eyes for a moment as if thinking.

"Siena!" called a male nurse in a blue coat.

"Yes, of course!" The young woman slapped her forehead with the flat of her hand. "The Sattelmachers are in the Siena Suite." Jenny Kring stepped closer and whispered: "May I ask if there's a problem?"

Pavel let his colleague answer because the woman's perfume bothered him. It smelled like an old-fashioned, heavy mixture of roses and violets, and didn't suit the young woman at all. Or had she chosen it to suit her clients?

Enna looked at him briefly. A flutter of her eyelids signaled confusion. Pavel looked up at the ceiling, where an unusually bright spotlight bathed the anteroom in warm light.

"I'm afraid we can't give you any information," Enna said finally.

It was normal for people to express their curiosity at times like this. But there was no harm in asking. "Have you ever had any problems with the Sattelmachers?"

Pavel studied the young woman's face. On the verge of a sneeze, he turned away and blew his nose with his cotton handkerchief.

"No, they're a very quiet couple."

"Do they get along well?" asked Enna.

"They go for a walk together every day, to the pier and back, no matter what the weather."

"That's true love, isn't it?" Enna nudged him with her elbow. Pavel jerked away.

"And with each other? Do either of them exhibit dominant behavior?" In his experience, it was extremely rare that neither partner took the dominant role in a long-term relationship. That even applied to professional relationships, but not to him, as he deliberately avoided such games.

"You mean who is in charge?"

"Yes, exactly."

"Well, you can't deny that Mrs. Sattelmacher is the more ... authoritative person. But I wouldn't call that..."

"Thank you, Ms. Kring," he cut her off. For some reason, people were embarrassed by calling others dominant. "Would you mind showing us where the Siena Suite is?"

"Uh ... yes, I'd be happy to. Please follow me."

"...and this is my colleague, Police Inspector Enna Koopmann," he finished the introduction this time.

Enna raised her hand in greeting. "Hello there."

She had entered the Sattelmachers' suite in his wake, and even now she didn't come forward to shake hands with the dead man's mother and father but kept a very low profile. Pavel was glad of that, for it allowed him to finish the greeting with an old-fashioned but neat bow. At the same time, he couldn't hide his astonishment.

Normal people, which he was not, tended to change their behavior from time to time, but when they did, there was usually a reason for it. Perhaps Enna knew the dead man's parents? Or maybe she was uncomfortable having to give them the news of their son's death.

"Enna?" Mrs. Sattelmacher suddenly approached them. Pavel felt the urge to retreat but forced himself to remain where he was. The old woman, however, wasn't moving toward him at all but was walking around him, clearly aiming for his colleague. She was dragging her left leg. She wore a combination of a white blouse and a long, light green skirt with a blue polka-dot apron. His ex-wife would have criticized the color combination, but since green and blue were close together on the spectrum, it made perfect sense from his point of view.

"Enna?" Mrs. Sattelmacher asked again.

"Yes, Mrs. Sattelmacher."

"Where is our Toni?"

Pavel furrowed his brow. What kind of question was that? Did the dead man and his colleague know each other well? "Mr. and Mrs. Sattelmacher," he began, "I have some sad news to tell you."

"Toni is dead, Mrs. Sattelmacher," Enna said in a strangely affected tone.

Silence. Pavel heard the sound of a ventilation system. It seemed to exceed the limits for low-noise systems, it was humming so loudly.

"What did you say?" asked Mr. Sattelmacher in a barely audible voice that couldn't compete with the noise of the fan.

Enna swallowed. "Toni is dead."

"But ... but he was here yesterday to visit us. Wasn't he, dear? Wasn't that yesterday?"

"Yes, he visited us yesterday," Mrs. Sattelmacher confirmed. Her eyes were glued to Enna, who had taken a step back. An emotion flashed across her face. Was it anger? Anguish? Incomprehension? Pavel wasn't sure what he was seeing. "What are you saying, Enna?"

A tear ran down her face. "Unfortunately, it is true. I pulled him out of the water myself today. My condolences, Mrs. and Mr. Sattelmacher."

The old woman frowned and looked at Pavel and Enna in turn. Something seemed to be going on behind her eyes. Perhaps the information had just registered. Yes, indeed, because suddenly she put her hands to her face and hurried back to the sofa where her husband was sitting. Like the rest of the furniture, it looked expensive—and ugly. She sank down next to her husband but didn't touch him. Then she shook her head in confusion. "But weren't you with him?" she asked.

"*Me*?" Enna frowned and narrowed her eyes. "What do you mean? I fished his ... his body out of the North Sea."

"But you're his girlfriend! You should have been with him."

Excuse me? Did he hear her correctly? Enna was the dead man's girlfriend? That was a good start. His new colleague hadn't told him about her relationship with the victim!

Pavel shook his head and said: "Enna, you're done here. You can't investigate this case." He had to get her out of the line of fire as soon as possible, not only to avoid jeopardizing the success of the investigation but also for her own sake.

"B-b-but it's not true, Pavel! I knew Toni, that's true, but I was never involved with him, you have to believe me."

She sounded desperate, but many suspects had lied to him with the same desperation in their eyes. Suspects, yes. Hopefully, she had only hidden the relationship from him so that she could continue to participate in the investigation.

"Enna, please leave the room now. I'll take care of this."

She started to object, but thankfully obeyed. Whew. He had feared he would have to escort her out. The heavy door closed behind her. That meant he had to take care of everything himself now.

"What about Toni?" Mr. Sattelmacher asked again. He didn't seem to have grasped what had happened.

"He was floating lifeless in the North Sea, Mr. Sattelmacher. I'm very sorry. We are now investigating the circumstances of his death."

"His death." Now Sattelmacher senior got up and started

pacing the room while his wife watched him. Pavel didn't know if the news had sunk in yet.

He left it at that and asked gently: "When exactly was the last time your son visited you?"

"Yesterday." Toni's father stopped and stared at Pavel, his chin trembling. "Is he really dead? My Toni?"

Pavel just nodded.

There were tears in Sattelmacher's eyes. "Oh God, it can't be! I should have been ... much nicer to him."

"Was there an argument?"

"No, not an argument. It was just about the bills for our apartment here. Toni always pays them, but some payments haven't arrived. I was angry with him because the management had threatened to evict us. We've settled in so well. Magda wouldn't be able to handle another move. She was so upset by the last one." Tears streamed down the old man's cheeks.

Pavel turned to the dead man's mother. She was leaning forward on the sofa and didn't seem to be listening at all. Had the apathy of shock already set in?

"When was Toni here, and when did he leave?" he asked emotionlessly.

Mr. Sattelmacher shook his head and sniffed. "That's a tough one. It was in the afternoon, before tea at three."

"Thank you. Did your son have any enemies?"

"Enemies? Toni? No, he was liked by everyone, unlike Heiner."

"Heiner?"

"Our other son. Unfortunately, he's quite... Well, my wife probably spoiled him. Toni is seven years older than Heiner, and he is not her biological son."

"Was." Pavel bit his lip, realizing the gravity of his correction. The old man had probably overheard his inappropriate remark. He now looked at his wife, who was still staring at the floor. Her shoulders were slumped. Not only was her age visible, but also the burden of her son's death. *Stepson*, Pavel corrected himself. They would have to check what had become of his mother. He added it to the checklist in his head. "Thanks for the information," he said. "We'll be in touch."

Mr. Sattelmacher just nodded.

Pavel thought of something else and raised his finger. "One more question, Mr. Sattelmacher." He whispered, afraid the woman would interrupt. But Toni's father didn't hear him.

"One more question," he said louder.

The man raised his tearful eyes. "Yes?"

"Toni and my colleague ... what can you tell me about that?"

At first, the man didn't seem to want to answer, but then he abruptly walked to the desk. Pavel followed him. There, Sattelmacher opened an antique-looking flat wooden box, leafed through its contents, and finally pulled out a photograph. It was yellowed and showed a young man and an even younger girl who only vaguely resembled Enna, but who was wearing shorts. It was impossible to tell if the socks were colored.

"That's Toni and Enna," Sattelmacher said. "They've been a couple ever since."

The photo was clearly more than twenty years old. He didn't need Enna to tell him that. Pavel shook his head. "Don't you have anything more recent?"

The man rummaged through the box. Suddenly he pulled out a photo that someone had cut. Then another and another. It seemed to take a lot out of Sattelmacher, because he threw the pictures on the table, sweating profusely and getting red spots on his face.

"Who is missing?" asked Pavel, pointing to one of the photos. He recognized a lighthouse on a rock and the two old Sattelmachers. "And please calm down. They're just pictures."

"Toni! Someone has cut him out! Everywhere!" Suddenly the man grabbed his chest, moaned loudly, swayed, and fell to the side.

With a lunge, Pavel managed to catch the slack body. The weight made him grunt, but he didn't let go and carefully laid Mr. Sattelmacher on the thick, almost new-looking carpet. "Get help!" he yelled, but Mrs. Sattelmacher was still sitting on the sofa, studying the carpet.

Crap. She wasn't answering. There must be a bell. There, at the entrance!

He ran to it and rang it several times. Somewhere in the corridor, a bell rang. The door immediately burst open and Enna rushed in. She saw Sattelmacher lying on the carpet and his wife sitting on the sofa. "What happened?" She hurried over to him and sank down on the floor beside him.

"Passed out."

"Okay. Get help! Quickly!" She was already bending over the unconscious man and addressing him. "Mr. Sattelmacher! Can you hear me? Hello?" Then she put her ear to his nose and looked at his chest, probably to see if it was still rising and falling.

Pavel remembered that she was a DLRG instructor. She knew what she was doing. That was good. He had practically no experience in CPR. When had he last practiced? Never mind. Get help.

He was about to walk out the door when two nurses and a doctor came rushing in. Damn, this place was well organized.

"He's breathing," Enna told the doctor. "But he's unresponsive. Pulse is weak."

"Okay. We'll take it from here," the doctor said. "Thank you."

Enna moved aside and puffed out her cheeks. Her eyes met Pavel's as the medical staff tended to Sattelmacher. They started an IV, got a gurney, and lifted him onto it. Then they pushed him out of the room.

Magda Sattelmacher did not follow her husband, but she had raised her eyes and watched what was happening. Her face was a stiff mask. Enna's face was rigid as well. Should he send her out again? No. That would be unfair.

"Mr. Neuhof," the old woman said suddenly. Her voice trembled slightly.

"Yes?"

"You shouldn't believe everything old people say. Some have forgotten the truth, and others don't want to know."

"What do you mean?"

"About Toni and Enna, that was a fantasy of Georg's. I don't think Toni was interested in women at all."

Pavel nodded to show a reaction. "Then why did you call my colleague his girlfriend earlier?"

A sigh. "I did it for Georg. I would do anything for him, and if the story that Toni is in good hands with Enna makes him sleep better—it doesn't hurt anyone, does it?"

"Well, Mrs. Sattelmacher. You should stick to the truth with us. A relationship between my colleague and your son could have had legal consequences for her."

"Really?"

"Yes. I'm glad you cleared that up for me."

Mrs. Sattelmacher just nodded, then got up and shuffled out of the room.

Pavel and Enna exchanged a long look, then followed her.

"Go ahead, Enna. I just need to go to the bathroom."

Enna simply nodded and walked along the corridor to the exit. The meeting with the Sattelmachers seemed to have taken a toll on her.

Pavel waited for the door to close behind his colleague. Instead of going to the bathroom, he went to the reception desk.

"Ms. Kring?"

"What a drama. Toni! That it happened to him of all people!"

"Should it have happened to someone else?"

The employee winced. She obviously remembered her official duties. "No, of course not. I meant that it happened to him of all people, with the emphasis on 'happened,' you see?"

No, she hadn't said it like that, but he couldn't coerce her into gossiping.

"One last question: have you ever seen Toni come here with anyone?"

"With anyone?" The young woman scratched her head. "Well, there was a lady about his age with him once. She seemed familiar somehow. But she didn't introduce herself by name."

"She didn't look like my colleague, did she?"

"The woman in the shorts? Haha, no, the other one was really dressed up. A woman of the world."

Pavel nodded. "Thank you." Then he followed Enna out of the retirement home.

As he did so, he realized that the case was gaining momentum. He liked that. Luckily, his colleague hadn't been involved with the deceased. That would have been unpleasant and complicated everything. They would figure out the rest. First, they needed Toni's cell phone number and contacts. Then they would see who he had been in contact with. And who he hadn't.

"What was that all about?" asked Enna when they were back in the car. She was sitting in the passenger seat as if she knew she was punishing him. Pavel only drove when he had to. Driving a vehicle on the streets was far too dangerous. It was enough that one of the many other road users might make a mistake, and then...

"Are you not talking to me anymore, Pavel?"

"I'm sorry, but it was necessary."

"Because a senile old woman thinks I'm her son's girlfriend?"

That was inappropriate language. Pavel swallowed, a bitter taste in his mouth. "She might have been right," he said. "You have to admit that." Anyway, it wasn't true.

"Look, Pavel. I've been in the service for fifteen years. I'm well aware that it would have jeopardized the investigation if I had been personally involved."

Maybe that was the case. But how was he supposed to know? "And who's going to tell me that?"

"I'm telling you. We have to at least trust each other."

Trust, there it was again. His ex-wife had thrown him out because he supposedly didn't trust her enough. But wasn't trust built on the consistency of actions and proof over time? He had tried that, but it hadn't worked out very well. Perhaps it was time for a new experiment.

"You're right, Enna. Let's try to trust."

As he spoke the words, they reminded him of the wedding vows he had once made. But his colleague didn't seem to notice.

"Fine," she said simply. "Let's go to the office."

Fine? Who said that? Pavel swallowed his answer. "Speaking of trust," he said. "I really don't like driving. Could you maybe..."

"Only if you don't tell me how to drive."

Pavel nodded. "Scout's honor."

"One more question," Enna said. "I saw a strange name on your ID when we met earlier."

Damn. He was getting hot. "Yes?"

"Waldemar. Waldemar Neuhof. Who's Pavel? Or did you kill Waldemar and take his place?" Enna winked, probably signaling that she didn't really believe he was Waldemar's murderer. But she wasn't wrong.

Pavel swallowed. Trust, what did that mean? "My mom called me Waldemar," he explained hesitantly, "but I don't use that name."

"Then why Pavel?"

She hadn't asked his reasons for not using his birth name. He liked that. But she must have heard of Pavel, the Pavel par excellence. "Pavel Chekov, surely you know him?"

Enna shook her head. "Doesn't ring a bell."

Unbelievable. She didn't know him! "Starship Enterprise?"

"I see. Heard of it, but never seen it."

"That's too bad. It's an interesting science fiction series from the 1970s. And the fictional Pavel is the navigator of the starship. Never in the foreground, but he tells them where to go."

"I see," Enna said, looking enlightened.

Pavel bit his lip and didn't ask. Hopefully she would soon forget the explanation.

Chapter Six

When they entered the office, her new boss went straight to the large window between the two desks and opened it wide. Enna shivered. The cold water of the North Sea still seemed to be flowing through her veins. But that was more likely due to seeing the dead man. She was used to examining corpses, but pulling Toni out of the water had really shaken her.

"You look pale, Enna. A little fresh air will do you good."

Enna stood by the open window. Maybe it would help. She breathed deeply in and out. Just then a ray of sunlight crept through two thick, blue-gray clouds and caught her eye. If that wasn't a sign! She smiled involuntarily. There were few things that gave her as much pleasure as sunshine on her face.

Neuhof gave her time. That was one thing in his favor. The dead man wasn't going anywhere. Nils had promised his final evaluation tomorrow. She turned around and looked at the office. Something was different. Ah, Neuhof had turned his desk a hundred and eighty degrees. Her former boss and she had sat back-to-back, both perpendicular to the window.

"You're right-handed, Pavel?"

He nodded. Of course, he couldn't sit with his right side facing the window, or he'd cast a shadow over himself. But he was now positioned so that he could always see her screen. Enna shook herself. She couldn't handle that. They would have to find another solution.

"So what do we have on the case?"

Enna didn't answer because she wasn't fully focused yet. Someone had tidied up her desk. The Dietrichsen files were neatly organized in the upper left corner. All the pens were in a jar that must have come from the cafeteria they shared with the City Council. The photo of her dog, Pete, who had passed away a year ago, was exactly parallel to the back of the desk. There was no dust on the keyboard of her computer. She opened the drawer, but its contents were as messy as ever. He hadn't gotten that far.

"Pavel? It doesn't work like this," she said. "My desk, my world, your desk, your world." She tried to speak without reproach.

"I get it," Pavel replied. "I was a little bored yesterday and the day before, so I used the time to tidy up. If I understand you correctly, you find my help intrusive."

Enna nodded. Yes, that was the right word. She looked at his desk. Except for the screen and the keyboard, it was completely empty. Where did he keep his mementos? He'd been with the police longer than she had. Surely he must have accumulated a lot? She sat down in her chair and turned it around to face Pavel. He lowered his eyes and adjusted his keyboard, which, to Enna's eyes, was already perfectly aligned.

"To avoid such misunderstandings, I am always grateful for feedback." Pavel spoke slowly, seeming to choose each word carefully. "Perhaps you've noticed, but my statements lack subtext. If you ever wonder what I mean, just look at the words. That's all there is to it."

Aha. That sounded simple. But did that mean he expected the same from her? That would make for a difficult relationship, and she had figured out the reason for his moving here—his colleagues in Kiel had probably not been able to deal with Neuhof.

"Your dilated pupils and silently moving lips indicate that something is unclear to you, Enna."

She smiled involuntarily. With Neuhof around, she didn't need to second-guess herself. He was a very keen observer.

"I was wondering if you expect me to do the same."

Pavel raised his hands. "Absolutely not. I can't apply my standards to the whole world. Besides, I hope we'll complement each other. It's seldom helpful to be too direct in an interview."

"That's true." Enna leaned back. She was beginning to like her new colleague. Boss—well, on paper he was, but he wasn't making it obvious. He also respected her feedback. They would get used to each other.

"Well, now that that's out of the way, shall we look at our case?"

Enna smiled and nodded.

"That's a good idea. Besides, you knew his brother and are from around here, so he will trust you." Pavel typed on his computer. A moment later, her cell phone vibrated. "I sent you his address and home number."

"Thanks. We'll leave the parents alone for now?"

"Yes. The father in particular seems very upset. You should have seen him when we were talking."

Enna raised her eyebrows.

"Sorry," her boss said. "We don't know anything about the victim's relationships at the moment, except that his stepmother probably thought he was gay."

"Did you order the cell phone records?"

"I ordered them, yes. They might arrive tonight."

"Excuse me?"

"Might be here tonight."

"I mean..." Enna smiled. Never mind. "Lucky you. Usually, it takes days."

"Old relationships."

Of course. Pavel probably had better connections at the LKA.

"I was told at the retirement home that the victim once

showed up there with a 'worldly woman' of about the same age as the deceased."

"A mysterious lover?" asked Enna. Toni had never given the impression that he would attract glamorous women. He always seemed rather unremarkable to her. Just normal.

Pavel shrugged. "We need to talk to the bank and the retirement home about the victim's finances and his family's."

"Tomorrow, after the pathologist?" Enna suggested. "Nils is expecting us at one."

Pavel typed again and then took a picture of his screen. "Then let's go take a look at his apartment now."

Damn. Why hadn't she thought of that? Without Pavel, she would have forgotten this important step. That was probably because she had never done a complete investigation on her own before. She needed to become more independent.

Her cell phone vibrated. She opened the message and found a section of Google Maps. The red marker was in a residential area just outside the city limits, near the dike.

Pavel seemingly thought of everything.

"Toni didn't have a family of his own, did he?" asked Pavel as they approached the address where the victim was registered.

Enna shook her head. The question was understandable since a lot of single-family homes had been built here in the 1970s, too big for a single person. It was also impractical for someone who worked downtown, since the local bus only ran three times a day, and during the summer months the main road to Fleetstedt was almost always jammed.

Why did Toni rent a house here? She drove the car down an S-shaped street. The houses were brick, with no plaster. The front yards were manicured to varying degrees. Where there was playground equipment, it was abandoned, the typical fate of a housing development where the children born when the families moved in had grown up, but had not yet inherited the little house.

House number fourteen stood out from the rest. It had the same boring façade, with the typical triangular roof. But a steel staircase led up to a gleaming white door. The roof was also freshly tiled.

Enna parked the car in front of the leftmost of the two garages that belonged to the house. The right-hand one was open. A small workshop was set up inside. A lamp was burning on the table, but no one was there. When they reached the fence, the first thing they heard was a dog barking. It was a shaggy Bernese Mountain Dog. It appeared friendly, but Enna still preferred to keep her distance. To the dog, they were intruders.

"Hello? Is anyone home? It's the police!" her boss yelled.

"Hello, someone's finally here!"

An elderly woman came around the house to the fence. She was wearing a blue coat and holding a scythe. Enna recognized a whetstone in her waist bag, which looked like a huge, horizontal penis underneath the fabric. She estimated the woman to be over seventy years old. Could this be the worldly woman who had been seen at the retirement home? Rather unlikely. Maybe she was prejudiced, but the woman didn't strike her that way.

Pavel introduced them and then asked: "Why 'finally'? Did you call us?"

"I certainly did. There's a smell coming from my tenant's apartment."

"You mean Toni Sattelmacher?"

"Yes."

"And who are you?"

"Elisabeth Thönissen, but I already told your colleague that, didn't I? Very nice to meet you."

The old woman held out her hand over the fence. The dog barked. Pavel didn't return the greeting. Was he pretending to be afraid of the dog? The old woman had a vise-like grip. She involuntarily imagined her strangling Toni and dumping him in the North Sea. She wouldn't have had to go far, but smelling unpleasant odors was a weak motive. She smiled, and Ms. Thönissen smiled back. No, she was a spirited but kind old lady who liked to have things tidy. In fact, the garden was very well-kept, and Enna could easily believe that she had extended the attic and re-roofed it herself.

"That's where the stench is coming from," Elisabeth Thönissen said, pointing to the stairs. "Don't be offended, but my knees..." She pointed at her legs.

"We need the key," Pavel said.

Thönissen reached into her pocket and took out a bunch of keys. She pulled one key off the metal ring.

"I have to tell you that we're not here because of your report," Pavel said. "That's why we'd like to talk to you afterward."

"I have no plans today. Shall I make some tea? Thiele, I'd better tell you now."

"Who's Thiele?" asked Pavel.

"Excuse me?" Thönissen replied, but certainly not because she hadn't understood the question. Thiele and Bünting were the two leading tea brands in the area. Actually, they were more in Bünting's territory here.

"Who is Thiele?" Pavel repeated.

"You'll have to excuse him," Enna said. "He's not from around here. I'll explain later, boss."

"Do you want tea now?"

"Oh, no need, Ms. Thönissen. We still have a lot to do today." Enna sighed. This was not how she had pictured her day off.

"Well, what I wanted to tell you, Ms. Thönissen: Your lodger won't be coming back."

"Is he in jail?" The woman clenched her hands at her sides.

"No, he's dead."

Elisabeth Thönissen put her hand over her mouth. "He's not up there, is he? I'll never get the smell out!"

"No, don't worry, the body is well refrigerated in the morgue. It would be very kind of you if you could come and identify him tomorrow."

Her boss had a very good idea. Thönissen looked much fitter

than Toni's parents, who would probably prefer to be relieved of this burden.

"That's ... interesting. Like on TV?" Enna could see that she was struggling with herself. "Can you pay for a taxi for me?"

"Even better," Pavel said. "We'll send a police car for you."

Ms. Thönissen's eyes lit up like a child's. Enna always liked it when people were happy.

"Do you think they could turn on the lights?"

She didn't think her new boss would allow it. But he surprised her: "Well, if there's a traffic jam on the highway and you're late..."

"You wouldn't believe how much I enjoy being driven with the lights on," he whispered to her as they climbed the steep stairs to Toni's apartment.

The source of the stench was in a bowl in the sink. It was red and bloody. Flies were buzzing around it.

"It's a steak," Pavel said and went to the window. When it was open, a gust of wind blew in and shooed the flies away.

Enna held her nose, which felt strange with rubber gloves on, and examined the meat. It didn't have the typical shape of a beef steak. She recognized the individual strands of muscle separated by white connective tissue and tendons. "A leg of venison, I'd say."

"Isn't that ... unusual?"

"You think we only eat sheep here, or what?"

"And shrimp or fish, of course."

"Haha, you'll find out what we have here. Deer too. But I'm afraid that won't help us."

"At least we can now almost definitely rule out the possibility that Toni went into the water on purpose. He started preparing this piece of meat, and then probably just left his apartment for a bit."

Pavel took down the left-hand curtain and used it to swat at the swarm of flies. He managed to drive three-quarters of them towards the window. Then he wrapped the stinking meat in the curtain and, after checking its contents, put it in the refrigerator. "It's well stocked," he called after her as she began to examine the small bathroom.

There was a tuft of hair in the shower drain, which she placed in a sample bag. She also added a hairbrush and a toothbrush. The selection of toiletries was limited to typical men's products. Either Toni had not been in a relationship shortly before his death, or he had been in love with a man. But there wasn't even a visitor's toothbrush.

In the closet, which was off the open-plan living area, were fifteen moving boxes stacked in three rows. Enna lifted the top one. They were filled to the brim. The sides were labeled with words like "nursery," "kitchen," or "basement," but all in different handwriting. Toni must have borrowed the boxes from somewhere.

"I've got his bank statements," she heard from the living room. "That's interesting."

Enna left the bathroom. Pavel stood in front of the desk with the drawer open. He held out one of the accounts toward her. There was a large minus sign at the bottom.

"Over a hundred thousand in debt," she said in astonishment.

"Unfortunately, only the last two months' statements are here."

Enna read the heading: "Ostfriesische Volksbank eG." There was a small branch in Fleetstedt, left over from the formerly independent Fleetstedter Volksbank. The bank's headquarters were in Leer.

"Do you know anyone there?" asked Pavel.

"What do you mean?"

"I mean, do you know anyone who works at the local branch?"

Enna smiled. "Possibly, but is it relevant? A letter from the prosecutor and we get access to the accounts."

Pavel remained serious. "I realize that. But that will take time. Toni is dead. Who would be harmed if someone told us about his financial position? We aren't investigating the victim."

That was an interesting legal opinion. Her old boss had thought similarly, but had kept her out of such investigations. She was surprised that the former LKA man was willing to do the same. Somehow it didn't fit in with the meticulously tidy desk.

"You look taken aback, Enna."

"No, everything's fine. I'm just thinking about who I might know." She thought about the two high school classes that had graduated with her, then the classes above them. "Michaela!" she exclaimed. She had started an apprenticeship as a bank clerk, instead of going to university like most people, because she didn't want to leave home. Was she still working in Fleetstedt? There hadn't been a branch here since the Postbank had a counter in the supermarket.

"Michaela's fine," Pavel said. "Can you call her?"

"Later, in the office?"

"No, best now."

Enna sighed, took her smartphone out of her pocket, and tried to dial, but the screen didn't respond. She left the apartment to take off her glove. On the landing, she almost ran into Elisabeth Thönissen.

"Watch out, young lady!"

Oh, had her knees suddenly gotten better? Enna suppressed a suitable retort. They needed some more information from her, and while she was here...

"Excuse me, but I can't let you in here, Ms. Thönissen."

"This is my apartment! Are you going to lock me out?"

"In half an hour a crime scene investigator will come and take a close look at everything," she said, but she meant *take everything apart*. "Only then will the apartment be accessible."

"So is he dead in the bathtub?"

Excuse me? Ms. Thönissen seemed to have gotten things mixed up. "I told you, Mr. Sattelmacher is lying in the morgue."

"Lying there? That sounds like he's on vacation."

Enna took a deep breath. "You can't say that in his condition. You will come tomorrow at one o'clock to identify him, right?"

"Oh yes, that's right, when the police car picks me up with its lights flashing."

"I'm sure your officer won't have the lights on the whole time."

"Your boss promised me!" That's what Pavel got. One shouldn't promise such things to elderly ladies. But that was his problem, not hers.

"Please tell me, when did Mr. Sattelmacher start living with you?"

"Living? But... Oh. Since... Since I had the attic converted."

"And when did he move in? Was it a long time ago?"

"No, about three months ago. And he still hasn't paid me the deposit."

That would not happen now. Ms. Thönissen could try to claim the money from the heirs, but if Enna understood the amount on the bank statement correctly—and there was little room for misunderstanding—Toni had been pretty broke. That was a possible motive for suicide, but they couldn't assume that. The question was whether he was killed because of his debts.

"How did you end up with him as a tenant?"

"I ... I don't remember. My age, Ms. Koopmann."

Thönissen remembered her name, which Pavel had mentioned only briefly as a greeting, but seemed to have forgotten how she had met Toni.

"Did you place an ad? We can easily check."

The old woman shook her head. "The roofer probably told him that an apartment would be available here soon."

The roofer? Why didn't she just say that? Something wasn't right. "What's the roofer's name? I'm sure he'll be able to confirm that."

"Fritz Si..." The old woman sighed. "All right. I don't want to involve Fritz. It went through Jette."

"Who is Jette?"

"Henriette Meier. I'm sure you know her, Frau Wachmeisterin. She sits on the town council and runs the Fleetstedt Business Association."

Enna didn't care what people called her, as long as they talked to her. Meier, Henriette. The name meant something to her. Not from an election poster, but from her private past. Right! That was the woman who had tried to persuade her to sell her parents' house, even though they were still living there. The head of the economic department later explained to her that the new owners could profit significantly from deductions for allowing her parents to live in the house until the end of their lives. Not only would the new owners get the house for less, but they would also benefit from its increase in value.

"Ms. Meier is a realtor, right?"

"Actually, she is a notary. But sometimes she brings buyers and sellers together, she explained to me. But please don't give her any trouble. It was just a favor, and she didn't charge me or Mr. Sattelmacher anything."

He could hardly have afforded it. But how had the notary found Sattelmacher? Most importantly, was this a motive? The Federal Law on Notaries forbade those in Ms. Meier's profession to mediate in real estate transactions or to participate in any kind of mediation of deeds. What if Toni had known something that would ruin Ms. Meier's career? A notary who violated the terms of her office would certainly be unacceptable to the city council.

"Thank you for telling me the truth. You know it always comes out."

"But don't tell Jette that you heard it from me. Please." Ms. Thönissen widened her eyes and looked at her.

Enna felt bad that an old woman was literally begging her. "I'll see what I can do. But will you come to see us tomorrow? We need your official statement as well."

"I will come."

The steps of the steel staircase squeaked as Ms. Thönissen descended them. Enna turned back to the apartment, which still smelled of rotting meat.

"When did Toni last leave the house?" she called after the landlady.

"The last time I saw him was four days ago. The day before yesterday I heard the stairs squeaking. I came right out to ask him about the deposit, but no one was there."

"And the smell?"

"Since yesterday. It gets hot under the roof in the sun, even with the new insulation."

She reached for the door again but suddenly remembered what she had forgotten to do: call her old friend Michaela. She looked up the number for the Fleetstedt Volksbank branch and dialed it. A man answered.

"Hello, you've reached the Fleetstedt branch of the Ostfriesische Volksbank eG. This is Otto Kammerer. What can I do for you?"

"Hello, could you please connect me to Michaela?" She tried to remain as non-committal as possible to make it as easy as possible for this Otto.

"She's not here. Who is this?"

"Police Inspector Enna Koopmann." Maybe that would help.

"Madam Inspector. Ah. Nice of you to contact me." Suddenly she remembered the face. Otto Kammerer usually sat at the counter when she came in to do business at the bank.

"I really need to speak to Michaela."

Kammerer sighed. "She's on leave because of the baby."

"Oh, when did that happen?" She hadn't heard about it!

"I've been here by myself for three weeks. The head office in Leer promised to send a replacement, but nothing has happened. And the holidays are coming. I'll be swamped with tourists."

"I'm sorry," Enna said. "Thanks for the information." She hung up.

Holding her nose, Enna ventured back into the apartment. The stench seemed to have increased. Pavel seemed to take little notice, leafing through folders he must have found in one of the moving boxes.

"So did you get through to your old friend? What did she say?"

"Nothing. She's been on maternity leave for the past three weeks. I'll talk to her tomorrow."

Pavel looked up at her briefly. Was he unhappy? If he was, he didn't show it.

"The landlady told me something interesting. Toni Sattelmacher was referred to her by a notary, Henriette Meier. She's probably in real estate on the side, too."

"Which she's not allowed to do." Pavel jumped up. "That's great! Our first viable suspect!" He patted her shoulder. Enna felt warm inside. The praise felt completely sincere. That was the advantage of sentences without subtext.

Pavel sat down again. "I think it's a bit early to arrest her."

Enna puffed out her cheeks. "Yes, my head is already spinning, and I don't think we'll get any further today. Without the pathologist's report, we're at a standstill."

"You're probably right. Let's leave it at that for today. You're still on vacation."

Enna smiled weakly. "That's why I'm going to have dinner at a very good Italian restaurant for the end of my vacation, and then have a nightcap at the Deichkante. Will you join me?"

Neuhof furrowed his brow. "Italian sounds nice. Deichkante sounds more like a lot of beer and schnapps."

"It sounds like that, but the name doesn't come from *getting wasted*. The Deichkante is a venerable, traditional pub, Pavel."

"I see. Thank you very much."

Enna didn't understand. "For what?"

"For keeping me from putting my foot in it."

"Oh, right, yes. My pleasure. Are you coming with me now, or do you want to continue watching that plant grow?"

Neuhof looked at the potted plant on the low coffee table as if he had just noticed it. Then he raised his finger as if to object, but lowered it again and nodded, to Enna's surprise.

Chapter Seven

When the door to the Deichkante opened, Pavel halted like a stubborn horse. It must be the cloud of smoke billowing from the room, as if a DJ inside had just turned on his fog machine. Enna tapped her boss on the shoulder as he turned to let a six-foot-tall man in a leather suit pass, a man who looked like he had a barrel strapped around his stomach. He was dragging a large beer banner behind him, along with two young women in blouses unbuttoned almost to their navels and short skirts. Enna followed them with her eyes; outside, the women joined the man, one on his left and the other on his right, and went merrily on their way.

Enna turned back. Suddenly she was alone. How had Pavel managed to disappear? He couldn't have escaped. Had he scurried inside? Unbelievable!

She yanked the door open, and an elderly gentleman in a suit with too-short pant legs, who had probably been leaning against the door on the inside, lurched toward her. She caught him by the arms, but the momentum was too much for him, so he grabbed hold of one of the high tables. Fortunately, the three men there reacted quickly, using their left hands to pick up their beer glasses and their right hands to hold the table in place.

It was a busy night at the Deichkante. It was already after 10

PM, and with closing time at midnight, the passionate beer drinkers were hurrying to reach their individual targets.

Enna was a little annoyed. They shouldn't have spent so much time in the Italian restaurant. The Deichkante also served food, but since it was a smoking establishment, the thick smoke quickly spoiled the taste. So they'd chosen to eat and talk in the Italian restaurant.

Pavel was quite entertaining if you let yourself into his world. He knew everything about new detection methods for all kinds of traces, everything about the Starship Enterprise, everything about the Swedish coins he collected, everything about every aspect of German law, but nothing about life.

Enna began to suspect that Pavel might be autistic. He seemed to see emotions like ... yes, like constructs. Like interesting concepts that controlled people. Cause and effect. He seemed to be devoid of emotions. That was why he spoke without subtext and analyzed everything in detail. She wondered if that was a good or even outstanding quality in a criminologist. Approaching a case without emotions and analyzing it thoroughly was always a promising and expedient approach. On the other hand, he probably didn't understand emotional motives, and the majority of cases ended up being crimes committed by people the victim knew, as the statistics of the Federal Bureau of Investigation showed. Pavel could only logically deduce such motives, not comprehend them.

Was that why he had spent the morning doing gymnastics on the Dietrichsens' roof beams, to get a "feel" for the crime? That would be like him ...

He had also told her in two sentences—between an anecdote about the Enterprise (the starship would weigh only a few pounds if one calculated its weight from the data in the series) and a crazy surveillance story in Kiel about a dealer—that his ex-wife had left him because of his lack of emotions. That also fit the picture. Enna couldn't imagine how someone could live with a man like Pavel. Although ... when she thought of the drama she'd gone through with her ex-boyfriend, who had been downright jealous of her job and the unpredictable overtime, perhaps cold logic was the better choice. Or maybe a predictable, reliable dog.

The thought of Pete started to bring on the grief again, but Enna pushed it away. After fifteen years of Pete accompanying her and sleeping by her side every night, she had mourned long enough. Slowly a space for something new was opening up again, Enna felt. Eventually, she would get another dog from the shelter.

Would Pavel be all right with her bringing a dog to the office? She thought about his show of fear at Toni's landlady's dog, but didn't know if he was really afraid of the dog or if he was just faking it to keep his distance. Distance seemed to be very important to him. Another reason why he would be difficult to live with.

It was always said that North Germans were reserved and cool, but once they let someone get close to them, they were warm and loyal for the rest of their lives. It sounded like a fairy tale, but it appealed to Enna. Did Pavel have those traits? Would he stay that way, or would he change his mind like a leaf in the wind depending upon his needs?

Only time would tell. He had talked about trust, but was he capable of it? He would nod, but what did he know about life?

Perhaps the thought was unfair and it was she who had no idea about life, or they both knew everything but lived in different worlds, or, and she had to admit this as well, they lived in the same world and neither had a clue about it.

But maybe she was already a little drunk from the delicious Italian red wine, a Nero Amaro from Apulia if she remembered correctly.

"Here, Enna, your beer," said Tina, the waitress who worked there almost every day.

"Wait, have you seen my boss?"

"No idea. Got special license plates?"

"Kiel number! He's tall! He looks like a tourist."

"Ahh! Is that him over there with the three Dutchmen?" Tina pointed to the other end of the bar, where four men were huddled together. The one sticking out the farthest was Pavel.

"Thanks," Enna said with relief, took a sip of her beer, and made her way over to the small group. Because of its small size, the Deichkante benefited from the special rules for one-room pubs when it came to smoking. But she didn't come here for the smoking—Enna had never smoked—but for the people. No one here had ever asked her about her shorts and colorful socks. The landlord, Andreas, could tell when a fight was brewing, and thanks to his broad build and a baseball bat under the bar, he had no problem getting the brawlers out into the fresh air. Even when she came here alone at night, no patron, no matter how drunk, had ever approached her in an unwanted manner.

Pavel also had a beer in front of him. The glass was half empty. Half full, he would have said. They had already worked that out. With the three Dutchmen blocking her way, she simply ducked under Pavel's left armpit to reach the bar, where he was using beer foam to draw the outline of the Starship Enterprise on the shiny gold surface of the bar. During the day, the edge of the bar looked worn, but at night it shone, precisely because the landlord, Andreas, only lit every second lamp on the walls. It also lit up the heads of the guests and the flashes of humor that constantly appeared at the few tables and made people laugh.

The DJ started a new set. It was a pop song. Enna felt like her head would burst if she had to remember the name of the singer —but since all the other customers were dancing, she couldn't resist. And, oh wonder of wonders, even Pavel danced along. "It's a Cha-Cha," he shouted in her ear, and it soon became clear that he knew all there was to know about standard and Latin dances, too.

"That was fun," Pavel said as they stepped out into the street, along with a throng of customers, shortly after midnight.

Enna nodded, laughing, and had the crazy urge to light a cigarette because she couldn't breathe without the smoke.

But Pavel didn't give her the chance to ask anyone for cigarettes. He pulled her along until they got to a street lamp, and looked at the other customers. Then he motioned to her and they walked in the opposite direction, where a dirty yellow Mercedes taxi was coming towards them. It slowed and stopped beside them as if by magic.

"You've done well with your shrewd foresight!" Enna laughed, exhilarated. "I think it would be a stretch for me to walk home tonight."

"I can see that. You've had a lot to drink, too." He gallantly opened the right rear door for her. Enna got in and slid over to the other side. Before she realized she was alone, the door slammed shut and the driver drove off as if he had read her home address from her mind.

"Hey, pull over! My colleague."

Enna turned around in the back seat to look for Pavel. His tall figure stood in the light of the lantern, waving goodbye. Then she realized. "Oh," came from her lips, followed by a burp and a giggle. She closed her eyes and said softly to the cabbie: "You'll wake me up, won't you?"

She did not hear him answer, "Yes."

Chapter Eight

The night was still young. While Pavel had been telling the Dutchmen about the Enterprise, an idea had occurred to him. He had thought about it the whole time, but hadn't dared to leave the corner.

The two beers had loosened his inhibitions.

At first, he hoped to avoid it. He had dutifully sent Enna Koopmann home and gone to the police station, which lowered his blood alcohol level to an estimated and manageable 0.8 per milliliter. But he had still hoped to be able to lie down under his desk with a blanket and go to sleep.

The two envelopes on his desk forbade him to do so. But he ignored them for now. That was what they deserved. When they had been sitting in the office, Enna had seemed somehow tense to him. It was almost as if she couldn't bear to have him looking at her back. He didn't want anyone to feel uncomfortable in his presence. He carried his computer over to the other side of the desk and pushed the chair behind it. The casters squeaked. He should oil them.

Tomorrow. Now it was the folders' turn. As instructed, Sergeant Berger had analyzed the navigation system of Sattelmacher's car, which the crime scene investigator had taken from the parking lot next to the widow Thönissen's house. The second folder contained the call records of Sattelmacher's cell phone. He placed the two lists next to each other and took a deep breath.

The phone list contained data from the last six months, almost five hundred calls. The list from the navigation system had only fifty entries, but with several stopovers. Pavel decided to merge the two. He entered the date, time, and destination of each call and trip into a chronological list, taking about twenty seconds per entry. After three hours of work, his back hurt and his eyes burned, but he had completed it.

But he wasn't done yet. He wrote a small script that visualized the data spatially, tested it, and finally ran it. The script drew a thick, red circle over an enlarged image of northern Germany. This was the central zone where Sattelmacher had spent the last six months and where he had been in contact. And that zone was not here, just beyond the dike, but in the comparatively distant city of Hamburg. Sattelmacher had refueled, eaten, phoned, and probably lived there, since a trip always ended at a certain location in Hamburg in the evening and began there again the next morning.

Pavel zoomed in on that section. He started with the captain's houses in Övelgönne, fancy old buildings where rich people lived. But Sattelmacher had only parked there occasionally. There was also an expensive retirement home nearby. Maybe he had met the worldly woman Jenny Kring had described there, if she wasn't the notary and secret real estate agent. No, Kring had said that the worldly woman was about Toni's age. The notary was out of the question. Henriette Meier had already been eliminated from his personal ranking of the most likely suspects, and Toni had often spent the night in the north of St. Pauli, Hamburg's notorious red-light district. Had he made contact with the underworld there? This case seemed to be much more complicated than he had thought. He didn't like that. Hamburg was in another state. They couldn't do an official investigation there. The fact that he was no longer with the LKA would probably make his life more difficult.

What would Koopmann think? She was clever and extremely adept at leading conversations. If Pavel could feel envy, he would have envied her this ability. But perhaps he could learn from her. They'd have to go to Hamburg together. Saturday would be a good day. Then they wouldn't arouse suspicion at the office. He didn't care about that, but he didn't want gossips making fun of his subordinate. He smiled, or so he thought. He quickly took the pocket mirror he'd bought especially for this purpose out of the drawer, but when he looked at himself in it, his face seemed quite normal. He pulled up the corners of his mouth, but that made him look like a clown.

Never mind. He put the mirror back, turned around so that he could see Enna's chair, and imagined that Toni Sattelmacher was sitting in it. While the dead man was obviously bored and jiggled his knee, he moved the mirror back and forth with a slight twitch in the corner of his eye. He saw a middle-aged man, born in Fleetstedt, who had achieved a lot in his youth. But now he had large debts, and he was also dead. What had taken him to Hamburg? Toni Sattelmacher didn't answer.

Pavel let his thoughts take over. He went back to the telephone lists. In the days before his death, Toni had spoken to his parents, once very briefly to his brother Heiner, to his landlady—who had called him, probably to ask for the deposit—and to a Danish number and another German number, but the provider had given faked data. However, as soon as he was in Hamburg, his contacts changed. From Fleetstedt, only his father kept in touch with him, albeit in a rather one-sided way, because Toni never called him.

Pavel thought about the cropped photos in the box on Sattelmacher's desk. His father had been very upset about them. Why would someone cut up family photos and remove Toni's image? It had to be someone close to him. But who? The mother? The brother? The father himself, without remembering? Had he been so upset because he suspected he had done it himself?

Pavel made a note to ask for the parents' medical records.

Then he tapped his chin with a pen. Why had Toni died? What was the motive? His instructor at the police academy had advised him: Follow the trail of either money or blood. Was this the result of a relationship? Or had Toni's life in Hamburg caught up with him? A landlady like Elisabeth Thönissen could be persuaded to wait for a deposit. Certain people from the Hamburg scene couldn't. That would fit in with Toni's mountain of debts.

Pavel zoomed out the computer-generated overview and tapped first on Fleetstedt, then on Hamburg. *Which one of them killed you?* In the big city, violent crime was the order of the day. In the tourist areas on the coast, women were beaten up just as often, but very few people were killed. But a lot of people here just pretended to Nordic cool. A hatred that had been repressed for a long time could just as easily find its final release here. Could, could, could.

He saved his map, turned off the computer, and went to sleep under the desk.

Chapter Nine

Fleetstedt had its share of public housing, but it was cleverly hidden behind dark red brick facades and black plastic window frames. The neighborhood was relatively new, built just a few years ago as more and more downtown apartments were repurposed.

Signs advertising vacation rentals were on every corner.

Enna was always surprised at how many there were. It felt like half of Fleetstedt was a vacation resort. But there were neither vacation homes nor tourists in the long stretch of row houses.

Enna parked right in front, looked around, and rubbed her temples. Her head was still throbbing from the red wine. Or from the beer and the loud music at the Deichkante. She had taken a painkiller with her porridge to be on the safe side, which hadn't really helped yet. But she had no regrets. The evening had been great.

Grinning, she got out of the car. Even on duty, she wore shorts—with the permission of her old boss, of course. Today her socks were decorated with green and gold pineapples.

She walked along the front of the apartment building and finally stopped in front of number eleven. *Sattelmacher* was written on one of the doorbells. She pressed it and waited.

After half a minute she rang it again, this time longer. She stepped back from the door and looked up at the windows. A child looked down from behind one of the panes and quickly disappeared. There were no other curious people to be seen, which surprised Enna. She would have expected a lot of older people in the apartment building.

When she rang for the third time, the door buzzed and she hurried inside.

Heiner Sattelmacher lived on the second floor. With disheveled hair and dark circles under his eyes, he stood in the doorway and looked visibly surprised when he recognized Enna.

"What are you doing here?" he muttered. "Are you on duty?"

"Officially." She showed him her ID, as per the rules. "Can I come in?" She didn't really want to, because the apartment smelled musty, sour, and of cold smoke, which reminded her of the Deichkante. Heiner probably hadn't aired out the room in a long time.

"Fine by me." He stepped back, clearing the way. Still, she had to squeeze past him, for Heiner Sattelmacher had grown quite a belly, hanging over his jogging pants. The fact that he must have been in good shape a few years ago was only visible in his massive arms.

Enna immediately regretted her decision, because the apartment smelled even worse from the inside. It looked terrible, too. Old pizza boxes were piled on the living room table next to an overflowing ashtray. Empty cans of Coke and beer from the discount store were everywhere.

Enna first opened a window, as Pavel had done in the office, then stood next to it with her arms crossed and looked at Heiner, who had sunk back onto the sofa. He was wearing a stained tracksuit that should have been washed—or better yet, thrown away—long ago. Heiner would have benefited from a shave and a shower, too. Toni's brother looked tired.

"What do you want?" he asked, grumbling and lighting a cigarette. "Did something happen?"

Either he didn't know or he was pretending not to. "When was the last time you saw your brother?"

Heiner snorted. "Just yesterday morning. Toni suddenly

showed up at the door. He'd called earlier, and I told him to go to hell."

Sounded like brotherly love. "What did he want?"

"I don't know. To discuss something."

"You don't know what?"

Heiner shrugged, took a drag on his cigarette, and blew the gray haze toward the yellowed ceiling. "What do I know? I yelled at him and wouldn't let him in when he came to the door. You know, he shows up after months and wants something, but otherwise, he never contacts me. That asshole. It's always about him."

It seemed that someone was angry with their older brother. "In what way?"

Heiner started to answer, but then he frowned. "Why do you want to know, Enna?"

She sighed. "Your brother was found dead yesterday."

Heiner narrowed his eyes. "Toni?"

"Do you have another brother? Toni was found floating in the North Sea."

"Shit!"

"That's one way of putting it." Enna pulled up an empty stool and sat down. "My condolences, Heiner."

He just shook his head. "Seriously? You're not bullshitting me?"

"Unfortunately not."

"Jeez. That's great." Heiner puffed out his cheeks and couldn't stop shaking his head. Ashes fell on his shirt.

Enna pursed her lips. "Should I leave you alone or would you like to answer some more questions?"

He growled angrily. "What do you want to know?"

"What did you mean about it always being about him?"

He waved it off with a snort. "It was always about Toni. Toni here, Toni there, Toni everywhere. I couldn't listen to it anymore."

"How did it come to that?"

Heiner shrugged, looking almost like a helpless boy who didn't understand it himself. "He was just better. In everything.

At school, at home, everywhere. No matter what I did, it was never good enough."

"And then you moved out?"

"No. Then I quit school and did my apprenticeship. With Tscherniak. Schwalbe Car Service."

Enna remembered seeing Heiner in the workshop once. But the garage had been closed for years after Tscherniak suddenly disappeared. Was that because of Heiner?

"I worked like that," Heiner continued. "Until it got to be too much for me to deal with my father. Then I moved out." He said it in a strangely sad way, which made Enna sit up.

"Didn't your family live somewhere near the dike?"

"Yes, in the old Gulfhaus."

Enna remembered that. It had been a beautiful, park-like property full of trees and bushes, in the middle of which had stood an old East Frisian Gulfhaus, nestled between the dike and the undergrowth. Yes, she had gone there as a child. A green paradise to play in.

Heiner nodded, but with bitterness in his moist eyes. "I loved it there. That's what broke me."

"What exactly?"

"Moving out. Somehow I left something behind and never found it again." He shrugged as if it wasn't important, then shook his head again. "Toni. Shit. When's the funeral?"

Enna raised her shoulders. "I don't know. He has to be autopsied first. That'll take a while."

Heiner's mouth tightened. An old scar appeared on his lip. "You're going to cut him open?"

"We have to. The circumstances of his death are still unclear."

"I see. Meaning what?"

"That we don't know how he died. But we're going to find out. So if you think of anything else that might help us, let us know." She took out a business card and placed it on the table in a reasonably clean spot. Ash immediately shimmered on the white paper.

Heiner looked at the card, then at Enna. Something flickered in his watery eyes. "Do you suspect me now or what?"

Enna shook her head. "We don't suspect anyone, Heiner. We don't even know if he died of natural causes or not. But it's reasonable to ask why he was floating dead in the North Sea. He could swim."

Heiner nodded. "Toni was a great swimmer. He was great at everything. I think he even belonged to a club in Hamburg."

"In Hamburg?"

"Yeah. He lived there. He used to come here for a week or two and then go back there. He probably makes good money too. No, he *made* good money, the asshole. Everything fell into his lap. Everything! Everything he touched turned to gold!" Heiner's voice grew louder as he worked himself into a rage.

Enna tensed. "Heiner."

"What?" he barked. "That's the way it is! You know it's true, don't you? Or what do you want to hear? That I had something to do with his death? Will you ask me about my alibi?" Heiner came out of his slumped position and sat forward on the edge of the sofa. Suddenly his arms seemed even bulkier. "Is that why you're here, asking me these nasty questions? What do you call them? Leading questions, right? Yes! That's what they call it. You're trying to trap me. Right?"

Enna stood up to look taller. "No," she said firmly. "I'm not accusing you of anything. I'm just doing my job."

"Yes, yes. Are you even supposed to be doing that? You've *officially* been Toni's girlfriend for twenty years. I know the story my mother constantly tells my father because he's somehow taken a shine to you. Policewoman. Pah! Is that why you're here? Did my parents send you? That would be just like them! Let little Enna kick the shit out of Heiner." He stood up and approached her threateningly. "Admit it! You're just trying to frame me!"

Enna snorted loudly. "You're crazy, Heiner." She flipped him the bird and headed for the door. "But the question of your alibi is legitimate. If I don't ask you, my boss will. You might as well talk to my boss if you're going to accuse me of shit."

Heiner glared at her, and for a moment she was afraid he was going to explode, but then he deflated like a balloon with the air let out and flopped back down on the sofa.

Enna looked at the pile of misery before shaking her head and leaving the room.

Suddenly she heard a soft "Enna?"

She stopped in her tracks. "Yes?"

Heiner's voice, now tired. "For what time period do you need my alibi?"

"From noon the day before yesterday until yesterday morning."

Silence, then a sigh. "I was here then."

"The whole time?"

"Yes."

"Alone?"

"Yes."

Not good for him. "All right. Thank you." She sensed he was going to say something else and paused. He whispered, "Will you let me know when the funeral is?"

Enna was about to say "No," but instead she said, "I'll try to remember, but I can't promise anything."

She heard the rattle of a lighter, followed by a deep breath. "Shit," he muttered. "Shit!"

Enna swallowed the bitter taste in her mouth, rubbed her throbbing temple, and then left Heiner Sattelmacher's stinking apartment.

She was just pulling into the parking lot in front of the police station when the harbormaster said over the speakerphone, "We've had no reports of abandoned boats in the last few days, Enna. I regret to disappoint you. And none have been reported by the Sattelmacher family either."

"All right! Thank you for the information."

"With pleasure and goodbye!"

Neuhof exited the office at that moment and came over to the car. He opened the door and sank into the passenger seat. He looked exhausted. He smelled tired, too. Probably like her.

"Hello," he greeted her dully. "Any new findings?"

"Not much. Heiner said he didn't know anything about Toni's death."

"Do you believe him?"

"Intuitively, yes. But don't hold me to it. It was interesting that Toni probably visited Heiner on the morning of his death, but Heiner didn't want to see him and kicked him out."

"Interesting. Possible motives for the murder?"

Enna spread her hands. "Well, Heiner got pretty loud this morning because he suspected I might blame him for his brother's death. So he did feel pressured very quickly."

"Pressured or treated unfairly?"

Enna hesitated. "That's a very good question. I think he felt that he was being treated unfairly. And that fits the picture. He's probably spent his whole life in his brother's shadow. Jealousy at injustice would be a possible motive in any case, but ... somehow Heiner didn't seem like a murderer to me."

"Even though he was aggressive?"

"Why do you think he was aggressive?"

"You said he got loud."

"Well. It's one thing to feel wronged and another to actively kill someone."

"That's just your subjective perception."

"Sure. Just throwing it out there. By the way, no abandoned boat has been found."

Pavel nodded thoughtfully and scratched his chin. "The weather was calm, too, wasn't it?"

"Absolutely. We only had a light rain the night he died."

"Is that why he was wearing that old-fashioned coat?"

"I don't know." Enna took a package of pink and yellow candies out of the glove compartment. She popped one into her mouth. The taste of raspberry and lemon burst on her tongue. She shook her head. "It doesn't make sense. A coat like that would have been appropriate in a storm, but not in a light rain. Would you like one?"

"No, thank you. So the coat question remains open." Pavel looked thoughtfully at his fingers and abruptly changed the subject. "You're a lifeguard, aren't you?"

Enna smiled. "Heart and soul."

"Very commendable. So you know the local currents."

"On the beaches, yes. Inside the bathing areas too, though they're more like microcurrents. Why do you ask?"

"Well, hopefully, we'll know after the meeting with..."

"...Nils Kessler..."

"...exactly how long Sattelmacher was in the water. That gives us time X. If we know the current conditions and extrapolate the corresponding drift speeds, we should be able to reconstruct quite accurately where Toni Sattelmacher fell into the water."

Enna puffed out her cheeks. "We won't be able to determine it that accurately. We're talking about a body in the open sea."

"Which has a weight Y and, given its size, a resistance to displacement. Weather data is available. Geographical conditions are known. Surely that can be mapped mathematically."

"Have fun with that!"

"You doubt it?"

"Yes. In practice, it can't be determined very accurately. The tidal range alone and the resulting currents are difficult to estimate. On the open sea, the speed of the tidal current is about one and a half feet per second. Near the coast, it can be up to sixteen feet per second. The boundaries are fluid. There's always a range."

"We could create a human-shaped package and lower it into the water. How heavy was Toni?"

"You want to simulate a body?" Enna didn't want to believe it. Her new boss was a bit strange.

"Why not? As long as the weather stays similar and we take the tides into account, it should work. Then we'll put a GPS transmitter on the parcel and find out."

Enna rolled her eyes. "Feel free to explore that yourself if you want. I won't stop you."

Pavel seemed to want to say something in return, but closed his mouth. "What do your thirty-plus years of experience on the ground tell you?"

"I think he went into the water east of where he was found, since that's how the current is flowing at the moment. I would walk the entire coastline from that location. It is a beautiful walk along the beaches and the dike. I highly recommend it."

"And how far would you want to go? One mile? Two miles? Three miles? Five miles? Ten?"

Enna sighed. "You always want to know exactly, don't you?"

"Yes."

"Okay. In Fleetstedt, according to the German weather service, we have an average current speed of about half a mile per hour. The weather has been very calm the last few days, so I would assume less. Maybe two and a half thousand feet per hour. So we're talking ... nine miles at the most. But since we found the body at high tide, it was probably drifting inland in the preceding hours. So not parallel to the coast. Depending on how long Toni was in the water, he could have drifted out at low tide and back in at high tide."

Pavel drew the shape of a wave on his thigh. "I see. So he could have been thrown into the water near the shore."

"Or had an accident there. If he was in the water for a shorter period of time, it's more likely that he fell into the water at sea."

"So you would make it dependent on time?"

"Yes. That's why we're leaving now. Kessler doesn't like to wait. And maybe it was an accident after all. It's still within the realm of possibility, even if it's unlikely." Enna started the car engine and drove off quickly. She deliberately ignored Pavel groaning softly. Instead, she grinned a little to herself.

Once they had left Fleetstedt behind and were heading for Leer, she asked: "Have you got any news?"

"Lots and lots. Toni Sattelmacher led a double life."

"How so?"

"Well, he spent a lot of time in Hamburg. I reconstructed that from his cell phone records and his navigation system."

"When did you do that?"

"Last night."

She narrowed her eyes. "*After* leaving the Deichkante?"

He nodded and continued: "Actually, Sattelmacher spent more time in the Hanseatic city than here."

"You were *still working* after the Deichkante?"

"Absolutely, but can we stay on topic?"

Enna couldn't believe it, but nodded. "So Toni had two lives. Fleetstedt and Hamburg. His brother mentioned that, by the way. Toni probably often went swimming in Hamburg. I assume that's where he worked."

"That still needs to be clarified. In any case, he spent most of his time there in a very expensive area. How does that fit in with his debts? We should take a closer look at that. I suggest we go to Hamburg as soon as possible and take a look around."

Enna looked at her boss, which made him visibly uncomfortable. "Could you please concentrate on the road?"

Enna maintained eye contact for a second before looking ahead again. "You do realize that we can't just go investigating in Hamburg. Jurisdictions and responsibilities and all that."

Pavel sighed. "I'm well aware of that. I will, of course, make an official request."

"All right then." Enna suppressed a shake of her head, which he would insist on interpreting. She wondered what he really meant. If his statements lacked subtext as he claimed, then he had just said that he wanted to go to Hamburg with her and look around. That was quite different from an official request, which might result in her receiving some information by fax.

Pavel Neuhof, the daredevil?

Suddenly she had no idea what to make of him. Didn't he care about rules? Had he left Kiel due to not following the rules?

She thought about him hanging from the rafters with a rope around his neck to simulate a suicide. It could fit.

God, this could be fun ...

Chapter Ten

But first, there was the morgue. The institute was housed in a venerable mansion near Leer. From the outside, no one would have guessed that behind the rusty brownstone facade were corpses stored in gleaming chrome refrigerators. Enna had even seen tourists taking pictures of the fancy house. If they had known what they were photographing, they would have deleted the pictures immediately.

But it was also idyllic. Peonies and sea buckthorn lined the driveway. On the second level, a magnificent elm tree rose into the sky. There was even a bench among the bushes in its shade, an ideal place to linger and read.

Pavel looked around curiously while Enna led him purposefully to the side entrance. There was a simple sign: *Forensic Institute, Branch Office*. Below it was a bell and a modern PIN pad.

"Nice place."

"Almost became a restaurant, but the license never came through."

Pavel laughed. "And then the dead came?"

"Something like that." Enna grinned, the door buzzed, and they entered Kessler's hallowed halls.

The contrast couldn't have been greater. Everything was in muted colors. Large anatomical motifs hung on the walls. The reception desk was deserted. There was only a coffee cup on the desk.

"You can only reach someone here in the morning," Enna explained, walking purposefully along the adjacent corridor. Gray, matte steel doors hung on the walls like modern works of art. The smell of fruit brandy sanitizer hung in the air.

Pavel seemed to be taking in everything at once. His eyes, now alert, darted everywhere.

Enna stopped at the third door. She knocked loudly. A muffled "Come in!" issued from behind it, and they entered.

Nils Kessler was still wearing his knitted cap. He had swapped his coat for a mint-green apron that always reminded Enna of a butcher's shop. His bare arms were covered in bloodstained gloves that extended to just below his elbows.

"Hello!" He seemed visibly pleased. He nodded at Pavel. "You must be the new guy."

"Neuhof."

"Kessler." The pathologist came around the stainless-steel table where Toni Sattelmacher lay and held out a bloodstained hand to Pavel.

He looked at it in horror and stepped back.

Kessler laughed. "Just kidding, Neuhof." He winked and stepped back over to the dead man. "Interesting case here, I have to admit."

Enna also approached the corpse. As always, it was disconcerting to see a body with a y-shaped cut open in front of her, but somehow, she could view the whole thing as a sort of composition, like a piece of abstract art. "In what way?" she asked.

"Well," Kessler began. "The dead man is revealing his secrets in bits and pieces." He pointed to several glass jars on a small cart to the side. One contained water, but whitish particles had settled at the bottom. The other contained a slimy mass.

"This is the contents of Sattelmacher's stomach," Kessler explained. "I found seawater in it."

"Which is not unusual for a body floating in water. After death, the automatic closing mechanisms fail and water seeps in." Curious, Neuhof peered into the open torso.

Kessler scrutinized Pavel. "You're right, Neuhof. But I also found water in the lungs. There is also an emphysematous change in the lungs."

"A distended lung."

Enna looked at her boss in surprise. What didn't he know?

Kessler nodded. "Also correct, Mr. Neuhof. I'm positively amazed. Do you have a medical background?"

"No, just a keen interest." He pointed to dark marks on the dead man's neck. "What are those? Hematomas?"

"Correct. They look suspiciously like evidence of a struggle."

"So it was murder."

Kessler shrugged. "I'll leave the interpretation to you. All I can say is that these bruises are very fresh, close to the time of death. I'd put it at about twenty-two hundred hours, plus or minus two hours. Back to the cause of death: At first I suspected that he drowned, as indicated by the water in his stomach and the distended lungs. But he didn't drown. He died from an external force." Kessler went to the dead man's head and pointed to the spot he had already shown Enna on the beach.

Pavel crouched down and examined the back of the head up close, as if it were an interesting piece of art. "Blunt force trauma?"

"Correct. Severe enough to cause an intracerebral hemorrhage that eventually increased the intracranial pressure. In other words, the pressure was compressing the surrounding brain tissue and interfering with normal brain function. I looked at the brain. The region of the brain that controls breathing was affected! So Mr. Sattelmacher didn't drown, he was beaten to death."

Enna cleared her throat. "And the water entered his lungs after he was dead?"

"I can't reconstruct that for sure. It could have gotten in from lying in the water, but he could also have tried to keep himself from drowning until his brain shut down. Unfortunately, he won't tell me that secret."

"That's not that important," Pavel interjected. "The important thing is that we now know there was a struggle and that he died as a result of an external force."

Enna again looked at the spot on the back of the man's head where Kessler had shaved off some of his hair. "That couldn't be from a fall, could it?"

"Probably not. There are no other injuries to indicate a fall, like abrasions or bruises."

Pavel nodded as if he was already putting the pieces together. "So there was a struggle, then a blow to the back of the head, and then either the body fell into the water or was dumped in the water."

Kessler smiled. "Those are the most likely scenarios, yes. I can also rule out the influence of alcohol. Zero point zero per mil. The drug screening came up empty—I'd have to do a basic toxicology report like Dietrichsen. But I wouldn't push for that under these circumstances."

Pavel didn't seem to like that. "I need the whole picture, Mr. Kessler."

He sighed. "We don't have the money right now. Budgets have been cut again. I'm afraid there's nothing I can do. You're welcome to pay for it out of your own pocket if you really want to."

Pavel furrowed his brow. "Is this another one of your jokes?"

"Unfortunately not. Either someone pays or there won't be an expert opinion in this case. I don't think it's necessary."

Pavel started to object again, but Enna squeezed his arm. "That's okay! The facts are clear enough."

"Good."

Pavel started to speak again, but Enna pulled him away from the autopsy table. "Thanks," she said to Kessler. "That helped a lot."

"Always a pleasure. See you next time."

"Yes, see you next time."

Then they were out the door, leaving Kessler and Sattelmacher behind.

"It's not my problem!"

"Yes, it is. We're lucky he still has a position here. Two years ago there was talk of closing the place down due to lack of funds. Is that what you want? I don't. Let's not get carried away, please. Sattelmacher was bludgeoned to death. It's highly unlikely that there were any fancy drugs or poisons involved, isn't it?"

"That's true, but..."

"No buts, Neuhof. That's enough for us." They walked out of the mansion and into the fresh air. Bees buzzed through the air.

Enna feared he would object again, but Pavel sighed. "I don't agree, but I understand the reasoning. So no toxicology report. All right?"

Enna smiled. "Thank you. Where do we go from here?"

Pavel looked at his watch. "We're waiting for Frau Thönissen. She should be here any minute."

"Right, that's something." Enna looked down the driveway, but there was no police car in sight. "Then we'll use the time until she gets here. Who do we look at next? We're looking for a suspect now."

"Or a murderer!"

"That's what I implied."

"But you didn't say that."

Enna closed her eyes. Pavel could be so finicky.

"It's okay," he said apologetically. "I understand."

"Thank you." Enna leaned against the hood and crossed her arms over her chest. Calmly she asked again: "How do we proceed now?"

"Well, I would like to gather more facts before we go after anyone. Acting with unclear facts is never a good idea."

"Because we run the risk of misinterpretation?"

"Exactly. The clearer the picture, the less room for interpretation. That's why I insist on details, Enna. It's just that no supervisor has ever understood that. They only have their budgets in mind."

"They run our system. Money makes the world go round."

Pavel waved her off. "Speaking of money, I'll go to the bank and check Sattelmacher's finances. His mountain of debt might have something to do with the motives of possible suspects. We need a complete picture there as well."

"Sounds like a good plan. I'll come with you."

"No, I can do it myself. You'd better take care of the land register extracts. I want to know if Sattelmacher owned any property." Pavel eyed her intently. "Why are you furrowing your brow? A thought?"

"Yes. I just realized that none of the Sattelmachers are living in properties they own. The old people in a home, Heiner in public housing, and Toni with Ms. Thönissen."

"What's unusual about that?"

"Well, the Sattelmachers used to have a big property right on the dike. An old Gulfhaus. Beautiful."

Pavel understood at once. "You're wondering why none of the family lives there."

"Yes. It was the Sattelmachers' pride and joy."

"Maybe they rented it out. Or sold it to pay for the retirement home. That didn't look cheap to me."

"Yes. Why do you say that? It takes money to run a place like that."

Before Pavel could respond, a siren sounded in the distance. It wailed for three seconds, then went silent.

A grin appeared on Pavel's face. "Ms. Thönissen."

Enna rolled her eyes. "Why does a little blue light and a siren get people so excited?"

"Not you?"

"Uh ... no." She pushed herself away from the car and stepped toward the street, where a patrol car was approaching, gliding into the parking lot.

Enna opened the door for the old lady and offered her a hand out. She ignored it and got out. Her eyes were bright with excitement. "That was great! Terrific!" She clapped her hands.

Pavel smiled engagingly. "That's good to hear, Ms. Thönissen. Would you follow me, please?"

The old lady became serious. "Of course, Inspector." With her head held high and her cheeks flushed, she followed Pavel, who led her to the entrance of the crime lab.

Enna let them go. She turned to the driver, Sergeant Berger, who had rolled down the window. "Are you all right?"

Berger shrugged in his usual manner, a gesture she had seen a hundred times before. "Everything's fine, Enna. Are you taking her back, or am I playing taxi again?"

"You're playing taxi."

"There are worse things." He leaned over to the glove compartment and pulled out a plastic bag. It contained a ham sandwich cut in half. He took out one half and offered the other to Enna. "Would you like some?"

She looked at the pink ham, thought of the cut-open Toni Sattelmacher, and shook her head.

Berger just nodded and took a hearty bite of his sandwich.

Since Enna didn't want to watch him eat, she walked over to the bench and sat down among the bushes. She waited there until Pavel returned with the old lady. She no longer looked so cheerful and enthusiastic, but rather green around the gills. Without a word of goodbye, she disappeared into the patrol car, which immediately pulled out of the parking lot.

Pavel stopped in front of Enna. "It's Toni Sattelmacher."

"Did you expect anything different?"

"No, but it would have given the case a surprising twist."

Enna laughed. "I suppose you're right. Glad it's him."

"You sound very relieved. Don't you like surprises?"

"Not so much, to be honest. I prefer things to be predictable."

Pavel pursed his lips and said nothing. Maybe that was for the best, because Enna couldn't shake the feeling that with Pavel Neuhof as her new boss, no case would ever be the same again.

Chapter Eleven

The Sattelmachers' Gulfhaus stood out with its huge, velvety red roof. One half of the house was two-story, the other one-story, with a roof that slanted down over the one-story section.

In the past, houses like this had been farmhouses with attached stables, which became widespread in northern Germany in the sixteenth and seventeenth centuries. Today they were known as East Frisian houses.

The Sattelmachers' was in excellent condition and, as Enna recalled, situated in a beautiful park-like setting. Mature trees lined the property. Everything was well-kept. The roof was newly tiled. The lawn was English and lush green.

As she parked in front of the house, the only thing missing was a tea party sitting on the lawn at a table covered with crocheted doilies, enjoying the afternoon. Children playing would have fit the picture too. People in general. There wasn't even a car. Instead, there were two wooden posts sticking out of a patch of grass. Apparently, a signboard had been taken down or was about to be put up. Currently, there was no sign.

Enna looked at the dark windows for a few seconds before getting out. The car door closing sounded too loud. It was extremely quiet. Not a dog barked. Not even a bird could be heard.

Enna shoved her hands into the pockets of her shorts and walked across the yard to the front door. There was no doorbell, either. Not even the mailbox was marked. Not a soul was in sight. But someone had to be living here. The grass was so short that it had to have been cut less than three days ago.

"Maybe a robotic lawn mower," she muttered, peering through the striped glass of the front door. It was quiet inside.

Enna rang and waited and rang and waited.

No one opened the door. Who would? There was no one there.

Enna decided to walk around the house. She set out at a leisurely pace and let her eyes wander. She recognized a tree she remembered from her childhood, but otherwise, nothing else. Then again, decades had passed since her last visit. The garden didn't bring back any other memories.

Finally, she ended up at the front door again. She was annoyed that she hadn't found anyone at the land registry office. They probably only worked there from nine to eleven. Had the Sattelmacher house been sold? Enna could hardly imagine it. Who would give up such a beautiful house and property? There was hardly anything else like it in the area.

The sound of an engine made her look up the long driveway. A dark Mercedes pulled up and stopped next to her car. A gentleman in his fifties got out. "Hello," he greeted her in a friendly manner. "Can I help you?"

"I hope so," Enna replied, pulling out her ID. "May I ask who you are?"

His face became serious. "I am Hinnerk Möller. Architect working for Norddeutsche Küstenkapital GmbH." He took a business card from his inside jacket pocket and handed it to her. "Any problems here?"

Enna studied the card. It looked like a group of investors. She shook her head. "I was actually here to see the Sattelmachers."

"They don't live here anymore. The house has been sold. I'm here because of the planned remodeling."

"I see. What's being planned?"

"Oh, the new owners want to remodel and expand the property. A big project."

Clearly a group of investors. "Is that possible? I thought Gulfhäuser were heritage sites."

"They are, but there are design options."

Enna nodded. "With necessary alterations, of course."

The architect smiled. "That's definitely an advantage. Is there anything else I can do for you? Otherwise, I must be about my business."

Enna shook her head. "I don't want to keep you. If the Sattelmachers don't live here anymore, I'm in the wrong place anyway. Do you know where I can find them?"

"I think at the retirement home. It was quite a drama, to be honest. Well, moving out. Mr. and Mrs. Sattelmacher didn't really want to leave."

Enna could understand that. "Sounds like they had to?"

"I have no idea. All I know is that their son sold the house. They probably had no choice. That can happen when you leave your house to your children."

That was interesting. "Why did Toni sell it? It was Toni Sattelmacher, wasn't it?"

The architect nodded and shrugged. "Don't ask me. I was surprised, too, because Mr. Sattelmacher had just completed extensive renovations. Normally, with today's construction costs, you would sell *before* the renovation, not *after*. But the new owners love it. And now I really have to go. I'm running late. Have a wonderful afternoon!"

"You too. Thank you!"

Enna watched the architect as he disappeared into the garden, then got into her car and replayed the conversation. It confused her. Why had Toni renovated the family home and then sold it to a group of investors? Why had Toni arranged the deal in the first place? Had the Sattelmachers signed the property over to him? It sounded like they had.

That was very interesting, because what about Heiner? Had he lost out again? That would be rough, since there was certainly a lot of money involved.

Enna turned the elegant business card between her fingers. The logo of Norddeutsche Küstenkapital GmbH was embossed in silver foil and shone brightly. The company was based on the island of Norderney.

Enna looked at the house again and estimated that it and the land were worth a million euros, probably more. Construction and renovation costs had only gone in one direction in the last few years: up. Had Toni overextended himself with the renovation? Was that why he had to sell and try to get the highest possible profit through a group of investors?

Too many questions, Enna decided. Pavel was right. They needed answers. Lots of answers.

Chapter Twelve

The Volksbank branch was located in a converted former brick warehouse. The owner had converted the upper two floors into vacation apartments. They must have a perfect view of the small Fleetstedt harbor. An "occupied" sign hung above the entrance. It seemed appropriate to Pavel.

The first floor was divided in two. To the left of the entrance to the apartments was a lottery shop. The bank branch was directly opposite. The arrangement looked like the work of a god with a sense of humor. Bank or lottery? Most people today could only hope to get ahead financially and socially by winning the lottery. Banks only managed what their parents and grandparents had built up and left behind.

No, it had to be a cynical god. Only the operator won the lottery. The chances of winning the millions advertised on the posters were so small! That should be clear to anyone who took a closer look. But many people probably managed to convince themselves that they had a better chance of winning the lottery.

But it was a big misconception that rich people had a monopoly on good fortune. Pavel had enough to do with them professionally to know better. It was the other way around: with money came greed and resentment, which increased the hidden conflicts in families to such an extent that they could apparently only be resolved by violence.

Or was this a *déformation professionnelle*, a professional miscalculation? He was about to open the door when his cell phone vibrated. He didn't recognize the number, but he could tell it was a cell phone. He hated talking to strangers on the phone. Without the accompanying facial expression, the seemingly inevitable subtext was even harder to discern. But something told him it was important. Even though he didn't like the feeling—he didn't care much for feelings—he pressed the green button on the screen.

"This is Doldinger from the crime lab," a woman said.

He still didn't know the name of the local crime lab. When he called her, she had come from Leer, but he had no idea if she was stationed there.

"Neuhof here. What is it, Ms. Doldinger?"

It was always good to call people by their names.

"It's about the samples Ms. Koopmann gave us, and the analysis of the evidence from young Sattelmacher's apartment."

"I'm busy at the moment, Ms. Doldinger. Would you let my colleague...?"

"I haven't been able to reach her yet. That's why I'm trying you."

Right, Enna had wanted to visit the victim's birthplace. "Of course, Ms. Doldinger. What did you find out?"

"You'll get everything in writing, but I thought you'd be interested."

"I can't judge that until I know what you're talking about, Ms. Doldinger."

"Oh, you don't say." Her tone had changed slightly. Somehow he must have annoyed her. That wasn't good. They had to keep the crime lab happy.

"Sorry. I'm very interested in your findings."

He heard a big sigh of relief. "Well, in the samples from the shower, in addition to traces attributable to the victim, we found female hair, head and genital hair from at least two individuals."

Samples from the shower? He hadn't even noticed Enna taking any. But this was exciting. Toni had had a visit from a lady. Was it possible that his landlady hadn't noticed?

"Thank you. And what else?"

"The evidence is confusing. There are a lot of fingerprints that don't belong to the victim. He must have had regular visitors. At least five different people. We found Kleenex with semen on them in the wastebasket."

"Did it belong to the victim? The mother indicated a possible same-sex sexual interest."

"We don't know that yet. We're still waiting for the DNA test results. But the appearance suggests masturbation. You have to imagine that..."

The door to the bank opened. A man stepped out, pulled a set of keys from his pocket, and started to lock up.

"I'm sorry, Ms. Doldinger, I don't have time to imagine that right now."

She probably thought he was a prude, but Pavel didn't care. Everyone had their own limits. But the man who had just come out of the bank had to be Otto Kammerer. He hung up without saying goodbye. "Mr. Kammerer?"

The man had a harried look on his face. He looked at Pavel but showed no recognition. He raised his hands defensively. "Please use the machine at the entrance. I have an urgent errand to attend to."

"Mr. Kammerer, I just wanted to ..." Should he show him his ID? The clerk was behaving very strangely. Well, he was probably alone in the building, so he had to lock up while he was gone. However, he was surely not supposed to leave his workplace during business hours.

The man did not turn around. Pavel looked at his office bicycle, which he had chained to a lamppost. If the man drove off in a car, he would not be able to follow. But Kammerer didn't. He started running down the street toward the market. After three hundred feet, he turned right onto the main road out of Fleetstedt. Pavel followed him after he disappeared around the corner. He ran to be on the safe side, and when he looked around the corner, Kammerer was striding purposefully down the street. After a quarter of a mile, they left the center of the village. Here, the houses looked much grayer. In summer, the main street was probably jammed with traffic, as it ended in a dead end that led to a large underground parking garage.

Still, the houses, mostly row houses that he estimated to be from the 1930s, were quite nice. They had small front yards, and the facades were decorated with maritime symbols. Although, as he had read in Wikipedia, no fishermen had ever lived here, the district was officially called Fischerpolder, probably just because it sounded good and the person in charge at the time had no idea what a polder was. Well, incompetent local politicians were not a new thing.

Kammerer stopped in front of a house that was narrower than the others and had no front yard. Pavel took out his cell phone and pretended to take a picture of something in one of the front yards.

"Get lost! Damn real estate shark!" a young woman with tattoos on her face yelled at him from an open window. Pavel decided to cross the street. Squeezing between the stopped cars was no problem. The view of Kammerer was better on the other side. Kammerer pressed the bell so hard that he could hear it even from this distance. Nothing happened at first, which seemed to make the bank clerk even angrier. Pavel moved a little closer to hear his words.

"...know you're here," he heard.

The door opened. It was narrow, like the whole house, which seemed to be built into a crevice. The woman who stepped out, on the other hand, was round as a ball. The combination made Pavel think of a work of abstract art, and he thanked a cynical God for it. If you walked through the city with your eyes open, you didn't need an art gallery.

Unfortunately, the bank clerk was speaking quietly now. Pavel bent down so that the cars hid him, which was tiring at his height of almost six foot four inches, and crept closer so that there was only the four-lane road between him and Kammerer and the stranger. Now he could at least make out a few words, except when the bored driver of a luxury car revved his engine. Yes, there was no rich and poor in a traffic jam. Pavel squatted down because his back hurt.

"...know what you arranged..." It was a man's voice. Probably Kammerer.

"...nothing at all. It was always just..." The woman.

"Don't lie to me! I have documents that show you..." Kammerer again.

"...suspicion. It was all fine and dandy until..."

The woman again, this time a little tearful. A suspicion or no suspicion? It was impossible to guess.

"...family. That was ... a serious threat!" The man became louder. Had someone threatened his family?

"...nothing for it. Toni didn't want..."

Toni? That could only mean Sattelmacher.

"...what I should do ... absolutely necessary ... believe me." Kammerer sounded truly desperate.

"...gone to the police." She was right, the woman. Why hadn't the banker come to them?

"Hey, what are you doing?" a man asked through the window of the car in front of him. "Are you taking a dump on the street?"

Pavel put his index finger to his mouth. "There are consequences," was the last thing he heard from Kammerer.

"Imagine, sweetheart, someone actually taking a dump in the street right here. I never saw that back home."

A tourist from the Rhineland, if he wasn't mistaken. Pavel fumbled for his ID and held it up.

"He's from the police, imagine that."

Pavel felt like groaning, but he was afraid that would only invite more comments. When you're on stakeout, you have to make sacrifices. He stood up. Kammerer and the stranger were done talking. The banker took off in the direction he had come. Pavel crossed the street. He photographed the doorbell sign as quickly and inconspicuously as possible.

Then he zoomed in on the image on his smartphone. "Michaela Wagner" was written under a red "No advertising" sticker. Should he question her now? No. It was probably the same Michaela Enna knew. She could get more information out of her.

"You again?"

What kind of question was that? Was this how you greeted a customer?

"Sorry, I'm a little stressed today," Kammerer said, trying to reassure him. "What can I do for you?"

"Hi, I'm Chief Inspector Pavel Neuhof." He waved his badge.

"I take it you don't want to open an account, do you?" Otto Kammerer got up from his seat behind the counter and opened a door in the barrier. He invited Pavel in and offered him a seat at a conference table.

"Tea? Coffee? Something stronger?"

Pavel shook his head. "I'm on duty."

Kammerer opened a door in his desk, took out a bottle of Jägermeister and a glass, and poured himself a glass. Then he walked over to the table, sat down, and toasted Pavel. He downed the liquor. Finally, he took a deep breath in and out.

"I'm not really a drinker, but today... Well, it's none of your business."

"Are you sure?"

The banker nodded, thrusting his lower lip forward. "Yes, of course. Unless you've got an official letter that legally compels me to disclose information."

"Ah, no, I don't." Not yet. "It's not about the bank. I got the impression I might be able to help you in some way. You personally, Mr. Kammerer."

The man winced when Pavel said his name. Then he grabbed his chest, a name tag was pinned to his immaculate dark blue suit.

"No, everything's fine. I'm fine. But thank you for your concern."

"Your family is fine, too?"

The man's right eyelid twitched as Pavel said the word "family."

"The little one is teething, something is always going on at that age." As he continued, he scratched his nose, so vigorously that Pavel started to itch as well.

Very well. He obviously didn't want any help. "Actually, I'm here about Toni Sattelmacher."

This time the crow's feet cleared around Kammerer's eyes for a moment. "Poor guy! Terrible."

"You know what happened?" Pavel wasn't surprised. Although Fleetstedt wasn't so small that everyone knew everyone else, word of a violent death would have gotten around even if Kammerer hadn't somehow been involved.

The banker nodded. "I'm really sorry for his parents. Children should never die before their parents."

He didn't feel sorry for the victim? "Did you know Toni?"

"Not personally. He had an account with us. But before you ask—I really need an official document to give you access. You know what I mean. We'll cooperate, of course, but we'd be opening ourselves up to prosecution if we didn't insist on a warrant."

Pavel reached into the inside pocket of his long jacket and pulled out the bank statements.

"These are from your bank, right?"

Kammerer took the papers from him and studied them. "Yes, they are. But if you are referring to the amount—this only gives half the picture." He put his hand over his mouth as if he had accidentally revealed too much.

"Is that so? So there was also a similarly large balance, perhaps in another account?"

"I'm not allowed to, you know, say anything." Kammerer leaned back and tapped the table.

Silence fell. Pavel didn't mind. On the contrary, it played into his hands, because very few people could stay silent for very long. Should he ask the banker about his visit to Michaela Wagner? If he did, Kammerer might warn her, and Enna wouldn't get anything out of her.

"You want to know something?" Kammerer leaned forward and lowered his voice. "Why don't you talk to the local notary about Mr. Sattelmacher?"

"Notary?" Pavel didn't want to tell Kammerer that he'd

already heard of her.

"Ms. Henriette Meier. She lives in Nordstrasse, I think house number eighteen."

Nordstrasse... That sounded familiar.

"It's right in front of the market," Kammerer explained.

Right, they had crossed the street after leaving the edge of the dike. After being surrounded by so many people for so long, his senses had gone into hyperfocus.

Pavel nodded. "Thank you. I'll see you tomorrow, then."

"Tomorrow? I don't quite understand."

"With the documents from the prosecutor's office."

"Oh, I'm sorry. We're closed on weekends. Please come back on Monday."

"Monday, then." Pavel stood and raised his hand in greeting. "I won't forget you."

Otto Kammerer could only nod, wide-eyed, in response.

"Could you perhaps visit your friend ... today?" asked Pavel, who had just informed Enna about his surveillance of the bank employee. He looked at his watch. It was late afternoon on a Friday. Hopefully he wouldn't spoil Koopmann's evening. But he had plans of his own.

"Of course, Pavel. One should strike while the iron is hot. That's what I always say."

An excellent work ethic. They would certainly get along well.

"I'm going to visit the parents again," he said.

"That's a very good idea. Why don't you ask them about their house?"

"Why?"

"I'd like to know who paid for the renovations and what happened. Since Toni handled the sale, he either had power of attorney or his parents had signed it over to him. That would be interesting in regard to Heiner. Did he get anything out of it or was he left out in the cold again? Oh, just ask her about her relationship with Heiner."

Heiner was her son. It made sense to ask about him. But why pressure the parents? "I prefer to question them gently. You can't force someone to tell the truth."

"No one is asking you to."

Hm. Hadn't Enna just...? Never mind. Each detective had their own methods. Enna must have gotten good results with hers so far. Her old boss never stopped raving about her.

"Good luck with Michaela," he said.

Should they arrange a check-in call in case one of them got into trouble? But he was certainly not going to be in any danger in the retirement home, and this Michaela was an old friend of Koopmann's. Pavel hung up, unlocked the bike lock, and got on the old bike he had fallen in love with on his first day.

He had to grin. His ex-wife liked to watch crime shows on television and had come up with a golden rule for all scriptwriters: If the detective falls in love with a female subject, she is always the culprit. *Well, you old rust bucket*? Pavel pedaled off. *If you're our killer, I will eat my hat.*

Chapter Thirteen

Michaela looked astonished to see Enna standing in front of her door. "Enna! What a surprise. What are you doing here?"

Enna thought back to Pavel's story and forced a smile. "I was in the neighborhood and thought I'd come say hello."

Michaela raised both eyebrows. They were plucked ruthlessly, but that only made her face look rounder. "Just like that? I don't believe you."

Enna grinned broadly. "You're right about that. I'm here on business."

"Oh well. Does it have something to do with Toni?"

"Yes. Who did you hear about that from?" Enna watched Michaela very closely, but she showed no interpretable emotion. She just looked tired.

"From the bakery." Michaela sighed. "It's the topic of the day! So you're investigating?"

"That's my job. And I have a few questions about Toni's finances."

"I'm not allowed to give you any information about that unless you have a warrant."

"We've applied for one from the prosecutor's office. We'll have it by Monday at the latest. But it would be very helpful if we could get an overview today." Enna smiled engagingly and Michaela waved her in.

"Tea?"

"Please."

Enna sat down in the kitchen. It was messy. There was baby stuff everywhere. Bottles were stacked in the sink. It smelled like burned milk.

"How's it going with the baby?" asked Enna while Michaela poured them some tea. A little small talk to get things started couldn't hurt.

Michaela shrugged and carried over two cups. "Exhausting. I really thought it would be different."

Enna pursed her lips. "I'm sorry about that."

"That's okay. The problem is more with my parents. At first, they offered to take Emilia three days a week so I could work, but they couldn't handle it. Now I've taken a leave of absence until I find a nanny or something. Hopefully I will. I also have to get used to everything. Right now I'm getting about two hours sleep. Which is not great. But I'm sure you're not here to hear me whine. So what would you like to know?"

"How Toni's finances were going. The bank statements in his apartment show debts. Substantial debts."

Michaela sipped her tea. It wasn't black tea, but something lemony. "He had debts, yes. Lots of them, actually."

"From renovating the family home?"

"That too. But the renovation was actually well financed. There were subsidies and loans with very good terms, because it was secured for old age and personal use. I signed the contracts with him myself."

"Okay, so why did he sell after renovating? That's unusual, isn't it?"

Michaela lowered her eyes. "He came to me, and he was pretty upset. He said he needed money fast. A lot of money. In fact, he wanted to take out another loan, but without giving a reason. So I couldn't give him good terms. My hands were tied."

"I see. And then he sold?"

"I guess he had no choice. He came back a week or two later, determined to sell the house. He had already been to the notary and checked everything. He wanted us to close the sale as soon as possible."

That sounded like a big hurry. What did he need the money for? "What kind of loan are we talking about?"

"Five hundred thousand euros."

"Wow. On top of the renovation?"

"Yes. That cost two hundred and fifty thousand. And then there was the five hundred thousand that the family home was mortgaged for. Oh yeah, and he had a personal loan in the low six figures."

"How much did the sale of the house net?"

"One and a half million, minus the notary and closing costs."

Enna was astonished. She sipped her tea to let the information sink in, then asked: "And he paid off his debts with the proceeds?"

"Yes, he paid off all his loans at once. And withdrew five hundred thousand euros."

"Wait a minute, wait a minute. You mean he had half a million in cash?"

Michaela grimaced and nodded. "I've never seen anything like it in my career. It was a suitcase full of money."

And certainly for something illegal. Enna puffed out her cheeks. "That's fascinating information. What did your boss say?"

Michaela looked up. "Kammerer? Nothing. He was just ... annoyed that Toni was handling sums of money like that with me, and not with him as branch manager."

That didn't sound quite like Pavel's observation. She scrutinized her friend, who quickly became uncomfortable under Enna's stare. Her fingers tangled and she picked at the edges of her nails.

"Is there something else?" Enna asked firmly.

Michaela lowered her eyes. She must have noticed that her fingers were restless and clenched her hands into fists. "There... there was an incident."

"What happened?"

"I think a guy came into our branch to see Kammerer."

"A guy?"

"Yes. He must have made threats. It was about Toni's house sale."

Enna's ears pricked. "Threats? A guy? Did you recognize him?"

"I wasn't there! Kammerer just told me. He came to see me today and gave me a good talking-to. What I'd done wrong and so on."

"And had you done something wrong?"

Michaela shook her head. "Not that I know of! The contracts were clean and notarized. I don't know who came to see Kammerer and threatened him and his family."

Enna would like to know that, too. "Why didn't Kammerer come to us?"

"I have no idea! He's his own man. He's also worried about the branch after so many in the area have closed. He doesn't want any publicity, especially bad press."

"That's all the more reason why he should have reported a threat against the bank! We'll have to talk to him again."

Michaela just nodded, her eyes downcast.

"It's okay," Enna said reassuringly. "I understand that you don't want to upset your boss, but if it's not reported, there's nothing we can do about it."

"I understand."

"Good. Was the sale made through Norddeutsche Küstenkapital GmbH?"

Michaela's eyes widened in surprise. "How do you know that?"

"They put a sign on the house. I was there earlier."

"Ah, I see. Yes, it's a consortium of investors from Norderney. A well-known company. They've been buying up land all around the North Sea to invest in upscale apartment complexes. Although..." Michaela fell silent.

"What?"

"Oh, I heard that Toni wasn't too happy after the sale. He even asked me if he could call it off."

"Why was that?"

"Apparently, Norddeutsche Küstenkapital GmbH wanted to make a lot more profit on the property. I don't know the details. I mean, of course, it's clear: they buy old properties, invest in renovations or new construction, and then resell at a higher price. They have to make a profit. And they take the risk. But yes... Anyway, I told Toni that it would be difficult for us to cancel the transaction, but it might be possible. Right to object and all that. But he would have to consult his notary, because the funds had already been paid, so the sale was legally complete. I don't know how to change that. I don't know enough about the legal stuff."

"I see. Real estate transactions are complicated."

"Yes, they are."

"Which notary was in charge of the sale? Do you happen to know?"

"Henriette Meier."

Ms. Meier again. Coincidence?

"But you didn't hear all this from me!" Michaela added.

Enna smiled disarmingly. "Don't worry, we'll have the information by Monday at the latest, after we've seen the data. You're just helping us to solve Toni's death faster."

Michaela suddenly looked very depressed. "Poor Toni. I liked him."

"Were you in contact with him?"

"No, not really. He was just one of our clients. But I knew him from before. He was friends with my brother for a long time until he moved away for his job. He was a really nice guy—unlike his brother Heiner." Michaela shuddered. "Now, there's a scary guy."

"Did he profit from the sale?"

"Heiner? No. He was not on the land register either. The house was transferred to Toni years ago."

So that was how it was. Very interesting. "That's strange. And his parents had to move out, too."

Michaela sipped her tea and sighed deeply. "Yes, I was very sorry about that. They did have usufructuary rights."

"So they were allowed to live there?"

"Of course. They didn't want to move into the retirement

home. That's why they renovated it, so they could have peace and quiet in their old age."

It sounded awful. Mentally preparing for retirement only to end up having to go to a retirement home because their son had accumulated debts. It was also very interesting information, since they had been extremely good to Toni. Good Toni, who always did everything right, had evidently made a real mess of things.

A child's cry came from the next room and Michaela sighed loudly. "Do you have any more questions, Enna?"

"No, thank you. And thank you for the tea."

"My pleasure. You can show yourself out?"

"Of course." Enna gave her old school friend a quick hug, finished her tea, and quietly left the narrow house.

Chapter Fourteen

The gravel crunched. Pavel had just passed the entrance to the retirement home, a golden gate. Now he pedaled with all his might, but he still got stuck. The gravel was too deep. Before he could fall, he dismounted and pushed his bike.

He leaned it against the wall in front of the gate. He tried to ignore the mismatched pillars, but he couldn't, and his hair stood on end.

You'll wait for me here, right? He hadn't spoken to his possessions out loud since he was ten. Some of his classmates had beaten him up for it. The bike didn't answer. He'd never gotten an answer, but that wasn't the point. Should he lock the bike? He looked around. He couldn't see the road from here. The locals wouldn't cross the gravel, and visitors certainly wouldn't need to steal his rickety old bike.

The half-hour ride had made him sweat. He took off his long coat and draped it over the handlebars. Then he walked up the ramp to the front door.

Jenny Kring was at the desk. Good. Not because it was Jenny, but because he already knew her. That would make his visit more efficient. He still had to convince Enna Koopmann to accompany him to Hamburg—or rather, to chauffeur him into the city. He liked trains even less than cars.

"The Sattelmachers?" he asked.

"Mr. Sattelmacher has been in the hospital since your visit yesterday," Jenny said, her eyebrows drawing together.

"Is he all right?"

"I'm not at liberty to give you any information about our residents. But why don't you ask his wife?"

"Thank you, Jenny. I'll find my way."

"Wait a minute. I saw her go into the park. She's probably still out there."

"Thanks." He turned and headed for the exit, but Jenny Kring called after him again: "The park entrance is past the dining room, through the double doors."

The dining room reminded him of an expensive restaurant. Two employees in fancy white uniforms were setting the tables for dinner. It was a pity that Jenny was so unapproachable. He really would have liked to know what the Sattelmachers were paying for this.

A double door stood open at the end of the hall. There was an almost transparent curtain in front of it, probably to keep insects out. Pavel stepped through. A cool breeze struck his sweaty face. He should have brought his coat with him.

The park was surprisingly crowded. Just beyond the exit, about twenty senior citizens were exercising under supervision. Two extremely thin women in tracksuits were jogging as fast as he could ride a bike between the spreading deciduous trees.

Pavel walked deeper into the park. It was noticeably cooler in the shade of the trees, which must be a hundred years old. He began to shiver a little. At the base of most of the trees were plaques honoring the tree's donor.

"This whole estate once belonged to Count von Wedel," said a woman who had just emerged from behind the thick trunk of an oak.

"I'm afraid that doesn't mean anything to me, Mrs. Sattelmacher."

Magda sighed. "You're not from around here, are you?"

"No, I'm from Kiel."

"If you like, I can tell you about the history of the castle. The blue marble floor in the vestibule, for example..."

Pavel felt guilty because Mrs. Sattelmacher obviously missed the company of her attentive husband, but not so guilty that he wouldn't interrupt her.

"May I ask how your husband is?" A little politeness was part of the deal.

She sighed again. "They kept him there. For tests, they said. I mean, we know his heart isn't very strong, he's already had a couple of stents put in. Nevertheless, we wanted to spend a few more years in this facility, until he died."

"Until he...?"

"Georg is fourteen years older than me. Of course, we both know he will probably die before me. But not now! If only Toni hadn't..."

"I'm very sorry." What was surprising, however, was that her husband's hospitalization had probably upset her more than the death of his son. An evil stepmother scenario, then? "I'm sure he'll be back soon." She looked startled for a moment, then quickly wiped her face and focused on Pavel's chin. "Your husband, I mean."

"Of course. I'm sure." Magda Sattelmacher looked much more reserved now. They walked side by side, but she stared stubbornly ahead.

"What would have happened after his death, if I may ask?"

"I would have moved back to our house, of course. You see, Georg was always careful not to be a burden to me. So Toni got us this very comfortable residence where he could be really well taken care of, where he had his diabetes under control, and so on."

"But you don't need all that."

"No. My mother lived to be ninety-six in perfect health. I intend to do the same. If I became an invalid, that would be another matter, of course."

Pavel remembered Enna's words. "Your house has just been renovated."

"Yes, isn't it great? Toni liquidated some investments to provide us with that luxury."

"Investments?"

"Please don't ask me the details. But he showed us the suitcase full of money."

A suitcase full of money? That was a sure sign that something was wrong. But he didn't want to worry Mrs. Sattelmacher.

"What does your son Heiner have to say about it? He would have been your main heir, right? Or had you adopted Toni?"

"I would have, but while she was alive his biological mother was against it, and later it would have been disrespectful. Toni was always like my own son. I treated them both the same. But Toni was always a little more capable than Heiner."

So Toni was not adopted. He would have inherited a quarter of his father's estate when he died, Heiner another quarter, and Magda half. Magda, who presumably already owned half, would end up with three-quarters of the family estate, meaning that Heiner would inherit 87.5 percent of the entire estate upon his mother's death.

"So Heiner is the main heir," Pavel said.

"No, that was Toni," Mrs. Sattelmacher corrected him. "We gave Heiner fifteen thousand euros three years ago as a prior heir. In return, he waived his compulsory portion."

"You disinherited him?"

Magda Sattelmacher stamped her feet energetically, and as if she were in league with the wind god, a violent gust of wind struck him at that very moment. "Of course not! You don't know him! He can't handle money. He would have frittered away every penny. We didn't want the brothers to quarrel after our death. Toni promised Georg that he would give his brother a fair share."

"Would you show me some family photos?" No one had ever refused Pavel this innocent request. Mrs. Sattelmacher smiled. "I would love to, Inspector. Would you come with me to our apartment?"

As Pavel opened the front door of the Siena Suite, another gust of wind blew the handle out of his hand.

"Please come in..." Magda Sattelmacher began, but then pointed to the chaos that had unexpectedly descended upon the living room. A window on the opposite side of the room was open.

"Did you leave that open?" he asked in a whisper, pushing the old lady, who shook her head, out of the room.

Damn. Pavel was already fumbling for his service weapon, taking it out of its holster and disengaging the safety, just in case. It looked like the burglar was already gone.

Pavel stepped into the room, holding the weapon in both hands. "This is Chief Inspector Neuhof. Come out with your hands up..."

A shadow emerged from behind the heavy cabinet. He was tall and thin. His face was covered with a Palestinian scarf. He, or she—it could be a woman, it was impossible to tell under the baggy black leather jacket—was wearing brown gloves.

"Stop right there!" shouted Pavel.

The burglar did not comply. Instead, he threw a book at Pavel. It flew slowly enough for him to make out the title—*War and Peace*, how appropriate—but fast enough that he couldn't duck. The book hit Pavel on the shoulder, forcing him to lower his weapon for a moment. Seizing the opportunity, the figure jumped onto the sofa, used its springs to land on the desk, jumped to the open window, and used the window frame like a gym bar to reach freedom.

By the time he heard a muffled groan from outside, Pavel was already on the move. He congratulated himself that he always wore a bulletproof vest under his jacket, because as he leaned out of the window, something hit him on the left side of his chest.

Pavel froze. The bastard had shot him! Good thing he was wearing the vest!

He stepped back, breathing heavily. He briefly examined the

damage. There was a hole in his jacket, just above his heart. The guy was a good shot.

But if he thought Pavel would give up now, he was wrong. He heard footsteps. They were coming from the right. From the right side of the house?

Pavel risked a glance out the window. There was the intruder, still alone. Pavel jumped out of the window and gathered his last reserves.

This was their chance to solve the case today! He knew it wouldn't be easy, but the mere prospect spurred him on. His chest burned like fire from the impact of the bullet. His legs moved automatically. All he had to do was keep his eyes open as he dashed around the corner. There was the exit! He could see his bike. Right next to it was a big motorcycle. Pavel memorized the details—chrome everywhere, numerous stickers whose motifs reminded him of the logos of well-known rocker gangs, a Kawasaki company logo, a license plate from Hamburg—HH, half a brain, they had always joked in Kiel. Did they say the same thing here?

The intruder had already gotten on his bike and started it. Pavel could have opened fire, but he hadn't become a detective to shoot people. You became a professional killer for that, didn't you? He preferred to convict them, and he would eventually do that with this person. But maybe he was in luck. The engine didn't start.

Second try, third try.

Ten feet to go.

Nine, eight, seven ...

Pavel imagined the audience of a cooking show cheering him on—four, three—but then the bike started, the intruder shifted into gear and sped off. Gravel crunched loudly and sprayed Pavel in a wide arc.

All he could see of the fugitive was a red taillight.

Pavel entered the foyer again, panting. He was exhausted and desperately needed to sit down.

"Oops, what have you got there?" Jenny Kring asked, pointing to his gun. "You better put that away. It will scare the old people, and you can imagine what will happen then."

Pavel put the gun back in its holster and sat down in the chair behind the counter. His mouth was sticky with saliva and his heart was slowly returning to normal. The guy with the Hamburg plates had actually shot at him! He took that personally. The shooter couldn't have known that he never forgot his vest.

Hamburg. Half a brain. Why had he talked Enna out of researching the Hanseatic city? He needed her, the flair for people and situations he had noticed yesterday. Maybe he could lure her with the promise of an exciting investigation. They weren't only investigating Toni's suspected gambling habit now. They also had a biker gang under surveillance, judging by the stickers on the motorcycle. Surely she would like that? Even if Hamburg was a place of interest, they couldn't investigate in the other state without making an official request. Surely he could sell it to the prosecutor as a team-building exercise—after all, they would be going on Saturday.

When his breathing had calmed down enough, he called Enna. "Have you finished with Michaela?"

"Yes, I was just coming into the office to give you..."

"I need you here at the retirement home. And bring a crime scene investigator with you, please."

"Uh, okay. Will do, boss." The connection was broken.

The receptionist was still standing next to him. "Jenny?"

"Yes?"

"Mrs. Sattelmacher needs another room for tonight. Her suite is now a crime scene, and no one is allowed to enter it except the police."

"But..."

"No buts. That's a police order."

"I can't..."

"Yes you can, or should I declare the whole building a crime scene?"

Jenny Kring surrendered, waving her hands and reaching for the lobby phone.

Pavel jumped up again. *Mrs. Sattelmacher*! Hopefully, she had weathered all the excitement. He ran to the suite.

Mrs. Sattelmacher was no longer standing at the open door where he had left her, her place taken by two curious old ladies whom he sent away with stern words. He looked into the living room. He hoped Magda hadn't started picking things up. The window was closed. No problem. Her fingerprints would be on everything anyway. Luckily, she wasn't tidying up. Mrs. Sattelmacher was sitting on her couch. She had a photo album on her lap and was slowly leafing through it.

Pavel approached cautiously. "I'm back, Mrs. Sattelmacher," he said gently so as not to startle her.

She looked up. Tears were streaming down her face. It must be from the shock. Someone had forcibly entered her home, her place of refuge. The loss of security alone would affect most people deeply. Even if he told her that the criminal wouldn't come back, it wouldn't help. The loss was irrevocable.

It would probably be best if the Sattelmachers moved to another room permanently. He didn't know much about their financial situation, but they might even have to move to another home. Toni would never be able to pay the rent again. Right here in town, a former hospital, which had been forced to close after the latest cutbacks, had been converted into an old age home. Maybe that was an option.

Pavel sat down next to her. It would be a while before Enna arrived, and even longer before the crime scene investigator arrived. The old woman turned the album so he could look at it. He saw a baby. The color pictures were a little yellowed, but the blue of the onesie was still clearly visible. So it was a boy.

"Wasn't he cute?"

DEEP WATERS

Pavel murmured in agreement. This must be Heiner.

"He babbled all the time, and was only quiet when I nursed him."

Pavel nodded.

"He was happy when I nursed him, you know?" Magda smiled at him through her tears. He could see the love on her face. It was a strange form of love, the nature of which he could only explain from a biological point of view. Some parents lied for their children even when they knew they were cruel murderers. He pushed the thought aside because it wasn't appropriate to the situation. Mrs. Sattelmacher wanted him to agree with her, to support her.

"And so complete," Pavel said, also smiling. That was what fascinated him about babies. They already had everything that made an adult human. It wasn't like that with other animal species. He had no children of his own. But wouldn't it be more exciting if humans had to pupate at least once in their lives? That way, the parents could always hope that the little rascal would one day transform into a butterfly.

"Complete," Mrs. Sattelmacher repeated thoughtfully. "Complete. Com...plete." She seemed to be listening to the sound. "That's an interesting way of looking at it. I'm not sure I quite understand it." She gave a short laugh. "When I was nursing him, he was quiet. Complete, you say? Completely full." She sighed. "Unfortunately, that too."

Now she sounded even more confused than he thought she was. At sixty-eight, most people weren't senile yet. Fresh tears streamed down her face. Pavel swallowed. He hoped Enna would arrive soon. He couldn't give Magda a handkerchief because she already had one in her hand. Touching her in any way was out of the question because she was incapable of giving informed consent in her current state. His options were limited. He could sit next to her and spend time with her.

Magda Sattelmacher turned the pages. The infant became a toddler. Magda seemed to be as surprised by the changes as he was, because she kept turning the pages back and forth, comparing the pictures. It almost looked as if the baby had secretly pupated in his crib at night, over and over again. And who could prove that he hadn't? No one watched their child around the clock, did they?

Of course, he knew that humans were not butterflies. Pavel clung to science the way science clung to him. Sometimes he let his imagination run away with him. That was why he had always been particularly annoyed when his ex-wife had accused him of having no imagination. Just because he preferred tried and tested strategies when in doubt?

"And then he does something like this," said Mrs. Sattelmacher, who had just come to a page showing a six-year-old boy in a colorful suit playing in the snow. In the background were high mountains that he thought were the Alps.

Pavel pricked up his ears. What had Heiner done? "What is that?" he asked.

The old woman pointed to the devastated room.

"You think he's responsible?" Pavel only knew Heiner from pictures. The figure earlier had been masked, so he hadn't been able to identify him. Could a mother be fooled by her own child? He didn't know. There were certainly characteristic movements that the parents would have unconsciously memorized. They wouldn't be able to describe them, but they would be able to identify them when they saw them.

But had Magda seen enough? He had immediately pushed her out of the doorway into cover, assuming the burglar was armed. Maybe she hadn't remained hidden, that was possible. All his attention had been on the chase. He felt his chest. His nice jacket was ruined. It was a good thing his coat was still hanging over his bike. If he had lost that too...

"What happened there?" asked Magda. She meant the hole the bullet had made.

"That? Oh, it's just a bullet hole."

"Did Heiner shoot at you?"

It must be the shock. It was impossible for her not to have heard the shot.

"Someone shot at me. But I don't think it was Heiner." Pavel failed to mention that the person had fled on a powerful motorcycle with Hamburg license plates. It didn't look like it, but he couldn't rule out the possibility that Heiner's mother was trying to protect him by lying for him, even if he couldn't quite understand her plan.

"It was him. No doubt."

He had never met a mother who openly accused her child of a crime. The gunshot had been attempted murder. Mrs. Sattelmacher wiped away a few tears with the back of her hand and stood up.

"Don't touch anything, please. The crime scene investigator needs to investigate this first."

"I'll just get my sewing kit from the bedroom."

The bedroom, of course. This was a suite, so there must be a second room. Pavel followed the old woman. One look through the open door was enough; the other room was untouched. Either the burglar hadn't had enough time, or he wasn't interested in jewelry or cash. Most people kept their valuables in the back of their sock drawer or in a bookcase. A professional burglar would know that. But this one had hardly taken any books from the shelves. What if it had indeed been Heiner? Then he must have been looking for documents, and probably had some idea where his parents kept them. The mess he had made might be just a distraction.

Sattelmacher returned with a small wooden box that folded out into three shelves on either side. "The jacket, please."

Pavel shook his head. "I can't do that, I'm sorry."

"I insist. If Heiner did it, it's the least I can do."

Could this be interpreted as a bribe? At least having something to do made Mrs. Sattelmacher stop crying. It had distracted her. He shrugged, slipped out of his jacket, and handed it to her.

It was fascinating to watch her fingers work. Though the skin on them was slightly wrinkled, they moved like ants, coordinated in a way he didn't understand, but which made sense nonetheless. That was how he sometimes felt as a criminologist. He collected facts that didn't seem to fit together, but in the end, they made perfect sense.

Why was Heiner's own mother, of all people, trying to make him look guilty? What did she know about him? He and Koopmann must have overlooked something.

"Why are you so sure it was Heiner?"

Magda Sattelmacher acknowledged his question by looking at him briefly. She continued sewing for a moment, then let the jacket fall into her lap. "It wasn't the first time."

Ah. Pavel took a rubber glove from his pocket and slipped it on. He hurried over to the desk, grabbed the flat wooden box with the photos in it, and carried it to the sofa. He sat down again and fished out some of the cropped photos.

"Was that him?"

Magda Sattelmacher nodded. "He broke in through the window."

"Through that one?" Pavel pointed to the window the burglar had used today.

"No, the one next to it. The caretaker fixed it."

Pavel stood up again and walked over to the window. One of the bars separating the panes gleamed a fresh white.

"And you caught him?"

"No, we had gone to a concert at the health resort. It looked like this when we got back."

"And the bedroom?"

"It was untouched."

A burglar who searched the suite the same way twice in a row? That seemed very unusual to him, unless the person had gotten new information in the meantime.

"You should have called the police."

"So you could arrest my son? He drinks too much sometimes and forgets his manners. But he's not a bad person. That's what I think, anyway."

"It's because of the cut-up photos, isn't it? You think Heiner did that, don't you?"

"He was always very jealous, although there was no reason for it."

Pavel shook his head. The Sattelmachers had effectively disinherited their younger son. How much was the house worth? Enna would surely be able to tell him soon. But it was certainly more than the fifteen thousand they had given him. He had probably needed the money urgently and had therefore signed all the documents.

But Pavel kept this thought to himself. He remembered all too well the old lady's stubborn reaction earlier.

"Did he leave any evidence?" he asked instead. "I mean, anyone who didn't like Toni could have come up with the idea of cutting his face out of those photos."

A police psychologist would probably have disagreed with him at this point. Cutting the pictures with scissors indicated certain destructive fantasies. In any case, it was more drastic than if Toni had simply been painted over.

"It was Heiner. Believe me. It is what it is. See all those books with red spines on the shelf? Open the volume *Me to Nt*.

He went to the shelf. An encyclopedia. His parents had owned one. The Google of the pre-Internet era. There were notes in almost every volume, most of them yellowed. He was familiar with that, too. His mother would update outdated entries when she came across a relevant article in the newspaper. The *Me to Nt* volume was bulging when he took it off the shelf. It contained numerous notes. One, however, was bright white, not yellow. Pavel opened to that page and found a sheet of paper that might be used in a printer or photocopier. It was folded. He unfolded it carefully.

"I WANT MY MONEY, OR ELSE..." it said in capital letters, cut out of some kind of newspaper. Only the three dots had been added with a blue ballpoint pen. What a cliché! Nowadays, blackmailers wrote anonymous emails or contacted people via Messenger. At best, he would have expected Magda Sattelmacher herself to write such an old-fashioned note. He looked at her. The old lady was concentrating on the damage caused by the bullet. She had pressed her upper lip slightly over her lower lip and narrowed her eyes.

Pavel shook his head. Why would the woman write such a

letter? To incriminate her son? Well, she and her husband had robbed him of most of his inheritance. But she was still his mother. If so, she might have felt guilty and unsuccessfully pleaded with her husband to undo the agreement.

He must have missed a crucial detail. But he would find it.

Pavel heard brisk footsteps in the hallway. The sounds were colorful and looked like socks. He wiped away the mental image. Enna had arrived at the perfect time.

"Can I get you anything?" the waitress asked, as if they were in a restaurant. They had retired to the retirement home dining room for their meeting, where dinner had just been served.

"Thank you, but we are not guests of your establishment," Pavel replied.

"Oh, I have specific instructions from the administration to provide you with whatever you need."

"But we can't..."

Enna nudged him. "I haven't had time to eat today," she whispered.

"You don't have to worry," the waitress explained. "Any leftovers from the buffet in the kitchen must be destroyed in accordance with the law. Which means they are only good for pet food."

"I think I'll have some, then," Enna said, "thank you."

"Good, I'll rustle up something for you. And the gentleman?"

Pavel shook his head. It was too complicated. He probably wouldn't be able to eat whatever they brought him. He wasn't that hungry. Maybe he had a bit of an appetite, but he could suppress it for a day.

While they waited, Enna talked at length about her visit to the victim's brother and her old friend Michaela. The sums involved were impressive, almost frightening. Almost one and a half million Euros! A policeman might be shot for that. And he knew the banker was hiding something. Why the hell didn't they call the police when they were threatened?

"Do you think Heiner is capable of committing murder?" he asked.

"He doesn't have an alibi for the time of the crime," Enna said.

"Neither do his parents. Hmm. They would hardly kill their favorite son, would they?"

Statistically, it was very rare. Children were more likely to kill their parents or grandparents, usually out of greed, but often out of hatred after years of abuse. In this case, it probably wasn't the latter. Greed? That was conceivable. Heiner had every reason.

"Remember, Toni wasn't Mrs. Sattelmacher's biological son," Enna said. "Conflicts between stepparents and stepchildren don't only exist in fairy tales."

"Yes, but parents usually stick together. And can you imagine an eighty-two-year-old man throwing his not-so-slim son into the water?"

In his mind's eye, he placed Magda Sattelmacher on the beach with the skinny old man, dragging her son into the water. There would have been drag marks and abrasions on the body. But neither the crime scene investigator nor the forensic pathologist had found anything like that. So the evidence wasn't helpful. They needed a way to kickstart the investigation. Preferably in Hamburg. Now all his new colleague had to do was agree to an unofficial trip.

The waitress brought a large plate with several sandwiches on it. Pavel recognized salmon, salami, shrimp, ham, and a reddish paste. There were two small bowls filled to the brim with a brown cream.

"That's chocolate mousse," the waitress explained and set a clean plate for each of them. There was already cutlery on the table, as well as an open bottle of sparkling water.

"Come on, don't make me eat alone," Enna said. "It tastes better when we eat together."

Pavel sighed. He stabbed a salami sandwich with his fork but realized he couldn't eat it. This was confirmed when he looked at the plate after removing the salami.

Underneath was a thin, white cream, definitely neither butter nor margarine, which would have been okay. He could scrape the stuff off, but some of it would have soaked into the bread, making it inedible.

He pushed the plate away and leaned back while Koopmann ate heartily. It was fun to watch. Pavel found it more amusing to watch others eat than to eat himself. The way a person ate revealed so much about them. How good was her self-control? Did she appreciate variety, eating everything in a random order, or was she systematic, and if so, in which order did she eat? What criteria did she use to make choices? Was she only interested in taste, or did calories or vitamins play a role?

"You're looking at me as if," Enna chewed and swallowed, "as if you are psychoanalyzing me."

Pavel grinned. She had him.

"Score!" she yelled. "At least tell me what you found out."

"There is a blackmail letter," he evaded.

"Man, Neuhof, you already told me that! What does the amateur psychologist in you say?"

He sighed. "All right. But don't hold it against me."

"I can't promise that. Anyone who says that is lying."

He disagreed, but that wasn't the point. "Well, you eat everything in a jumble, and never two bites of the same thing in a row. You're curious and enjoy eating, with curiosity being the predominant factor. Your weakness, and I hope this doesn't sound like a cliché, is your lack of strategy."

"Is that so? Is there an optimal strategy for eating?"

"Absolutely. If we assume a random, equal distribution of food, it would make sense to choose purely at random. But you emptied your plate from right to left. That shows me you also have a preference for order."

That was probably the only thing they had in common, but that was okay. He'd never felt this much of a connection with anyone before, and he didn't particularly like it. It certainly wasn't easy to deal with someone like him.

"Interesting." She took a bite out of a carrot, causing it to snap. "But why would I hold that assessment against you?"

"Self-image and the opinion of others rarely coincide."

Enna laughed. "That's another one of your characteristic phrases. So I'm not the way others see me. So what? Who cares how others see me? Only I know who I am."

That was an interesting way of thinking. But wasn't it typical of assholes who didn't care about others? His colleague didn't give that impression, and that confused him. It would be best if they talked about work again. He was more familiar with that.

"I wanted to ask you how you would feel about a personal trip to Hamburg. My associates there haven't contacted me yet, and I have a feeling that the details we're missing are buried there."

"I hope not." Koopmann laughed.

"Oh, hidden, that's what I meant."

"I'm game. To be honest, I thought about injecting you with sedatives and taking you to Hamburg, but then I remembered that I'd have trouble getting you into the patrol car without your help."

Pavel's eyes widened. Surely she was joking?

"You still have a score to settle with the shooter, don't you? So as far as I'm concerned, we should leave first thing in the morning."

He nodded. A score, yes. Attempted murder. "Not in the patrol car, of course."

"No way, what do you think? I'll pick you up in my personal car. At eight o'clock."

"Please don't forget your bulletproof vest, Enna. Magda Sattelmacher will repair any holes in your clothes."

"Okay. But if we're going to Hamburg tomorrow, we have to visit the Norddeutsche Küstenkapital GmbH on Norderney on Monday. After I visited Michaela, I did a little research on the Internet. They seem reputable, but I found several complaints about the company, saying they take advantage of people's misfortunes by buying land cheap and then selling it at a much higher price."

"Could that have happened here?"

Enna nodded meaningfully. "Michaela mentioned that Sattelmacher tried to rescind the sale. Maybe he discovered something like that and wanted to capitalize on it."

"A motive for the investment group?"

Enna growled. "It's one thing to take advantage of people and rip them off, and quite another to murder a man."

"But they no doubt didn't like the fact that Toni wanted to rescind the sale."

"Certainly not. We should talk to the notary as well. Preferably on Monday. She has her fingers in too many pies, despite the fact that she shouldn't be involved in these kinds of transactions."

"Just earning some pocket money."

Enna looked grim. "She earns enough as a notary. But let's check out Hamburg first, then do the rest on Monday."

"There's just one small problem," Pavel said.

"Yeah? You only have one suit and you don't want to show up in front of the Hamburg moneybags in the one with a hole in it?"

Pavel looked at his colleague. Of course he had more than one suit. But if you wanted to be taken seriously in Hamburg, appearance was very important. How would Koopmann dress? He'd better not ask that question.

"Mind if I interrupt you two lovebirds?" They were joined by a woman in her forties, wearing a cleaner's smock, her arms at her sides.

"Oh, Maria, are you ready to go? Would you like some? I can't eat all of this."

"No, thank you, Enna. More than anything, I want to get home to my wife."

"I understand," said Koopmann. "Are you ready to go? By the way, this is Maria Doldinger, the head of the crime lab. My new boss, Pavel Neuhof."

Pavel stood and shook the woman's hand, bowing briefly. "We spoke on the phone this morning."

"I hope you won't make a habit of this, Enna. It's no fun

having to come all the way from Leer to Fleetstedt on a Friday afternoon."

"It's not my fault that we don't have a crime scene investigator here."

"Well, don't allow so many crimes to take place."

"Okay, we'll send the criminals over to you."

"That's kind of you."

Pavel was getting restless. The two women had been talking for several minutes without exchanging any information. "Have you found anything yet?" he asked.

"Fingerprints galore. Not surprising under the circumstances. A print from the motorcyclist's boot on the desk. If you bring us the boot, we'll nail him with it. The bullet was probably fired from a Jarygin PJa, caliber nine by nineteen millimeters, but I'll have to confirm that before it goes on file."

"Jarygin?" asked Enna.

"Replaced the old Makarov nine by eighteen millimeter in the Russian military in 2003. It's still relatively rare in Germany, but it has the advantage of being able to use NATO ammunition."

"How convenient. That makes it more flexible to maintain," Pavel said.

"You had a guardian angel, by the way. The Jarygin was developed because the Russians found the good old Makarov to be ineffective against bulletproof vests."

"It was the distance," Pavel said, trying to hide his shock. "The kinetic energy of a nine-millimeter bullet..."

"Yeah, I know," Doldinger interrupted. "Is that it, then?"

The head of the crime lab was putting a lot of pressure on him. He couldn't think straight. What else had he wanted to know? "Ah, signs of forced entry on the window?"

"Yes, one of the windows was forced."

"Did you compare that with the damage to the other window?"

"Judging by the repair, the other one was smashed and then forced open."

"So a different approach." It could have been Heiner last time and someone else this time.

"Or he learned from the first attempt," Enna said. "It makes a lot of noise when you break a window."

"Your colleague is right," Doldinger said.

"The letter I put on the desk..."

"I bagged it. It was from a daily newspaper."

He had already established that. "Which one?"

Doldinger sighed. "I knew you would ask that. All right, I'll find out, but give me until Monday. My weekend is sacred. And don't you dare dig up another body before then!"

Pavel narrowed his eyes. Was she serious? He was expected to wait until Monday for this important information? It had to be a joke. But he wasn't sure, so he winked at Koopmann. She obviously knew the crime lab boss. Couldn't she convince her to work a few extra hours? She could make up for it on Monday.

But Enna didn't react. She just winked back, which didn't tell him anything.

"Um, Ms. Doldinger," he began, while Enna shook her head inconspicuously. "Could I ask you," Enna kicked his shin under the table, "could I ask you to let me see the letter again? I just want to take a photo."

"All right," she said, and Enna relaxed noticeably. Doldinger held the letter out to him and he took a picture of it with his cell phone.

"Then I'm off. The suite has been cleared."

"Thank you, Ms. Doldinger."

Enna jumped up and said goodbye to the crime lab boss with kisses left and right. You rarely saw that up here. They seemed to have known each other for a long time.

"She used to be in love with me," Enna explained when the crime scene investigator had left. "Unfortunately, I'm not in love with her. She's a friend you can steal horses with."

"Stealing sheep might be more popular here."

Enna raised her arm and pretended to tickle herself. "Ha-ha-ha."

"Hello darkness, my old friend," Pavel hummed as he entered the dark office. He had let Enna drop him off in front of his boarding house and then cycled here. He didn't want her to feel bad because he still had things to sort out. Pavel turned on the small desk lamp and undid the top button of his pants. Then he removed his beloved jacket. He stroked the hole that Mrs. Sattelmacher had darned. It was barely visible, but he could feel it. Did the family actually make saddles? The old lady must have learned how to use a needle and thread so perfectly somewhere.

Don't digress, he reminded himself. Now he had *free time*! He hung his jacket over Koopmann's chair and made himself comfortable. It wasn't work he had in front of him, but a puzzle. It consisted of twenty letters and four punctuation marks. He thought he had a good chance of solving it faster than Doldinger from the crime lab. But first, he had to transfer the photo to his computer. He rummaged through his things for a data cable and plugged it into his cell phone, but found it wouldn't work on the computer. The computers here still had the old USB-A ports; at the State Criminal Police Office, they had brand-new models with the flatter USB-C ports.

He turned one hundred and eighty degrees in his chair and scooted over to his colleague's desk. Surely she would have the right kind of cable? But there were none plugged into her computer. Would his research fail because of a missing cable? That was out of the question. He opened the drawer carefully. He didn't want to look inside, but he had to if he wanted to find the cable. There was a jumble of coins, a condom, at least two pairs of earrings (he hadn't even noticed she wore any), numerous pens, a broken geo triangle, some photos he ignored as best he could, a driver's license, and, hoorah! a USB cable.

He quickly pulled it out and used it to connect his phone to his computer. He downloaded the photo of the note and opened it.

"I want my money, or else..."

Pavel zoomed in on the image and counted. It consisted of six individually pasted pieces: I, want, m, y, money, or else, and the separately pasted comma, which he would ignore. The font and the colors—blue and red—indicated a newspaper. There were two newspapers in the area: BILD and Morgenpost, or Mopo for short.

Unfortunately, he had forgotten to ask Mrs. Sattelmacher for the date of the burglar's last visit. That would cost him a lot of time. He assumed that the author of the letter had used a fairly recent issue. The extravagant font size indicated that the words must have been cut from the front page. So the first thing Pavel did was to go to the online archive of the Mopo, which had been published weekly for a while now. He then entered the word "money" into the archive search and selected all front-page articles no more than six months old.

It worked! But the editors seemed to have a fondness for the subject. Money appeared in all its variations: less and more money, too much or too little, as counterfeit money, people's money, change, housing money, welcome money, holiday money, dirty money, monetary policy, fines, ATMs, money down the drain, money worries, money laundering, and Bob Geldof.

However, on none of the corresponding front pages did he find both "I" (which had to be capitalized) and the number word "one". Several times he was on the verge of jubilation. However, he had overlooked the fact that the cutout "one" had significant white space on either side. The blackmailer could have cut "money" out of compound words, but not "one" out of "one", "ones", "one in a row", "stone", "honesty" or "zone"—or, for that matter, "money"—and certainly not out of "phone" or "pioneer", although that would have fit his crime.

Surprisingly, the intruder did not seem to attach much importance to this, which was a pity, because it would have increased the intellectual value of his search for clues if he had discovered such hidden messages. Wouldn't a clever criminal get a certain thrill out of it? But such a person wouldn't have shot at him, but would have sent a cleverly programmed drone after him, or wouldn't have been caught at all.

Well, if he wanted such criminals to exist, he would probably have to become one himself, and what prevented him from doing so was not so much his sense of law and order as the fact that the chance of meeting an investigator who would appreciate it was very small, or close to zero if he crossed himself off the list.

So the Mopo turned out to be a bust. Perhaps that was what had cost it so many readers—the overuse of the word *money* when its readers didn't have it in sufficient abundance. A conflict of interests.

Competitor BILD seemed to suffer from a similar problem. Since it was published six times a week, there were many more places to find information. In his opinion, money appeared more often in negative contexts than in positive ones, but this could be due to the editorial line.

It took Pavel an hour to work his way through the connected instances of "I" and "one". It went faster when he realized that "I" correlated with the presence of a person's photo. That meant he could quickly scroll through the front pages with "money" in the headlines, reducing the number of possibilities by half.

But now manual work was required. The front pages scrolling across his screen looked very different at first but turned out to be quite similar. He quickly found the first combination of "I", " want", "else" and "y". The "m" was also there. However, the font sizes did not match his pattern.

On he went. The second hit didn't match either, but the third did. The cover story accused some politician of having the wrong monetary policy. *Money* was printed in large type. The article "He won't work for free" described the daily life of an unemployed man who refused to retrain. At the bottom right was an article entitled "I love my chicken", from which Pavel was able to extract the two missing words. However, the protagonist did not love chicken but instead was probably referring to his wife. Since the text was continued on page four, which he didn't have to hand, Pavel was satisfied with the incomplete information. He used the screenshot button to cut out a suitable "M" and put the ransom note together.

"I want my money or else"

He printed out the sentence and put the three dots at the end with a pen, just like on the original. At the bottom, he wrote "Found in BILD, Hamburg edition" and added the date of publication. Then he put the printout in an official mail envelope and addressed it to the crime lab in Leer. What would this mean for their investigation? It was a clue. The person who wrote the letter must have been in Hamburg almost exactly three months ago. They could probably rule out the parents of the dead man. They had to find out what Heiner had been doing. Pavel checked the phone records he had sorted yesterday. Toni had indeed been in Hamburg on the days in question. But why would he have broken into his parents' house? Pavel shook his head and was startled when he looked at the clock. Four-thirty in the morning—he'd better get some sleep under his desk.

Chapter Fifteen

Pavel woke up to icy air. He crawled out from under the desk. Enna Koopmann was standing at the window. She had her arms at her sides and was staring at him grimly. Uh-oh.

"What were you thinking, Neuhof?"

He zipped up his pants, turned to the desk, and held up the printout of the replica blackmail letter like a white flag.

"I found out what issue it was from!"

"We were supposed to meet at your guesthouse at eight. When we didn't find you in your bed, I was about to report you missing!"

"I'm very sorry about that." Pavel shivered. Couldn't she at least close the window?

Enna's mouth twisted. "I might just send you to Hamburg alone."

"Please don't. I need you."

Pavel was serious. They would have to talk to a lot of people and wouldn't be able to rely on their badges. They weren't worth much more there than in Tijuana or Moscow, at least if the people they talked to knew anything about the law, and professional criminals would be bound to.

"Please, Enna," he added.

She turned around. Did he hear a giggle? "Take a shower first. Then we'll have to get you some fresh clothes."

Pavel looked at his watch. It was ten past nine. At least he had slept nearly five hours. That was more than enough.

"In the back, please," Enna demanded as they stood in front of the car. Pavel raised his left arm and sniffed. Koopmann was right. Two nights in the same clothes, plus a car chase, had left an odor. He pulled on the handle, but it stuck.

"Wait, I have to do it from the inside." His colleague reached through the window from the driver's seat. She didn't aim for the lock button, though, but gave the lever that opened the door a good tug.

"Thanks," Pavel said and got in. It was a red Volkswagen Polo. He saw a lot of red inside, too, which made him tense. Today Enna's socks were orange with purple flowers. Quite pretty, but the contrast to the interior of the car was painful. He pressed the lock button, but it was jammed.

"The door is always locked unless you open it," Enna explained.

That was reassuring in that he could still get out of the car himself in the event of an accident. However, the fire department would have to cut the door open from the outside.

"At least this way you can't forget to lock the car," Pavel said. In the shower, he had decided to go easy on his colleague today and only disagree with her when it was a matter of life and death.

"I can't lock the car," Enna said. "The central locking system hasn't worked properly for years. That means it locks, but it doesn't open. By the way, I have to warn you: don't use it to lock the car! The doors can only be opened from the inside."

"That means the car stays open when we get out?" Pavel jiggled the black lock button again. It was stuck like King Arthur's sword in the stone. He turned the window handle. At least the window opened. That was very reassuring. It was still chilly this early in the morning, but if he left a gap, the fire department would have an easier time rescuing him. Usually, the window could just be pushed down.

"Yeah, why? It's not a problem."

"But then anyone can get in. And these old models must be really easy to start."

"That's never happened to me, and I've had the car since I was eighteen."

Don't argue. If she was happy with the old Polo, so was he.

"That's good," he said. "We can go whenever you are ready. Just be careful, there's a bike path right behind the gate."

"Of course, boss. I've known about it for fifteen years."

That was wrong, but he had made his rules for today. After almost colliding with another cyclist on his first day, he had checked with the highway department. The bike path had been built eight years ago and was not an area of frequent accidents, as he had assumed.

Pavel started as Koopmann took off like a shot. Fortunately, she stopped at the gate before joining the flow of traffic, using her turn signal as required.

They stopped briefly at his guesthouse. In his room, Pavel undressed completely. He took a fresh T-shirt and clean underpants from the pile his landlady kept adding to, laundry service being included in the rent. The dirty clothes went into the laundry basket. Then he took the two stiff plates out of the bulletproof vest. Even though it was only Class 1 protection now, it was much more comfortable to wear. He pulled a long-sleeved shirt over it and chose another suit.

Pavel really liked suits. They made him look conservative, which he wasn't, but he didn't care. He made sure his pants and jacket matched. His ex-wife no longer picked out his clothes for him, and he had given up trying to learn the supposed rules that had to be followed to be considered well-dressed. Especially since they changed almost every year!

He adjusted his suit in the mirror. The bulletproof vest was barely visible. Only someone who knew that he didn't have that broad a chest could tell. He almost always went without a tie. Very good. Pavel started for the door but then remembered something. He opened the closet a second time, took out his spare vest, and tucked it under his arm. After all, the man they wanted to see was armed.

"That was quick." Enna smiled. Was that meant ironically? After all, it had taken him seven minutes, but he couldn't see any signs of irony in his colleague's face. Pavel grabbed the handle of the back door.

"No, come around to the front." Enna took a large black handbag from the passenger seat and opened the door. "It's easier to talk this way."

Pavel got in. The seat back was upright. He fumbled with the lever to move it back a little. "You don't mind, do you?"

"Go ahead."

The lever was a thin metal rod running crosswise. He pulled it and fell flat along with the seat.

Enna laughed. It was contagious, and even though he had to assume she had anticipated this outcome, he laughed along with her. When he straightened up again, the backrest followed.

"You have to push the lever back, but not lift it," Enna explained.

He tried to follow the instructions but fell back again. No matter. He had enough room for his legs. Pavel picked himself up and took a deep breath. At the same moment, Enna reached between his legs and the seat slid smoothly back a few inches. Pavel froze—his colleague was already on the main road and they were approaching a pedestrian crossing.

But Enna turned back to face traffic fast enough for him to refrain from reprimanding her. He dropped the spare vest he had picked up on the floor behind the driver's seat.

"For me?" asked Enna.

"Better safe than sorry."

"Does the State Criminal Investigation Department issue those?"

Pavel sniffed. Bulletproof vests might be worn by SWAT

teams during an operation, but they weren't part of their standard equipment. "What do you think? I bought them myself."

"Is Kiel such a dangerous place?"

"Not Kiel, Fleetstedt! Did you know that the concentration of firearms in Germany's federal states is much higher than in the city-states? In Lower Saxony almost nine out of every hundred inhabitants own a gun, in Hamburg only two."

"Hunters, right?"

"Not only that, but also because of tradition. Many villages have their own rifle club."

"Then I wonder why we're taking vests to Hamburg of all places."

In principle, Enna was right. To be consistent, he should have left the vests at home. But statistics never applied to individual cases. They were dealing with a trigger-happy intruder. Better to be prepared. What was the kindest way to say it?

He decided on "I just don't want to lose you, Ms. Koopmann." Then he took his cell phone out of his pocket, which showed an incoming message. The sender was Berger. Great. The message contained an address and a name. The suspect's name was Harry Küster, and he lived at 22 Danziger Strasse.

"We'll go to Danziger Strasse first," he said. "That's where the guy with the black Kawasaki lives."

Enna immediately started typing on her cell phone, which was illegal while driving. Pavel looked away and compared the address with the data he had extracted from Toni's cell phone and navigation lists. He had created his own map overlay, which now floated like a shadow over the center of Hamburg. There were location tags mainly on addresses in the trendy district of St. Pauli, but there was one tag in the rather poor and less touristy St. Georg, where Danziger Strasse was located. And where had Toni been? On Danziger Strasse near number 22. The city map showed him that there was a shisha bar there, called *Saphir*.

"And what about Toni?" asked Enna. "It looked like he had an apartment in Hamburg."

"Unfortunately, the registry office had no record of it. But he often stayed near Bleicherstraße 70. That's in St. Pauli."

"Expensive area."

Pavel nodded. Not that he knew his way around St. Pauli very well. He knew no more about the notorious district than any other tourist. Maybe they should have investigated along with their counterparts in Hamburg.

Enna stopped the car in a no-parking zone of all places. He looked at her. She probably just wanted to talk to him about what to do next. But his colleague turned off the ignition and removed the key. Then she turned to the back seat, shoved the vest down into the footwell, and picked up her purse.

"Look, there's twenty-two!" She pointed to a square sign.

Pavel pointed to the other, round sign with a diagonal line through it.

"Eight to six on weekdays," Enna read aloud.

"Saturday is a working day."

Many people didn't know that. But Enna worked as a policewoman. She should have known.

"There's not a single car in front or behind us. We're not blocking anyone."

As if that was a valid reason!

"Yes, because there's no parking here. The others respect that."

"And what about the motorcycle in front of us?"

Oh, a black bike. Pavel's eyes scanned for the license plate. But they couldn't ...

"If we didn't have to discuss our parking space, we'd already be on our way."

"All right, then. But let me just check the license plate quickly. Then we'll drive on."

"Agreed." Enna grabbed her bag and slammed the door. Pavel was gentler with his door, just pushing it against the body so that it bounced back and stayed open.

"More force, boss!" yelled Enna.

He put his finger to his lips. They had agreed to travel incognito. He sighed. He took long strides toward the motorcycle. There it was again, half a brain. The license plate matched. He scanned the vehicle. The engine was cold and the seat was covered with pollen. The owner hadn't ridden it since yesterday. Pavel looked ahead along Danziger Strasse, shielding his eyes with his hand. There seemed to be a small park about six hundred feet to the left. Maybe there were parking spaces there?

When he looked back at the red Polo, Enna was gone. He fumbled for his gun and ran in the direction she had been going earlier, until he spotted her in front of the building. Whew.

"What are you...?"

Enna looked at him sternly, shook her head, and leaned over to the intercom. "Hi, Mrs. Krüger, I need to talk to Harry for a moment."

"Hi, Harry's not here."

"We have an appointment for one o'clock. I'm sure he'll be back for that."

Pavel looked at his watch. It was ten to one.

"All right," the voice on the speaker said. "Come on up."

The stairwell was clean and smelled of cleaning products. Mint and something artificial. Ocean freshness, perhaps, something clever marketing departments had come up with.

They climbed to the third floor. Behind one door they could hear a television, behind another children's cries. Krüger's was quiet, but a child's bicycle leaned against the wall in the hallway. The front door was ajar.

When they reached the door, it opened fully. Mrs. Krüger was in her mid-thirties and wore an apron over a brightly colored bikini.

"Hello," she said again. "You don't want to talk to us about God, do you?"

What made her think that? Pavel often wondered how he came across to people.

"No, I'm Enna Koopmann. I'm a colleague of your husband's. We need to discuss something."

"A ... colleague? I didn't even know he had any. And who is this?" The woman pointed at Pavel as if he was a non-entity.

"This is Mr. Neuhof. A rather important client."

The woman's face tightened as if she had bitten into a lemon. With her shot in the dark, Enna had probably missed whatever the target was.

"But you're right," she said quickly. "Mr. Neuhof was just curious to meet Harry. He'll wait for me in the car."

Would he? Pavel looked at Enna without understanding. But Krüger's face relaxed. That was understandable. The woman was alone. Who would want to let two strangers into her apartment? Enna in her shorts and colorful socks was no threat in comparison. His colleague must have thought this through in a flash and acted strategically.

"You're right, Enna," he said. "I need to go over some strategy reports anyway." He turned away, but out of the corner of his eye, he noticed Enna gesturing discreetly to Mrs. Krüger, who smiled in response. He started downstairs and heard the apartment door close.

Slowly he became restless. *Oh no, slowly my ass.* He'd been trying to convince himself of that all along. But he had been restless from the beginning. Not because of Enna. She would get along well with Mrs. Krüger. But it was already ten past one, which meant that they had been parked here for at least twenty minutes. That couldn't continue much longer. He was sitting behind the wheel, but if someone asked him to drive on, he would only be able to shrug his shoulders because he didn't have the keys. In his imagination, he would be asked for his driver's license and registration, which he didn't have either, which would lead to him being taken to the police station. Well, yes. Maybe his badge would help in that instance.

Suddenly a shadow fell over him. A surprisingly large finger on an even larger hand tapped on the passenger-side window. Pavel was startled but calmed down when the grinning freckled face of a young boy of about eight to ten appeared next to the hand. He stuck out his tongue. Kids liked that, didn't they?

"Hey, bro," a deep male voice said without looking into the car. "Do yourself a favor and get out of here. They're really strict with their checks. Twenty-five euros minimum. But parking is cheap over there by the Alster."

"Thanks, bro." He had to stifle a laugh as he said the word for the first time in his life. There was something magical about it, the harsh vibration of the "r" and the open "o" after it...

"Harry, the man stuck his tongue out at me," the boy said.

Since when did children call their parents by their first names? It seemed strange to Pavel. Only then did he realize what the boy had called the man. Harry. Harry Krüger?

Sure enough, the man walked to the entrance, unlocked the door, and stepped into the elevator, which Pavel could see through the glass. He managed to dash over and stick his foot in the gap before the front door closed. Then he ran up the stairs to the third floor, but arrived just as the apartment door was closing.

Pavel put his ear to the door.

"Can I play PlayStation?" he heard the boy say.

"Only with headphones, honey. We have a visitor."

"Thanks, Mom!" Pattering feet.

"Don't let him..." the man began.

"There's a woman in the living room who says she's your colleague."

"My what?"

"Colleague."

The man laughed. "You know where I work."

"But she doesn't, apparently."

Crap. Koopmann had probably been found out without realizing it. If only he hadn't talked her into this trip. And she hadn't even put on her vest!

He heard a metallic click.

"What are you doing?" asked Mrs. Krüger. They were still

whispering near the entrance. Hopefully, Enna would get suspicious!

"I wonder why?" Another click, as if the man had released the safety on a gun.

"Not in front of the boy! Or I'll throw you out!"

Very good, a brave woman. The boy was probably playing in the living room, where Enna was waiting.

"He has his headphones on. Very clever of you, Dani."

"Out of the question. Give me that gun, come on!"

Yeah, give it to her, dummy. You want to save your relationship, don't you?

"What are you doing?" a woman asked. Pavel turned around. He took his badge out of his pocket. The woman came closer, looked at him, and seemed satisfied as she walked past him up the stairs.

"Shh," said Harry Krüger. "There was a car downstairs with the license plate WTM. There was a man in it. Maybe he's outside right now?"

Pavel ducked. Someone was probably looking through the peephole right now.

"There's no one there," said Mrs. Krüger. "You're getting worked up for nothing. If you ask me, you should never have given that man the money."

"It was a sure thing. Fifty thousand in, five hundred thousand out."

"Well, where's the five hundred thousand?"

"You're right, Dani. You're a sweetheart."

"Then give me the gun."

"Nah, I'm leaving. They don't want anything from you."

Suddenly the door opened outward, so violently that Pavel was knocked off his feet. He couldn't stop himself from hitting the wall, but he managed to get back on his feet.

"Don't!" the woman shouted, and only then did he realize that Harry Krüger was aiming at him. Pavel trembled, but the man obeyed and put the gun in his wife's hand.

"I can take you, you worm," he growled.

"Just watch the walls. The landlord will charge us for every stain," Mrs. Krüger scolded, as she leaned against the wall and watched with her arms crossed. It looked like she had experience watching her husband fight. Where was Enna? Surely she must have heard something.

Pavel was on his feet again. He loosened his limbs and prepared to fight. The referee had just said *Hajime* in his head. The fight was on.

Harry Krüger came straight at him. At the last second, Pavel dodged, seizing his arm and utilizing his momentum to execute a *hiza-guruma*—a full-body turn initiated with his left foot

Krüger crashed headfirst into the concrete but got back up. Blood dripped from a cut on his head.

"You stupid bastard!" Krüger shouted. There was a lot of anger in him, too much for a fight like this. He could probably massacre a hundred Spartans by himself right now, but he was no match for an *O-Soto-gari*. Pavel liked the German name—outward sweep—and that was how it worked. It was pure physics. He preferred to fight heavier, faster opponents. Mass and speed provided momentum, and if he was smart, his opponent provided the momentum for his own defeat.

Harry charged in, and found himself on the ground again. His face shone red as he glared grimly at Pavel. A vein of rage throbbed on his forehead. "So you want to do this the hard way!"

Pavel just waved his fingers.

He caused Harry Krüger to struggle to his feet twice more. His wife didn't seem to notice how things were going for her husband, or she didn't care. At least she hadn't given him the gun back, for which Pavel was grateful.

Finally, he had enough of fighting and held the sweating Krüger in a *yoko-shiho-gatame*, a four-point side control, which gave him the opportunity to bind his wrists with the plastic handcuffs he always carried in his jacket pocket. It worked just like a zip tie, but had rounded edges to minimize injury if worn for long periods.

"Ippon," he said excitedly. That meant victory. The referee raised his arm and the crowd cheered.

Harry Krüger gasped against the concrete floor. "What do you want?" he asked, straining.

"To talk."

A snort. "Talk?"

"Just talk." Pavel loosened his grip, and Harry nodded. Pavel released him completely and the loser scrambled to his feet.

"You assholes have messed up the wall," Mrs. Krüger said, pointing at the wall. "Who did that?"

There was indeed a large scuff mark on one of the walls. There was also blood dripping onto the concrete.

"I'm sorry, Mrs. Krüger," Pavel apologized.

Harry suddenly looked dejected as well. "Sorry, Dani," he said meekly and slipped into the apartment.

"What happened?" asked Enna Koopmann as they entered the living room. She spoke unusually loudly because she was wearing headphones. She also had a controller in her hand. On the television, a grim, half-naked, blood-spattered warrior held a sword aloft. She was frozen in mid-motion.

"Enna fights pretty well," the boy said. "Can we play a little longer?"

"Max, you fought well too," Enna said, taking off her headphones.

"We adults need to talk for a while," his mother said. "You better finish your homework. Dad's picking you up at three and then you won't have time."

"I'll do it Monday before first period."

Dani Krüger didn't argue, which was probably the best strategy, and her son left the living room.

"You're the one who chased me yesterday, aren't you?" asked the man, who was still tied up.

"You shot at me, Krüger."

"I only wanted to slow you down. A blind man with a cane could see you were wearing a vest!"

"Jeez, Harry, you promised me you'd only use the gun as a

threat," Dani Krüger said. "I'm telling you, if you get more than a year, I'll find someone else."

"I'm not going to jail," Harry Krüger said.

"We'll see about that," Pavel objected. "Assaulting a police officer, attempted murder..."

"Oh, and why is there a red Polo with Wittmunder plates parked downstairs instead of a green squad car?"

That was a clever interjection. They were not yet legally investigating here, at least not through official channels. He could hardly speak of imminent trouble.

"The gun is definitely illegal," Enna helped him. "I don't know what you do for a living, but that's a problem for most employers."

"I work behind the bar at the club around the corner, over there by the rainbow crosswalk."

"That's why I didn't believe you that you were a colleague of Harry's from the start," said Dani Krüger.

"Why? Don't any women work there?"

"Drive past there later and you'll see."

"You probably want to get going now, anyway," Harry said.

"Now, slow down. I'm not leaving until I know why you made such a mess in Fleetstedt, and what you had to do with Toni Sattelmacher's death."

"Death? What are you talking about?" Dani Krüger's face turned red again. She seemed to get upset very quickly. "Harry, say something! You said it was all legal!"

"I had nothing to do with it. I didn't even know the guy was dead. Otherwise I would never have gone there! I'm not stupid."

It was strange, but Pavel was inclined to believe the man. He might be a bit reckless, but he didn't seem to have anything to do with organized crime.

"There are two options. I call our counterparts in Hamburg and hand everything over to them. The illegal weapon alone would lead to unpleasant questions and proceedings. Or you can tell me exactly what is going on, and if I'm convinced that you only got involved by chance, you can make an official statement to us in Fleetstedt, and that will be it."

"I have to go back into your territory?"

"You know the way."

"Harry, tell the gentleman what you know," the woman said. "Sounds like a fair offer. You'll never get the briefcase anyway."

"A briefcase full of money?" asked Enna. "Half a million, by any chance?"

"At first it was only about fifty thousand. Toni needed money," Harry Krüger reported.

"How did you know him?" asked Enna.

"From the bar."

"Okay. And what did he need the money for?" asked Pavel.

"He said he had a sure way to increase the amount twentyfold."

"That's what whetted your appetite."

"Hell, he was going to give me five hundred thousand. You don't say no to that!"

"Why was he so generous?"

"Because he had nothing left. He showed me his bank statements. I asked him why his parents couldn't give him anything. He said they had just had their house renovated for two hundred and fifty thousand, and he didn't even know how he was going to pay for their retirement home. But the fifty grand would bail him out."

"What was he going to do with it?" asked Enna.

"He had a notary on hand. She had probably found an investor who wanted to convert Toni's parents' property into a residential park for rich people. So he got that started—only the building authority wouldn't approve it. I think it was about monument protection. The fifty thousand euros solved that problem."

"Bribery," Pavel noted. That was something that would not go over well with her superiors. Accusations of corruption always cause bad blood.

"Who was bribed?" asked Enna.

"I don't know. He just told me that everything would go smoothly and that I would soon have half a million in my pocket."

"But nothing came of it."

"Exactly, Inspector. So I tried to put some pressure on him. With the bank, with the notary, with his parents..."

The notary? She hadn't reported any threats either. Was everyone in Fleetstedt so tight-lipped? Or was Henriette Meier dirty? Had she orchestrated the bribery? That would be a serious matter!

"I even tried to get information from the buyers, but they claimed not to know Toni Sattelmacher at all and not to know anything about a bribe. So, yes. It became clear to me that they didn't have the half million."

"Because they had paid one and a half million."

"That's what the guy from the bank told me when I twisted his arm a little."

"Then you got mad at Toni for betraying you and killed him."

"I told you, it wasn't me. Are you even listening to me, Inspector?"

Pavel took a deep breath. The story sounded plausible. But for an otherwise peaceful bartender, Krüger had really gone out on a limb.

"That was quite a gamble, wasn't it?" he asked. "I mean, it was an investment of fifty thousand, that's a lot, but what you were willing to do for it..."

"I had nothing to do with Toni's death! I swear on my mother's life."

"You'd better leave your mother out of this. Where did you get the fifty thousand?"

"Yes, I would like to know that too," Dani said.

Harry Krüger looked at his wife, or girlfriend, and Pavel thought he saw fear in the grown man's face. He had intended to question her separately as a witness later, but apparently her presence saved him from having to put the screws on her husband.

"How else? I took out a loan from Volodya."

"Volodya? You must be crazy! Do you want to get us all killed?" Dani Krüger took off her right shoe and whacked the man with the pointed heel until Enna took the fake leather weapon away from her.

"You should leave now," Pavel said.

Dani Krüger snorted but obeyed.

"Thanks," Harry said as the door to the hallway closed.

"Who's Volodya?" asked Enna. "Russian mafia?"

"Another customer from the bar. But yes, rumor has it that he has certain contacts. And he lends money, even without collateral, and without asking what it's for."

"Now he's putting pressure on you, isn't he?" asked Pavel.

"When I didn't pay right away, he threatened to kidnap Dani." Harry grew silent. Something was bothering him. A guilty conscience for putting his family in danger?

"He stopped?" Enna asked.

"Yes, he's leaving me alone now. I'm afraid I got Toni into it."

"Got him into what?" asked Pavel.

"Well, into getting killed. I told Volodya what the money was for. Otherwise he would have done something to me. I haven't had any trouble from him since."

Had this Volodya taken the money from Toni, along with the accumulated profit? Did the Sattelmachers' son die because of that—or in the process?

"Does your friend Volodya still come to your bar?" asked Pavel.

Krüger shook his head. "I haven't seen him since."

"He went into hiding with half a million," said Enna.

"Or all of it. We're not going to find him. It is above our pay grade. The FBI would have to get involved."

"If it's true."

As always, he had to agree with Enna.

"Do you believe what Krüger told us?" asked Pavel.

Enna steered the Polo through the afternoon traffic, which was quite heavy in Hamburg even on a Saturday. She downshifted before an intersection, then replied, "It all sounded plausible. But that guy Volodya could have been made up. He sounds a bit random to me. Mafia, you can blame them for everything you don't want to admit to."

"We won't find out if he went underground or never existed."

"That's why we have to find witnesses to corroborate Krüger's statements."

To do that, they now had 70 Bleicherstrasse on their agenda. But it could also be 72, which was next door, or 77, which was across the street. Toni had only entered the street name in his navigation device, and the cell search was not that accurate. That was why they were going to split up and use the picture of the dead man to question the residents. Someone had to know him. He had spent a lot of time there, more than in Fleetstedt.

"Did you see the crosswalk?" she asked, "Very colorful."

"Hm, not really up to code."

"It's pretty, though. Oh, there's that pub the Krügers were talking about."

Pavel read the name and looked it up on his phone. "It's a gay bar. Does that mean Toni was gay? His mother hinted at it."

"Does it matter now?"

Pavel thought about it. "No." It had no relevance to the case. So far they hadn't found any jealous lovers. On the contrary, they hadn't found anyone who had had a relationship with Toni. But murders were often crimes of passion. "But we should find his boyfriend."

"Or his girlfriend. Remember the hair from the shower."

That was also a possibility. Maybe the victim wasn't only interested in men.

Good. They had a plan. Unfortunately, that gave his tireless mind the opportunity to dwell on the past.

"Was it a mistake to just let Krüger go?" he asked.

"We'll have to see."

"Maybe you can tell me if it was the right decision."

Enna laughed. "Oh, is that how it works for you?"

Unfortunately, it wasn't that simple. They had taken the illegal weapon from Krüger, so the man couldn't use it to rob a bank or sell it to a terrorist. But there were still a lot of stupid things he could do, and when it came out that they had questioned him without a warrant...

"I'm sure Dani will keep an eye on him," Enna said. "She promised me she would when we said goodbye. By the way, she thought we were an item."

"What?" Pavel snorted until he noticed a small crease in Enna's forehead. She tried to hide it, but she had to make an effort, and it made her features look harder.

"Yeah, a stupid idea," Enna said, "a really stupid idea."

He didn't like the way she emphasized *stupid*, but of course, she was right. The age difference alone! Or maybe his colleague was interested in women? They hadn't discussed that yet. No, he had told her about his ex-wife. Enna had never talked about her ex-whatever.

"How did Dani Krüger come up with that idea?"

"She saw you fighting with her husband. He used to be a soldier in the German army in Afghanistan, so he's not completely inexperienced. But she said you took him down effortlessly."

"Effortlessly? I wouldn't call it that," Pavel said. A pleasant feeling flooded his stomach. *Ippon*. Was there a judo club in Fleetstedt?

"Anyway, Krüger thought you were fighting like a lion for me."

"No, that wasn't the case. I knew you weren't in any immediate danger, Enna. The two Krügers were with me in the corridor, and little Max was no match for you."

For some unknown reason, Enna sighed. Perhaps because he had mentioned the child. Women and children were a strange combination.

"Oh, Max really beat me at that game," she said.

Chapter Sixteen

"Let's go," Enna said and got out of the car.

Pavel got out and followed her to the meter. "Two euros per hour with a maximum of three hours!" he grumbled as he inserted two two-euro coins. "We have a hundred and twenty minutes." He placed the ticket on the dashboard. Hopefully, no one would steal it. The car was unlocked.

The neighborhood was pleasantly quiet, even though they were in the middle of the city, very close to the cesspool that was St. Pauli. The sound of traffic could be heard in the distance. On the even-numbered side of the street were apartment buildings built in the 1970s, clad in clinker brick with wide, red balconies. The apartments were probably perfect for families. The other side was dominated by buildings that looked more like office blocks. They had no balconies facing the street. But Pavel saw curtains and lights, and there was a long nameplate at the entrance. Single people probably lived there in small apartments—people like Toni. According to his calculations, the only possible addresses were seventy, seventy-two, and seventy-seven.

"Will you take seventy? I'll take number seventy-seven."

Enna nodded.

Pavel fumbled for his cell phone, which had a picture of the victim on it. "Be careful," he said. Harry Krüger's attack was still fresh in his mind. Were they right to leave such a dangerous guy alone? But as a first offender and with a good record, he would probably get off with probation; besides, a prison sentence rarely reformed anyone. Koopmann shouldn't have any problems in the building with the family apartments.

The panel of doorbells for house number seventy-seven was very long. He started with the top one.

"Who is it?" asked a man.

"Delivery!" shouted Pavel. The door buzzed, and he stepped into a tiled hallway that smelled of food. It wasn't even appetizing, but his mouth watered anyway. It was way past lunchtime.

He ran up the stairs to the third floor. One of the four apartment doors was ajar. He read the name on the doorbell—Müller—and knocked. A man in a muscle shirt stretched over a huge belly opened the door. Pavel took a step back. The apartment reeked of fish.

"Paul, did you check the potatoes?" a woman's voice called in the background.

"Hello," said the man. "Delivery? One *mooomeeent*, darling!"

"Good day." Pavel shook his head and showed his ID, then Toni's photo on his cell phone. "Do you know this man?"

"Of course I do. That's Rio. Rio Reiser. Anything else? My wife..."

"Like the singer?"

"Like the King of Germany. He always sings when he's full. Do you know the song?"

Pavel nodded. "Do you know where he lives?"

"Well, not here in this building. On the other side."

"In the seventies?"

"Is that across the street?"

Pavel nodded.

"Shahatz, where does Rio live?"

"Well, over there, you know. Remember the potatoes! I'm still on the toilet."

"*Seventy or seventy-two?*"

"I don't know. The potatoes!"

"I have to go," said the man.

"The potatoes, sure. Thank you very much."

The door closed behind him. Pavel dialed Enna's number, but she didn't answer. He sent her a text message: "They say Toni lived on your side."

⁂

No one opened the door to the apartment next door. It was dark behind the peephole. He put his ear to the white-painted wood. Silence. Should he not bother questioning the rest of the residents? He shook his head. Worst case they would find Toni's apartment, but wouldn't be able to get in. They couldn't just break in, in the course of a private investigation. What were they thinking? He had never had such ideas while working at the State Criminal Police Department.

A door opened behind him and a little boy in rubber boots scampered out.

"Stay here, Marco!" shouted his mother, a young woman in jeans and a t-shirt who had just appeared in the doorway and jumped when she saw him. The boy braked and hid behind Pavel, holding onto his legs.

"Sorry," the woman said. "He really wants to ride his tricycle, but we're about to have lunch."

"I tricycle!" the boy shouted.

"No problem. I'm Police Chief Inspector Pavel Neuhof." He held out his badge to the woman. "Can I ask you something?"

"Leave the man alone, Marco!" the woman yelled. "If it's quick..."

He showed her Toni's picture on his phone.

"I know him. Always partying at night. We've had to call the police twice. Unfortunately, the children's room faces the street. Has he done anything wrong?"

"When was the last party?"

Little Marco crawled between his legs, but at least he stopped saying "tricycle" all the time.

"Wednesday, I think. Or was it Tuesday? Yes, Tuesday!"

"Was he alone?" Pavel looked down at his shoes. Marco had loosened the strap and was untying the laces.

"Alone? Haha, there were at least twenty people there."

"I mean, did he usually live alone. When he wasn't having a party."

"How should I know? I only noticed he was there when there were parties. Marco, don't do that!"

"No problem. Cute little guy." Fortunately, his face never betrayed the fact that he was lying. "One last question—which apartment did the noise come from?"

"Across the street, second floor."

The little boy held up a shoelace, stood up, and then ran to his mother. "Look!" he shouted.

"Give it back to the gentleman," said his mother.

"House seventy or seventy-two?"

The woman closed her eyes for a moment. "Diagonally left, looking out Marco's window. It must be seventy-two."

"Thank you, you've been very helpful."

The woman nodded and took the shoelace from her son. "I'm sure you need this."

˞

This time Enna answered. "Sorry, I just had to listen to an old lady's life story."

"A little boy stole my shoelace. But now I know where Toni lived."

"Yes, Hamburg boys are extremely dangerous," Enna said, her smile carrying over into her voice. "House number seventy-two, second floor on the right."

Crap. One for one. "I'll come over, then."

"The old lady suffers from insomnia, loneliness, and boredom. So she kept a record of who left which apartment and when."

"Very practical. She could see all that?"

"She probably questioned everyone, too. Toni didn't live alone, by the way. He's had a steady girlfriend for years. She came to the house for the first time on March third, two thousand and nine."

The old lady was very thorough. "Do you know what that means?"

"Yes, we'll probably find her there."

According to the phone records, the cell phone number Toni had used for his last five-minute call belonged to a certain Lisa Munterer. She was registered in Hamburg, but not in this area. They had not yet been able to reach her by phone.

"I really hope so," Pavel said. "She might be the last person our victim spoke to on the phone. Are you waiting downstairs in front of the apartment?"

The doorbell panel at number seventy-two was arranged systematically, showing four apartments per floor in a rectangle, but without names. The apartment where the victim lived was on the right, so Pavel pressed the appropriate button.

"Let me talk," Enna said.

Pavel nodded. Woman to woman, she probably had a better chance.

There was a crackle in the intercom. "Who is this?" a female voice asked.

"This is Police Inspector Enna Koopmann."

No answer. Enna pressed the button again.

"What do you want?"

"It's about Toni Sattelmacher. You didn't answer our calls."

"Oh, that was you! I thought you'd found..." Pavel noticed how the rest of the sentence died away in a sudden wave of suspicion.

"Will you please let us in, Ms. Munterer? We have something to tell you."

The woman replied by pressing the open button.

"Hello! Oh, you're not alone," the woman said from the open door of her apartment. Lisa Munterer was in her late thirties. She was slim, but had a prominent bust, which, combined with long blond hair and full lips, made her a stereotypical St. Pauli beauty. What was considered a worldly woman in Fleetstedt?

"Hello, this is my colleague Pavel Neuhof. We're investigating a case together."

Well, technically he was her boss, but he refrained from correcting Enna.

"Would you like to come in?"

Enna shook the woman's hand. Pavel noticed gold rings on Munterer's fingers. "That would be great, Ms. Munterer."

The woman stepped into the room. It smelled like an Indian restaurant, but not like food—more like perfume. Abstract paintings in warm colors hung on the walls. Dark red and burnt sienna dominated the color scheme.

Ms. Munterer pointed to the closet. "If you want to take off your coat."

Pavel shook his head. He wasn't hot. Enna took off her jacket and hung it on a hanger.

"May I?" She pointed to a fur coat.

The woman nodded. Enna felt the garment. "It's so soft!"

"Sable collar, the rest is nutria." The woman's eyes lit up.

"A very nice coat," Enna said as the woman led them into the living room.

There was an interesting contrast here. The sofa, armchair, and coffee table were black and had geometrically precise shapes. On the other side of the room, the wall was covered with a colorful patterned tapestry. There was a plush chaise longue. A bottle of wine with a cork and a half-full glass waited on an ornately carved side table. A book with an opaque dust cover lay upside down on the chaise longue.

"What did you want to tell me?" asked Munterer.

"Won't you sit down? How well did you know Toni Sattelmacher?"

As agreed, Pavel left the questioning to his colleague. He sat down on one of the low chairs. Perhaps the woman would follow his example.

"Very well. We've been together for over fifteen years. We intend to get married next year."

Pavel thought about the women's hair in the shower in Toni's apartment. What if he had dumped his Hamburg girlfriend unexpectedly? Or at least wanted to, and she had suspected it for some time? Jealousy was always a strong motive.

"And Toni Sattelmacher feels the same way?"

"Yes. We love each other. He just wants to... What about him?"

It seemed to dawn on her that something must have happened. That made things interesting. Did she know about Toni's death because she was involved, or would it come as a shock? The love story sounded a bit one-sided. He had heard it before. In many a long relationship, one partner couldn't imagine life without the other, while the other had long since moved on, but didn't have the courage to officially end the relationship.

"Sit down, Ms. Munterer," Enna said, and this time the woman obeyed. "I'm sorry to tell you that your boyfriend was found dead."

"What? That can't be..." She jumped up again. "We already set the date! Just two weeks ago ... Toni just wanted to..." She broke off, sat down again, and put her hands over her face. Pavel heard a soft whimper that he wasn't sure was real.

"What did Toni want?"

"Money, Inspector. It's always about money. Toni always needs a lot of it. That's the way he is. Our honeymoon is supposed to be in Tahiti."

Needed, was, and *was supposed to be*. People were surprisingly slow to react to such information. The more important the information was, the more important it was to react to it correctly, the longer it took to penetrate their consciousness. Sometimes it seemed to Pavel as if most people had lead pipes in their heads, clogged with memories and eaten away by desires.

"How is Toni going to solve the problem?" asked Enna.

Now his colleague had also entered the realm of ignorance. He had to stop himself from correcting her.

"It's his parents' house, which they signed over to him. He must have found the perfect investor."

"But there are still some problems."

Lisa Munterer shook her head vigorously. "No! It's all taken care of. The investor paid on time. He just has to get his parents to agree to the sale."

"They're not very happy about it. When they transferred the house, they registered a usufruct for the rest of their lives. Somehow that was gone."

Gone?

"Gone?"

Pavel smiled. Enna was already thinking the same thing he was.

"I don't know much about it." Lisa Munterer quickly wiped away a few tears. Was she trying to distract from her face? "Toni has a notary for the legal stuff. Had, I have to say now." Fresh tears streamed down her face.

This was all well and good, and it confirmed what they knew. But it didn't get them any further.

"May I tell you my own theory?" he asked. Enna shook her head, but he wasn't deterred. The sympathy tactic had failed.

"You visited him on Wednesday."

"On Wednesday... I was here on Wednesday waiting for him."

"Are there any witnesses to that?"

"No."

Of course, there were no witnesses, because Lisa Munterer had arrived in Fleetstedt some time before.

"You waited in his apartment. Do you know which apartment I'm talking about?"

The woman nodded.

"You found something there. Proof that he had someone else. Don't deny it. We found hair from two different women in his shower. I bet some of it is yours."

"I'm sure it is. I was there often. But I..."

"You called him that night. We have his cell phone records. Your call ended at 8:03. In it, he told you he was leaving you. With the money. Not only were your big plans in tatters, but your future lifestyle was in jeopardy. It was too much. You met him on the beach and there..."

"Pavel, wait," Enna interrupted. "We've been questioning Ms. Munterer as a witness. Before we question her as a suspect..."

Damn. He was getting ahead of himself. That hadn't happened to him in a long time. "I'm sorry about that. You don't have to answer my question. Enna, would you please advise Ms. Munterer of her rights?"

"That won't be necessary. Yes, I called him because I wanted to know how he was doing after talking to his parents. But he was still busy. He promised to call me the next day. He didn't."

"And you weren't worried?"

"Of course I was. I've tried to call him several times since Friday, but there was no answer."

Lisa Munterer stood up, walked over to him, and showed him the list of calls on her cell phone. She was right. Was it possible to fake a story like that? Probably, but he didn't think she had. He had only analyzed the call data up until the victim's death. That list showed who had called, but not from which cell. Munterer could still have been in Fleetstedt.

"You're welcome to look at my phone records," said Munterer, who must have realized he was not convinced. "I'll give you all the authority you need."

It was a decent offer. That way he wouldn't have to declare her a suspect and everything that went with it, but he'd still know her whereabouts up till Wednesday night at the latest.

"That's a fair offer, Lisa, and we'll gladly accept it. Please excuse my colleague. He's a little ... awkward sometimes."

Lisa Munterer wiped away more tears. Her makeup was already smudged. But that didn't mean she was innocent. Culprits were often just as distraught as all the other relatives. Who was to say that the suitcase with half a million in it wasn't in the bedroom next door? As soon as they left the apartment, the girlfriend would take it to a safe hiding place. Jealousy and greed were a perfect match.

"Did you ever wonder what your boyfriend was doing all alone in Fleetstedt?" he tried again.

"His parents live there. He's done some business there, too."

"And other women, what about them?"

"We loved each other. That doesn't mean he couldn't have sex with others sometimes!"

"Doesn't it?" asked Pavel.

"Of course not. What century were you born in?" asked Enna.

"The twentieth," he replied, though he didn't quite understand the question. Koopmann and Munterer were born in the same century as he.

"If I can trust you not to report this to management, I'd like to show you something," Lisa Munterer said, standing up.

"You don't have to," Enna said.

"I want to clear up any suspicions about me." Toni's girlfriend hurried to the bedroom door and opened it. Behind it was a fantasy room, bathed in warm shades of red. Next to a velvet-covered bed with a canopy, a large X-shaped cross was nailed to the wall. There was also a dentist's chair, just like the ones Pavel had seen in the dentist's office. Who would put such an instrument of torture in their bedroom?

"An interesting setup," he said.

Suddenly his mind pulled aside a curtain that must have gotten stuck somehow. Lisa Munterer was a sex worker!

"Before you think badly of me—I'm registered with the authorities, of course," she said. "Only the neighbors don't know about it."

"Thank you, Ms. Munterer," Pavel said. His face felt as hot as if he had caught a cold. "You didn't happen to have a visitor Wednesday night, did you?"

If so, they could cross the woman off the list of suspects right away.

"No. I only have two or three clients a week. My services are exclusive."

"I see. Since you knew Toni Sattelmacher well—we've heard that he often visited a gay bar."

Lisa Munterer nodded. "And why not? He's very versatile." She closed the door and sat back down on her chaise longue. "Was. He was. I still can't believe it. Could you leave me alone now? I want to call his parents in private. We need to make funeral arrangements."

"Do you believe her?" Pavel asked as they got into the Polo in front of the house.

Enna sank into the driver's seat and looked at him for a few seconds with a furrowed brow. "Pavel, what was that? We had an agreement." The look on her face indicated that she was annoyed. On the other hand, she was using his first name instead of distancing herself with "colleague" or even "Chief Inspector Neuhof". He should give her permission to use his first name soon. That would give Enna more linguistic differentiation possibilities, from *you are a prince, Pavel*, to *Neuhof, you disgusting cretin*. Not that he expected to be addressed by one of these extreme variants. Thanks to the broader spectrum, he would just have to guess which wrinkle, twitch, or flutter in her face belonged to which emotional expression.

"Are you even listening to me? That was totally inappropriate. You can't go changing the nature of the questioning without informing the woman of her rights."

Pavel nodded. Of course, Enna was right. It would be a relief if Lisa Munterer was innocent. Then there would be no problems. But did Koopmann have to harp on it like that?

"I am sorry. I don't know what came over me. The mixture of greed and jealousy is such a perfect motive. Seven figures. If I experienced jealousy, the combination might even make *me* a murderer. No, maybe not."

"You don't experience jealousy?"

The change of subject worked. When he mentioned it, most people, men and women alike, picked up on it.

"No. But most people really are jealous, even if they say they aren't. That's why Toni's girlfriend is still on my list. He promised her marriage and half a million. If something like that suddenly goes away..."

"There is no evidence of that. In fact, it looks like he still had the suitcase with the money."

Pavel nodded. Harry had fruitlessly searched for the case. What about the Russian, Volodya? Someone like that wouldn't just let fifty thousand euros go. He must have made a deal that satisfied him. But why would he have killed Toni? Murder would only mean more money and risk. Toni's deal with the investor—if Harry Krüger was telling the truth—was so shady because of the bribery of the building authorities that Sattelmacher couldn't go to the police to seek justice.

"What do you think of the notary?" Pavel asked as he buckled his seatbelt.

"She did something she wasn't supposed to do. But that would probably just land her in trouble with the notary's office. The contract would be void and she would lose her commission, but she would still be allowed to continue working as a notary. Unless she knew about the bribe. That's a different story."

Enna was right. But Pavel didn't believe the notary would be willing to take such risks. An invalid contract? The investor, Norddeutsche Küstenkapital, would probably have suffered the greatest loss. It was a pity they couldn't contact the notary or the investment company today. How could he tolerate the uncertainty until Monday?

"Tell me, Enna..."

"Yes?"

"How would you like to go for a walk on the beach tomorrow? You've done a lot of research on currents, which will be helpful."

"We could also get the crime scene investigator from Leer to come."

Was she torturing him on purpose? He couldn't let a crime scene investigator do the work for him!

Enna seemed to notice his horror, for she smiled disarmingly. "I was only joking, Pavel. We can search the crime scene tomorrow morning. I don't have anything else planned anyway."

Was she serious? He didn't ask. "Good. Hopefully we'll make some progress."

She nodded thoughtfully and put the key in the lock. "Yeah, somehow I feel like we're finding motive after motive, but not getting any closer to the killer."

"That's not entirely true. We're tightening the noose slowly but surely."

Enna gave him a look, this time more reflective, but said nothing. Instead she started the car. Back to Fleetstedt. Pavel was glad. He was still annoyed about his slip-up. On the other hand, the day with Enna had gone very well. They were a good team. He liked that. Very much.

Chapter Seventeen

Enna had her hands in the pockets of her shorts. With her right hand, she played with her house key. A fresh breeze blew in from the north and brushed against her bare legs. She was wearing red socks today, with golden-yellow French fries shining on them.

She glanced at her watch and stifled a yawn. Was Pavel sleeping under the desk in the office, and would she have to wake him up again? He was a strange guy, but somehow she liked him. She had the feeling that things could be just as good with him as with her old boss—different, sure, but good. She liked that; a good work environment was very important to her, and one of the reasons she loved the little office in Fleetstedt so much.

She thought back to their trip to Hamburg and grinned broadly. She liked the way Pavel had handled Harry Krüger. Too bad she had missed the fight. It could have been legendary, but Enna couldn't tell anyone about it. They hadn't been there officially.

In the distance, she saw a tall figure. It was walking along the wooden path from Fleetstedt to the beach. It was the slender silhouette of Neuhof.

Enna grinned involuntarily and sauntered towards him. She was in no hurry. It was Sunday morning, the sun was shining, and they had a long walk along the beach ahead of them.

It was said that Norderney had the most beautiful beach in Germany, but Enna was convinced that Fleetstedt did. The white dunes literally glowed in the sun, along with the sparkling water and rippling grass. Enna loved mornings by the sea. She could taste the salt air on her lips. The tourists would come later, after they'd had their fill of breakfast in the hotels and guesthouses. Only a few joggers and dog owners were out this early to walk their four-legged friends.

Enna suddenly missed Pete acutely. How often he had scampered across the beach, running in circles and scratching like crazy. She loved to watch him chase the ball "Balla" and bring it back to her, well-behaved and proud.

A sigh escaped her lips. She would talk to Pavel and see if he could handle an office dog. He would probably need a little more time. And it wasn't necessary to settle everything straight away.

"Hello!" she heard Neuhof call. He even waved.

Enna waved back. "Did you sleep well? Hopefully in your bed."

Pavel laughed. "I did this time!" He looked around the beach and grinned appreciatively. "Really beautiful here."

"At least as beautiful as California. You'll love it! Come on. We'll start right down here."

Together they walked over the rumbling wooden planks to the dune, then across the beach to the water's edge. Just above it, where the sand was still wet and hard, they turned east.

"So this is where you fished the body out of the water?" Pavel fumbled with the straps of his backpack. He obviously had equipment with him—for whatever reason. He always seemed to be prepared for any eventuality.

Enna pointed to a hollow between two dunes. "This is where we put him down. He was floating about six hundred feet further out."

Pavel glanced at the razor-sharp line of the horizon, then across the beach and back to Enna. "I wouldn't have thrown a body in the water here."

"Neither would I. Too conspicuous."

"And too far. You'd have to drag or carry him a long way

across the beach, which would be exhausting with Toni's two hundred-plus pounds, and—if it happened here—you'd still have the problem of not knowing whether the tide would carry the body out to sea. That was probably the intention: to make his body disappear. Much more time would have passed before his death was discovered. The evidence older, colder, maybe even gone altogether."

Enna nodded. "Off the top of my head, I can think of two possible places to dump a body."

"Sounds good. Let's get started."

They started walking. Their uneven footprints could be seen stretching far behind them on the wide beach.

Enna squinted into the sun, loving the moment. It was another beautiful Sunday morning, once again reminding her that you didn't need much to be happy. Sun, beach, and shorts.

Pavel also seemed lost in thought as he walked beside her, gazing into the distance.

Suddenly he said: "We missed an opportunity." He raised his forefinger admonishingly. "Kessler said Sattelmacher could have been alive when he fell into the water, and drowned after being hit on the back of the head."

"But that wasn't the cause of death."

"Correct, but there could have been a struggle at the water's edge, then a final blow that ended the struggle."

"That would remove the *intention to make the body disappear*."

"Yes. In that case, the parties involved might have met on the beach for other reasons."

"Sounds like a crime of passion."

"And the North Sea was simply the best body disposal option."

Enna shook her head. "You and your vocabulary. Body disposal option. I'll have to write that down."

He stopped, took the backpack off his back, and fumbled with the buckles.

"What are you doing?" Enna wanted to know.

"Getting you a pen and some paper."

"For what?"

He looked up, puzzled. "You wanted to write it down."

Enna's mouth opened and closed. Then she burst out laughing. "I meant that... never mind. Thank you, Pavel."

He nodded like a turtle, visibly confused, then took out a pen and paper and handed them to her.

Enna wrote down *body disposal option*, folded the sheet, and put it in her pocket with a grin. Then they walked on.

The beach extended for two miles to the east in the form of an elongated bulge, until the white sand ended in higher dunes. Enna pointed up about thirty feet and began to climb.

A little out of breath, she reached the top and took in the view of the old fishing port. A few boats were anchored in the shelter of a storm break. Their masts swayed gently to and fro. A few seagulls circled.

Pavel stepped up beside her and looked around curiously. "Do the Sattelmachers have a boat? You checked, didn't you?"

"Yes, I did. And no, they don't."

"Too bad. That could have been the crime scene."

Enna nodded, and they walked down the well-worn coastal path to the harbor on the other side. There, Enna started to walk toward the storm break, but Pavel shook his head and pulled her toward the harbor. He pointed to a security camera at the entrance to the breakwater.

Enna understood; no one would be that stupid. Then again, she hadn't noticed the camera. Pavel really noticed every detail—it was crazy.

"I would rule out the harbor as well," Pavel said, pushing forward with his long stride. "And if Sattelmacher was in a boat with someone else, we probably won't be able to find that out now anyway."

"We could ask for all the security camera footage and give Berger some popcorn. He likes jobs like that."

"Was that sarcasm?"

"No. He really likes doing it."

"Good to know."

They reached the access road to the harbor. Pavel studied the road for a few seconds before crossing it and following the coastal path.

"I checked Sattelmacher's navigation data again this morning," he said. "He didn't drive the night he died. Did he have a bike?"

"Not that I know of. He wasn't really the bike type."

"Which is not valid information."

Enna waved it off. "Was he on the phone with anyone other than his girlfriend before he died?"

Pavel pulled out his cell phone and briefly studied a list. "Just the call to his brother Heiner before he went to see him. Nothing else after that."

"So he obviously didn't make an appointment with anyone. At least not by phone." Enna sighed. "Although we don't have all his messaging apps. That's how most things work these days."

Pavel threw up his hands apologetically. "It's not as easy to crack a password-protected cell phone as it looks on TV."

The path narrowed, so they had to walk one behind the other. Knee-high grass lined the path to the left and right. Sand crunched under Enna's sneakers. She found it strange that Neuhof had taken the lead when he didn't know his way around here. But he was doing well; he followed the path that led down to the beach and then back up to the dike. There the path widened again and they came to the luxury Seestern Hotel. They had to go around it, but Toni probably hadn't been there either. Again there were security cameras.

Pavel surveyed the hotel before saying, "You said something interesting earlier."

"Ah, and I don't usually do that?"

He stumbled, but immediately regained his composure. "You were talking about an impulsive act. That's an interesting approach, because it would make it more of a crime of passion."

"With Heiner at the top of the list, because of the house sale and the lost inheritance."

"Then the girlfriend, who also lost money."

"Although she might be earning enough with her special business."

"Yes, but that's not an argument. In their eyes, it would be Toni's fault that they lost the money."

That might be true. "But I think it's plausible that she was in Hamburg, which would eliminate her as the culprit."

"I agree with you. Her cell phone data will confirm that."

Enna scratched her chin. "That just leaves the parents, who I'm sure were also angry with Toni. They didn't want to go to the retirement home. I wonder how Toni managed to hide his double life from them. He was the sweet golden boy. The model son. It must have been a shock to his parents."

Pavel was silent for several minutes. They had passed the *Seestern* and turned back down onto the public beach. It was especially wide here, stretching into the distance, bordered by shimmering sky-blue water.

Enna kicked a stone away. It disappeared in the sand. "What are you thinking about now, boss?"

"About the parent-child relationship. The father doesn't really know what's going on anymore. His reaction to the photos, the story about you being Toni's girlfriend, and then his breakdown..."

"What are you getting at?"

Pavel suddenly raised his hand and stopped. He narrowed his eyes and pointed with his index finger into the distance.

The Fleetstedt lighthouse stood there, a red and white striped finger in the cloudless sky.

It jutted out into the North Sea on a protruding cliff.

"The lighthouse!"

"That's Fleetstedt Lighthouse. You like facts, don't you? I can give you a few: It was built at the end of the nineteenth century. Worth seeing. There's still an old five-wick kerosene lamp in the town hall. Today, it uses a Fresnel lens that can be seen for almost twenty-five miles."

"Interesting, but I saw a photo of it at the Sattelmachers. In the photo box. It was one of the photos that Toni was cut out of. Come on, come on! I want to get a closer look!" Pavel hurried off with long strides.

Enna looked after him, shook her head, and followed at a brisk pace.

The lighthouse loomed above them, but Pavel had eyes only for the surroundings. He kept stopping and looking around as if searching for something. His lips moved silently.

Enna left him to it. In this state, he wouldn't answer her anyway, or just ask her to be quiet. So she made use of the time to walk up to a railing that blocked the way to the lighthouse from the general public. Below her, the North Sea lapped leisurely against the wall that stretched eastward from the rock. It smelled of seaweed and fish.

"We have to go further east!" he shouted suddenly and hurried on.

Enna sighed and followed him. He would explain eventually. On they went, along the wall, then a left turn, on and on, to a plaque on a boulder with the year the lighthouse was built, a shake of Pavel's head, then on and on, to the other side, a look back at the lighthouse and a nod.

"Come on!" Pavel ducked under the barrier and hurried onto the adjacent dune. The terrain sloped down again towards the third Fleetstedt beach, at the end of which was the old lighthouse bay.

Enna had to hurry now to follow her boss. She ran after him, down to the water. Pavel had halted on the rocks. He held his thumb and forefinger out in front of him, forming a rectangle that framed the lighthouse.

"This is where the picture was taken!" he exclaimed enthusiastically. "Right here!"

Enna climbed up the rocks towards him. Shells and algae clung to the edge. "And what does that tell us?"

"That an important moment for the Sattelmacher family was captured here and then destroyed—at least photographically."

"Which tells us nothing at all."

"No, but it was a *crime of passion*! Maybe Toni met Heiner

here for a discussion. That would fit. Neutral ground. Or even positively charged ground." Pavel looked around even more attentively. His forehead was furrowed. A vertical crease ran from his eyebrows to his receding hairline.

Enna examined the spot as well. "Do you think this could be the scene of the crime?"

"Why not? There are no witnesses here. They knew the place. People tend to return to emotionally charged places like this over and over again."

"Okay. Let's assume that. Toni talks to his killer here. There's an argument, then a fight."

Pavel staggered on the rocks as if he'd been beaten. "I'll fight back. Ha! No! Stop it! Stop it! Then comes the blow. I'm slipping on the seaweed." He sank to his knees at the edge of the rock and looked down into the water.

Enna also looked down into the dark blue and nodded. "And a plunge into the tide. Yes ... quite possible."

Pavel nodded in satisfaction. "We'll do a thorough search. Maybe the murder weapon was also disposed of here."

"It could be anything!"

"All the same. Let's go! Let's search!"

So they searched. Enna crawled around on the rocks for over half an hour, peering into crevices. She found beer cans, seashells, and lots of plastic waste, but no murder weapon. What did Neuhof expect to find, especially after days of high and low tide?

Then she paused and looked closer. Something copper-colored shone in a crevice. Enna bent down and took a latex glove from her jacket pocket. She slipped it on and pulled a thumbnail-sized button out of the crevice. It was copper-colored and embossed.

"Boss! I think I've got something!"

He was by her side immediately. "Yes, and look at this! This is very interesting." He had his phone in his hand, scrolling through photos until he held one up triumphantly in front of Enna.

It was a photo taken by the crime scene investigator of the antique coat Toni Sattelmacher was wearing when he died.

A copper-colored embossed button was missing from the collar.

Chapter Eighteen

As the ferry pulled away, a slight vibration ran through the ship. Pavel held on to the railing so tightly that his knuckles were white.

Enna grinned. She hadn't been on the island ferry from Norddeich to Norderney in a long time, but there was certainly no need to hold on like Pavel when there were no waves.

"As exciting as a trip on the Enterprise?" she asked jokingly.

Pavel grumbled and tentatively let go of the railing. "Ships aren't really my thing," he admitted.

"Neither are cars. Do you like any form of transportation?"

"The office bike."

"Heino."

"Excuse me?"

"It's called Heino. We used to call it that."

Pavel seemed about to say something, but then he walked past her to the foredeck. There he sank down onto one of the wooden benches. He didn't look relaxed, but he didn't look tense either.

Enna sat down next to him and checked her phone. She had received an email from Maria. Enna said to Pavel: "The crime scene investigator just wrote that no other usable evidence was found at the crime scene."

Pavel sighed. "I almost expected that. What a pity. The find at the lighthouse was really amazing."

Enna pointed at Pavel. "You deserve the credit. I would have walked right past it."

"You didn't see the pictures in the box either." Pavel scratched his chin. "Everything points to there having been a relationship."

"Sounds like a *but*."

Pavel nodded. "We still haven't spoken to the notary. And the fact that Sattelmacher wanted to rescind the purchase wouldn't have made the investors happy either. We have all sorts of motives, but how does that relate to the crime scene?" Pavel answered himself: "Difficult, or do you see it differently?"

Enna shrugged, her eyes fixed on the gray horizon.

Pavel raised his hand. "How should I interpret the lifting of your shoulders now?"

"As you wish. I don't want to commit yet. I still somehow lack a gut feeling about the matter. Something..." Enna raised her shoulders again. "Would you like something to drink? Some tea?"

"Uh, no, thanks."

"Whatever you say." Enna straightened her socks – today they were navy blue with white anchors – before going inside to get something to drink for the remaining fifty minutes of the trip. She chose a hot chocolate with cream.

Norddeutsche Küstenkapital GmbH had its headquarters on Norderney, right on Kaiserstrasse behind the beach promenade. It was a fancy office building with a dark granite facade and lots of glass. From the second floor, the view of the beach and the North Sea was probably spectacular.

"Pretty fancy," Enna said as they stopped in front of the building and looked up. Clouds chased across the sky and were reflected in the windows.

"The biggest pile gets shat on again."

Enna laughed. "Rarely do such crude words come out of your mouth."

"It was a quote. In the vernacular." Pavel walked to the automatic doors and disappeared inside.

There they were greeted by a lady in a chic suit. The fabric clung to her body like a second skin. Her smile could have come from a catalog.

"Can I help you?"

Enna and Pavel pulled out their badges in sync.

The smile disappeared. "Do you have an appointment?"

"We do now. We're investigating a murder."

The receptionist went green around the gills, nodded, and stalked behind her desk to make a phone call. It took her less than twenty seconds to say, "Mr. Christiansen will see you in a moment."

He was part of the management team, as Enna had researched beforehand. She nodded politely and waited. She would rather observe now anyway. Pavel had worked in white-collar crime for several years. He knew best how to talk to bosses like this.

Enna looked at her boss. He was looking at the large-scale artwork hanging on the anthracite-colored exposed concrete walls. They looked like abstract beach scenes, probably created by a local artist. The light effects were well captured, so you could make out the beach and the sky, but nothing more.

Brisk footsteps sounded behind them.

A broad-shouldered man in a gray suit came toward them. He wore glasses with thick plastic frames. "Ms. Koopmann? Mr. Neuhof?"

"Mr. Christiansen?"

"Yes, please follow me."

He led them up a broad flight of stairs. They went up one floor to a conference room.

The view of the ocean was phenomenal.

Juices and fresh fruit were on the table.

After closing the door and directing them to empty chairs, he asked: "How can I help you? I heard there was a murder! How terrible!"

"It is. Tragic." Enna said. "We are investigating the death of Toni Sattelmacher from Fleetstedt. You should be familiar with the name."

Christiansen nodded hesitantly. "Mr. Sattelmacher is one of our clients. Is he really ... dead?"

"Unfortunately. And our investigation raises questions. Questions about your seaside property."

The managing director's eyes twitched slightly, but otherwise he remained calm. In fact, he leaned back and assumed a confident posture—chest out, legs wide. He knew how to direct a conversation. "I'll give you as much information as I can, of course."

"Good. I'm sure you won't mind if we record the conversation?" Pavel took over as agreed and took out a Dictaphone.

The lines around Christiansen's eyes tightened again briefly, but he nodded. "Of course."

Pavel smiled kindly. "Thank you." He activated the recorder, dictated the date, place, and people present, and began the interview.

"According to our research, Toni Sattelmacher sold his family home to your company for one and a half million euros. Is that correct?"

"Yes. I can produce the contracts, if you like."

"That would be very nice."

Christiansen disappeared for a minute before returning with a folder and leafing through it. Then he nodded again. "The amount is correct. The sum has also been transferred to Mr. Sattelmacher, so the sale is legally binding."

"However, according to our research, Mr. Sattelmacher wanted to back out of the sale. He made accusations against Norddeutsche Küstenkapital GmbH that they had bought the property below market value."

Christiansen snorted. "That old sob story. We hear it all the time. People see a property bought for a million and sold for ten, and they smell injustice. But we're putting most of the money into new development. That costs money. A lot of money, given the rise in construction costs and material prices. We are taking a risk. That has to be calculated. In the end, we won't have much left."

Enna wanted to say something sharp in reply, but Pavel waved her off with a curt gesture. "So Mr. Sattelmacher didn't try to cancel the sale?"

"Not with us, he didn't."

"Okay. Then what do you make of the fact that the Fleetstedt building department wouldn't approve the new construction? The house is a listed building. Besides, the seller's parents had a lifelong right of usufruct. Their son would not have been allowed to sell."

Christiansen drummed his fingers on his knee until he noticed and stopped. He seemed to decide on a strategy and sighed. "We're probably the wrong people to talk to. These matters would have been handled by the notary."

"Henriette Meier?"

"That's the one. I remember there were *concerns* from the building department, but they were resolved."

"Because money was paid. Fifty thousand euros to Roland Bramberger of the Fleetstedt town council."

Another shrug. "That would be extremely troubling, but as I said, as a serious group of investors, we are not involved in such machinations."

"You're passing the buck to Ms. Meier?"

Christiansen's face turned red. "I'm not going to answer that question, Mr. Neuhof. All I know is that Ms. Meier got the zoning changed. We didn't check how she did it. That is not our concern. We generally assume that our business partners are reputable. We also checked the final contracts, and they were in order." He placed the contracts on the table in front of them.

Pavel didn't reach for them. He just looked at Christiansen. "And yet there is a legal right of rescission. Mr. Sattelmacher could have backed out of the contract. That would be a bitter blow for you. A motive for murder, so to speak."

Christiansen snorted like an ox. "That's far-fetched. We make dreams possible! Residential dreams! We don't murder our clients."

Pavel shrugged. "That remains to be seen. According to the facts, you, or rather your company, have a motive. We will request the relevant documents and investigate your company. That will take weeks and months and..."

Christiansen raised his hand. "Ms. Meier did it."

Enna frowned. "What did Ms. Meier do?"

"She arranged the bribery of this Bamberger and informed us afterward."

"I don't understand."

A loud sigh. "Sattelmacher probably went to her to rescind the sale. The two of them argued. He wanted a lot more money, but Henriette Meier blew him off. She probably saw her commission and her job in jeopardy and didn't think Sattelmacher could go to Bramberger. Suddenly he got cold feet and wanted to withdraw the zoning change."

"I thought you knew nothing about it."

"We didn't know until Ms. Meier told us. If we had known, we would never have made a deal with her."

Sure. "So you're saying the baby had already fallen into the well?"

"Yes. What else could we have done?"

Enna folded her arms across her chest.

"Report Ms. Meier, for one thing."

Christiansen laughed bitterly. "Would that have changed anything? No. We even considered increasing the amount to avoid bad press. We could have gone up to two million and still made a small profit. We take our work seriously, I can assure you."

Enna didn't believe a word of it, and neither did Pavel, but neither of them said anything. Enna expected Pavel to return to Sattelmacher, but to her surprise he thanked the man for talking to them and ended the recording. Then he shook Christiansen's hand and walked out of the conference room.

Enna got up as well and took one last look out to sea before following him.

Outside the building, Pavel waved the recorder like a trophy. "This conversation is gold."

"Really? It may get Henriette Meier into trouble, but it hasn't gotten us any further with Toni."

"Yes, it has. It takes the focus off Norddeutsche Küstenkapital."

Enna grumbled. "I didn't believe a word of what he said. They knew about it from the beginning, I'm telling you!"

"Of course they were in on it from the beginning, but with Sattelmacher they would have killed the wrong person. From their point of view, they should have threatened Bramberger and, worst case, killed him, so that he wouldn't make the desired change. Toni was not the problem. At best, he would have been a happy winner and made two million. Or even more, if he'd had the nerve."

Pavel was right. As Heiner had said: Everything Toni touched turned to gold.

This time it would have happened again, if someone hadn't killed him.

Chapter Nineteen

"We shouldn't have gone through Emden," Enna said.

Pavel took a deep breath. The shortest route his phone had shown him went through Emden – and then onto the A31, where they were now stuck in a traffic jam.

"There shouldn't be a traffic jam here," he said, showing Enna the screen. "Look, it's all green."

"But there is a traffic jam."

"It must have just formed."

"Unfortunately, that doesn't help us."

The ferry from Norderney had been delayed. They'd gotten back on solid ground just after three, and Henriette Meier would be closing her office at five. Her secretary had told them that they would be standing in front of a locked door after that, because her boss had to prepare for the city council meeting. Another wasted day. They were forced to admit that they had made no progress in their search for the killer. The noose had not tightened.

They couldn't bring Ms. Meier in easily, either. She seemed to have her fingers in almost everything, and probably played golf with the prosecutor. He had already warned them not to mess with the head of the Fleetstedt Business Association.

"We'll make it," Enna said, "if you don't mind me driving fast on the main road later."

"If you have to..."

Her colleague tapped the analog clock above the air conditioning vent. The little hand immediately jumped forward a few minutes, taking away more precious time. Pavel had to force himself to stop rubbing his knee.

"We should have visited her first," he said.

"But then we wouldn't have what we got from Norddeutsche Küstenkapital."

That was true. The only question was whether it would help them.

With a screech of brakes, Enna stopped right next to a garbage can. Pavel jumped out of the Polo, bent over the trash can, saw a dead pigeon on the ground, and threw up.

"The fish sandwich on the ferry must have been bad," he said afterward, wiping his mouth with the handkerchief Enna had given him.

"So there you are, drinking in broad daylight," said an older gentleman with a goatee and a brown leather hat, who walked past them at a brisk pace and disappeared into the modern house in front of them.

"You're good," Enna said. "I know my driving style takes some getting used to. You need to practice more. But we got here in time. We even have fifteen minutes to spare."

She handed him a bottle of tap water. He gargled with it for a moment, spat it out, and then took a sip.

"Thank you. Let's go."

"I'm sorry, but Ms. Meier has another appointment," the secretary said. "Would you mind taking a seat in the waiting room?" She pointed to a transparent door behind which a silhouette could be seen. Entering the room, Pavel recognized the man with the beard and hat. He immediately looked for a seat as far away from him as possible. He checked his breath but didn't find it unpleasant.

"Do I have a bad smell on my breath?" he asked Enna quietly.

She moved her head closer until he could smell her perfume, sniffed, and then shook her head. "All good. Just a bit of anxiety sweat." She laughed. He liked her laugh because it didn't sound malicious.

His cell phone vibrated. It was Berger. Pavel answered the call and walked out the door. After all, his phone call was none of the man in the hat's business.

"Berger, what do you have for me?"

"The details from your witness's cell phone number."

"And?"

"She made the call from her apartment in Hamburg."

Too bad, Lisa Munterer would have fit the bill. Instead, the noose was tightening around the other suspects. "Thank you, Berger. Good work!"

Pavel took a few more steps. The fresh air did him good. At five o'clock on the dot, he re-entered the notary's lobby.

"Didn't you say this place closes at five?" he asked the secretary. "Ms. Meier has to get ready for the city council meeting," he teased, knowing that the secretary was merely Ms. Meier's spokesperson.

"I'm sorry," the secretary said, piqued. "As soon as Mr. Michelsen has spoken with Ms. Meier, you can..."

Pavel pulled out his ID and placed it boldly on the counter. "She'll see us now," he said, startled that he had spoken so loudly. What was wrong with him? Was it still shock from the fast ride? No, it was the stress of many interrogations and conversations. Too many people and too much excitement had robbed him of his discretion.

A glass door next to the counter opened with a squeak. Ms. Thönissen stepped out. They greeted each other, and Thönissen blushed as if he had caught her doing something criminal. Behind her was Ms. Meier. He recognized her immediately from the pictures hanging outside.

"You can send Mr. Michelsen in now..."

"I'm sorry, but a gentleman from the police would like to see you..."

The color drained from the notary's face for a moment before she regained her composure.

"And a lady," Pavel said, opening the door to the waiting room and motioning to his colleague.

"You found Mr. Sattelmacher Norddeutsche Küstenkapital GmbH to invest in his property, and received a huge commission for it." There was no need to beat around the bush.

"That's nonsense," Meier countered. "And an insult to my intelligence."

"You were in contact with both parties involved."

"I had to be, as a notary. There's nothing illegal about that."

"We are investigating a murder. If you insist, we'll check all your accounts. We'll find evidence of the sums paid somewhere."

Henriette Meier crossed her arms and yawned. "Certainly not. Is that all?"

"No. I just wanted to give you the opportunity to clear yourself. Are you sure that a thorough review of your books wouldn't reveal any irregularities?"

Pavel had worked in the Economic Crimes Division for six months. There wasn't a company in the world that accounted for everything correctly. He smiled. He would really enjoy bringing Henriette Meier down. Hopefully, she wouldn't cooperate.

"Just think of the damage that would be done to the Entrepreneurs' Association if its chairwoman ..." Meier threw a dirty look at Enna.

"Save the veiled threats," Pavel said dryly. "I am not impressed, neither by the Entrepreneurs' Association nor by any other titles or threatening gestures."

"He's probably right," Enna whispered in agreement.

Meier looked at her, then waved her off. "Well, let's put it this way: maybe I was trying to do the Sattelmachers a little favor. I've known Mr. and Mrs. Sattelmacher for a long time. Nice, good people. I didn't know I was going to receive a commission. Of course, I'll pay it back as soon as I can."

So she did receive the money.

"The Sattelmachers?" repeated Enna. "You're lying, Ms. Meier."

"Toni Sattelmacher was the one who wanted to sell," Pavel added. "The parents were surprised when they found out. They never wanted to leave their home. They had a guaranteed right of usufruct when they transferred the property."

The notary shook her head vigorously. "The three of them came to see me together. Sattelmacher senior had the usufruct canceled to allow the sale to Norddeutsche Küstenkapital. I can show you the deed. It's signed by both spouses."

Meier stood and walked to a cabinet that turned out to be a safe. She opened it and took out some documents.

"I'm giving you this voluntarily and asking you to take note of my cooperation in solving the murder."

She handed the letters to Pavel. They contained what the notary had promised.

But they still had an ace up their sleeve. "The recording," Enna said with a cold smile on her lips.

"Of course." Pavel took the recorder out of his pocket and pressed the play button. "You recognize the speaker."

Henriette Meier nodded with pursed lips, then listened with a focused expression.

The more Christiansen spoke, the grimmer Meier's features became.

Finally, Pavel stopped the recording. Meier's face had turned dark red. "That coward," she growled.

"Coward?" Pavel asked.

"Bramberger from the city council just wanted to raise the price. I would have taken care of it. Who do you think I am meeting tonight?"

The price, of course. It was all about money. Sometimes Pavel missed the days when people killed for love. Then again, one was as wrong as the other. But hadn't the notary just confirmed that she had a motive to kill Toni? No, it was useless. They had no proof that Toni Sattelmacher had tried to rescind the contract. Henriette Meier was corrupt and greedy, but she could always come up with a reason for her actions.

"Did Toni or the Sattelmachers really want to rescind the contract?" asked Enna.

"No, why would they? With half a million, Mrs. Sattelmacher could stay in that fancy retirement home for the rest of her life. Georg and Toni were happy that she would be so well taken care of. Georg has a heart condition and probably doesn't have long to live. Why would Magda want to live alone in the old Gulfhaus without the money to afford decent care? I was there myself when the money was paid out, and lent him an old briefcase."

"What did the briefcase look like?"

"Like this." Meier showed him a picture on her cell phone. Pavel took a snapshot.

Henriette Meier was still a money-grubbing swindler. But she had no reason to kill Toni. They had to find someone else.

"You will hear from our people in the economics department." Pavel put the documents back on the table and stood up. "I'm sure they'll appreciate your cooperation as well."

Chapter Twenty

"Here! The call details for Heiner Sattelmacher."

Berger stepped into the office and held up a stack of papers. Enna jumped up and grabbed them out of his hand. She pulled out the last page and ran her finger along the last lines.

"Ha, I knew it!" she exclaimed.

As Berger left the room, Pavel stood and took the photo of Toni's brother from the circle where they had arranged all the suspects.

"Where was he Wednesday night?" he asked.

"At home."

"Are you sure he didn't just leave the cell phone lying around?" It was a routine question. Enna was smart enough to have considered it.

"Yes. He made two calls of about fifteen minutes each to a premium rate number."

"Premium rate?"

"Those are rip-off numbers. Call – me – on the phone. You know the kind? They're advertised on TV."

Pavel didn't watch TV, but he could guess what Enna meant. Heiner must be very lonely. A lot of people had that problem. Why didn't he just visit his brother? Then they wouldn't have a case now.

Pavel looked at the large table. There was only one photo in the center of the circle. It showed Georg and Magda Sattelmacher standing next to each other. Magda had her hand on her husband's shoulder as if to steer him in a certain direction.

What had Jenny Kring, the receptionist at the nursing home, said? He could still hear her voice. *You can't deny that Mrs. Sattelmacher is the more authoritative person.* What had she made her husband do?

"That leaves the parents," Enna said.

Pavel sighed. Parents who killed their own child. A tragedy with a history. What had that been like?

"Toni was always the favorite, apparently," Pavel said.

"It's understandable that he was Georg's favorite as the firstborn," Enna said. "But why would Magda, his stepmother, choose him over her own son?"

"For Georg's sake, perhaps? He must have been a widower when she met him. It's easier with divorcees. There's a separation first. But Magda had to compete with an ex who was taken from Georg by breast cancer."

"So she betrayed her own son?"

Betrayal was a harsh word. She probably didn't see it that way herself. Toni was more successful in school than Heiner, which would have demoralized his brother right from the start. No one could have guessed that Toni had accumulated a mountain of debt over the years. His business seemed to be going well. The last deal almost worked.

"Families develop a certain dynamic," Pavel said. "Once you set something in motion, it's almost impossible to stop it. You roll toward the abyss with your eyes open, but you can't jump off."

That was how his marriage had ended. They had both been smart enough to see how things were going, but neither had the strength to end it before the crash.

"Who do you think did it?" asked Enna.

"Georg. It was his son. If Magda had killed him, he would never have forgiven her."

Enna pursed her lips in disapproval. "I think it was Magda. She is stronger than her husband. Look at the photo. Georg almost looks like a puppet, guided by the hand on his shoulder."

"And the motive?"

"Disappointment. Boundless disappointment. The three of them proudly collected the money from the notary, and then Toni told them that he had to hand it over to the Russians. One and a half million melted away like ice cream in an oven."

"If the notary isn't lying," Pavel pointed out.

"It's Berger's turn. There are plenty of security cameras in the center of Fleetstedt."

There was a knock. Berger opened the door. "I have the bank statements from the bank."

"Finally!" This time Pavel hurried to get them from their co-worker, but again Enna was faster. She flipped through the statements and let out a cry of triumph.

"Ha! There it is. Magda transferred ten thousand euros to Heiner's account on Wednesday, which she had previously deposited in cash."

"And the rest of the money?"

"Nothing. The Sattelmachers' accounts are practically empty." Enna leafed through the thick pile of paper. "Toni had almost cleared his account. A million in several installments."

"So there's half a million missing," Pavel said.

"Which Harry Krüger was looking for. Then he told Volodya about it, and it's been quiet since then."

Something was wrong with the order of events. But there were two people who could explain it to them.

"I think we should pay another visit to the parents," Enna said.

One last visit, yes.

"Oh, this is exciting," Pavel said into his cell phone as Enna turned the police car onto the gravel road leading to the retirement home. "And all three are clearly recognizable?"

"Yes, I'll send you the picture. It's a frontal shot, taken from slightly above. There's a diner across the street that's been broken into a few times, so the owner has a camera on the roof."

"Berger found footage of the three Sattelmachers," Pavel explained. "Excellent work, Berger."

"Should I ... I mean, the camera. After all, it is filming public places. And he kept the footage much longer than necessary. That's illegal."

"Camera? What camera?" asked Pavel.

Berger laughed. "I see."

"Please don't take this the wrong way, but the owner of the diner was kind enough to help us, so we shouldn't thank him like that. That's the job of law enforcement."

"But that makes it difficult to use the footage in court."

Berger was undoubtedly right. A smart lawyer would question the source of the images. But Pavel didn't expect it to be that difficult. An emotional relationship makes a deep impression on everyone and changes people.

"Don't worry, Georg Sattelmacher will confess," he said, ending the conversation.

"Magda," said Enna. "I'm betting on Magda."

Maybe they were both right. That was the only problem he anticipated. They had to prove one person guilty—the culprit, not a person who claimed to be the culprit.

"Hello, Ms. Kring," Enna said. "We need to see the Sattelmachers again."

"All right. But Mr. Sattelmacher is still in the hospital."

Hmm. Was that good news or bad news? Perhaps they should have called ahead. Enna had even suggested it, but in Pavel's experience, such an announcement led to people memorizing a very specific version of the story and then continually repeating it.

"Give me a minute, please, Enna. I'll call the hospital. We probably need to speak to Mr. Sattelmacher today, too." Maybe even before talking to his wife, because, in Pavel's mind, the sick man was the culprit.

He walked into the dining room, where the staff were setting the table for lunch. He looked up the number of the hospital and asked to be transferred to the cardiology department.

"Cardiology department, head nurse Ricarda. What can I do for you?"

He introduced himself. "I need to see Mr. Sattelmacher as soon as possible." He didn't ask. Anyone who asked risked a no.

"I'm sorry, but I have to check with the attending physicians first," the head nurse said.

"How long will that take?"

"They're on rounds. Give me half an hour."

"Thank you very much. Could you call me back then? It's really urgent."

"Hang on, I'll write down your number ... Done."

The connection went dead. Ricarda didn't bother with niceties. He liked that. He didn't need greetings if people were willing to help him do his job.

As he left the dining room, the receptionist pointed inside the home. Enna had obviously gone on ahead. He found her in the living room of the suite, where she had taken a seat at the large round table. A cup was steaming in front of her. He smelled the aroma of black tea. Magda Sattelmacher was sitting across from Enna. She was wearing a black dress, but no makeup. There was a cup in front of her, and one in the empty space between the two women.

"Hello, Mrs. Sattelmacher," he said.

"Cup of tea, Mr. Inspector? I was just telling your colleague about my childhood in Holland."

"Oh, you're from Holland?"

Pavel made a detour. He walked past the desk where the box of photos still stood, picked it up, and carried it to the table.

"Yes, my parents moved to Germany when I was..." Magda's voice trailed off. She must have recognized the box.

"Go ahead," Pavel said, picking up the cup and blowing across its surface. The steam dissipated like the fog on the North Sea in a storm. He tried a sip. The tea was unsweetened and strong.

"I bet you don't like sugar in your tea," Enna said.

Pavel nodded. "I prefer things pure and simple. An egg without salt, coffee without milk, and tea without sugar. That's the real deal for me.

"What do you think, Mrs. Sattelmacher?"

He didn't like pressuring old ladies. Maybe she would take the opportunity to get things off her chest.

"I prefer tea with milk and honey," Magda said.

Too bad. What now? They had to get the woman out of her defensive mode. Why hadn't they discussed strategy in the car? Pavel looked at his colleague, but she didn't seem to have any ideas either. He opened the box of photos and fumbled for the cropped pictures. They were at the bottom of the box, which was different. But they were still there, even though they were evidence because of what they revealed about the relationship between the people involved.

Pavel took out one of the pictures and traced the cut edges. Toni had been removed with amazing precision. Photoshop couldn't have done a better job. He thought of the nimble fingers that had mended the hole in his jacket. Their interplay had seemed magical. Had he really believed that Heiner could have cut out those figures?

"You ... fixed these photos," he said. "You couldn't throw them away, because then you would be throwing away your life with Georg."

Magda Sattelmacher put down her teacup and swallowed. Pavel took out one photo after another. "Toni here, Toni there. He takes up most of the space in almost every picture. Your husband took these pictures, didn't he? You were jealous. But you couldn't show it. Because of Toni. Because he was the golden boy. You must have noticed how your biological son was suffering, too."

"Heiner," Magda said, "leave Heiner out of this. He hasn't done anything wrong."

"Mrs. Sattelmacher? I must interrupt my colleague for a moment," Enna interrupted. Pavel leaned back. She was right. He had almost made a grave mistake in suspecting her husband and not her. "We will now be questioning you as the accused. You don't have to talk about yourself or your husband. But anything you say can and will be used against you in a court of law. You have the right to an attorney." Enna placed the recorder on the table. "I'm going to record the rest of our conversation." She pressed the record button, naming the place, the time, and the people involved. "Pavel, please."

"Thank you, Enna." He tried to put as much gratitude into his look as possible, but he wasn't sure if it would come across.

"Mrs. Sattelmacher?" he asked, and the old lady flinched as if he had hit her. At that moment, she barely looked younger than her husband. "Is there anything you want to tell us?"

"No."

"Good, then I'll tell you." Pavel sorted through the photos until he came to the one with the lighthouse. He picked it up, and Mrs. Sattelmacher recoiled from it the way the poor victim at an exorcism shrinks from a cross. He felt no less sorry for her. But only she could put an end to it.

"You like this place a lot. Your whole family does," Pavel continued. "Toni invited you and Georg there on Wednesday night last week. You assumed he wanted to celebrate with you on the beach. After all, you had just brought home a suitcase full of money."

Pavel took his cell phone out of his pocket and showed the old woman the picture from the surveillance camera.

"But Toni didn't want to celebrate. He wanted to confess to you. The money that was supposed to secure your retirement was gone. Toni had more debts than anyone suspected, even more than the bank knew about, and owed to people who were no fun to deal with. Your husband Georg is a very even-tempered person. But this was too much. He pushed Toni. There was a scuffle, and unfortunately, he fell. A button came off Toni's jacket, which we found at the scene."

He reached into his pocket and pulled out the button. Then

he leaned over the table and placed it directly in front of Magda Sattelmacher, who closed her eyes for a moment.

"And then you made the mistake of your lives and carried Toni into the water together. Georg couldn't do it alone. You had to help him. Anyone would have done that. After all, you're his wife. Everyone will understand that."

Magda pressed her lips together and stared at the edge of the table. Her fingers were under the table. Pavel heard soft noises. She was probably kneading her hands.

But she didn't say anything.

Pavel took a sip of tea. He no longer needed to blow on it to cool it. And now? He exchanged glances with Enna, but she seemed as perplexed as he was. Should they take the Sattelmachers to the morgue? Seeing the victim sometimes worked wonders.

His cell phone vibrated. "Excuse me," he said as he picked it up.

"Head nurse Ricarda again. The attending physician has agreed. You can question Mr. Sattelmacher for twenty minutes. But no more!"

"Thank you, Head Nurse. I'll see you later." He ended the call. "Did you hear that, Enna? Georg Sattelmacher is fit for questioning." He turned to Magda. "Would you like to come with us?"

Suddenly all strength disappeared from Magda Sattelmacher's voice as she said, "Please don't."

"I can't do that to Georg." Magda Sattelmacher got up and walked around the living room as if looking for something. Here and there she took a book from the shelf, straightened a blanket, or wiped the dust off the old-fashioned radio.

"What can't you do to your husband?" asked Enna.

The old lady paused. "Make him face this again."

"What is it, Mrs. Sattelmacher? We would like to help you. You seem ... desperate."

Enna was doing a good job. Pavel decided not to interfere.

"This ... situation. The bay in the photo."

"We don't need to talk to Georg about it today."

Very good. She didn't promise anything she couldn't deliver, but still managed to ease the woman's intense fear. At some point, they would have to ask Georg Sattelmacher about it.

"But you have to tell us what happened," Enna added. "We have to solve Toni's case."

Magda Sattelmacher winced. It was probably a bit too much.

"I can explain," Magda said.

It hadn't been too much.

"It was just as your colleague described. Toni invited us. It's such a beautiful view. We thought he wanted to celebrate with us."

"But he didn't."

"Yes, he did—he even brought champagne. He wanted to celebrate with us that he was finally out of debt. Debt-free! There was nothing left of the million and a half!"

"That made you angry."

"Yes, but my husband even more so. They were yelling at each other and then Georg pushed him. Toni fell pretty hard, with his face right in the water."

Had she just accused her husband of killing his own son? However, the sequence of events did not match the injuries Kettler had reconstructed. The dead man had water in his lungs, but he had died from a blow from a blunt object. A blow, not a fall.

"That's the way Georg will tell the story," the woman said. "He'll leave out the end to protect me."

"And what's the real end?" asked Enna gently. She got up, walked around the table, picked up the coat button and the photo, and put them both in her bag. The old woman slumped as if the sight of the evidence had made her muscles go slack.

Enna put her hand on the woman's shoulder. She gave a short sob, but quickly regained her composure.

"The real ending, yes." She sighed. "Georg pulled him out of the water. I was amazed at how much strength he suddenly had. Then he yelled at me for not helping him. Toni would have done it for us, he said, despite everything. That was so wrong! His son never thought about us, only about himself. We gave Heiner peanuts, but he was still our child! Georg probably didn't want to admit that Toni, his Toni, had taken everything from us. I think, inside, he always loved his dead wife. That made me so angry that I took a heavy stone and threw it down on Toni's head."

"You were beside yourself with rage," Enna said.

Enna was putting words in the suspect's mouth, but Pavel didn't correct her. An argument that got out of hand was a typical sequence of events in a murder case. He couldn't see any sinister motives. Magda Sattelmacher would have to serve at least five years in prison, but would be eligible for parole after serving two-thirds of her sentence. Her husband was at least guilty of assault, but given his condition, he could probably avoid a trial.

"I don't remember," said Magda Sattelmacher. "I just remember being very calm afterward. I convinced myself that he was dead. Then we carried him into the water together. That was the hardest part, getting him to a place where the waves would not wash him back on shore."

"You know we have to take you with us once you have finished your confession?" asked Enna.

Magda nodded. "I have only one request: I would like to go to Toni's funeral with my husband. Can that be arranged?"

"I think special permission can be given for that," Pavel said. "But only with a police escort."

"You need to consider that word will get out about what happened," Enna said. "People who don't even know you will come. Just out of curiosity."

"Toni would have liked that, I think. He always wanted to be famous."

"But he'll be in a coffin. They'll be staring at you."

"That's okay. I'll be able to walk next to Georg. Who knows how long I can be with him?"

Would the victim's father want his killer to walk beside him? But that wasn't Pavel's concern. Georg would probably have lied for his wife and taken the blame. He was eighty-two and had a heart condition. He wouldn't even be able to leave her anything because his son had ended up losing everything.

"May I ask what happened to the suitcase with the money that you took from the notary?" Even though Magda had confessed to everything, they still needed proof. Heiner had an alibi, but it was always possible that she was protecting someone else.

"The empty suitcase is in the bedroom," Magda said. "Toni brought it with him. He wanted us to return it to the notary, since he was going back to Hamburg. Imagine, he wanted to get married there—leaving us in misery."

Enna got up and went into the bedroom.

"In the big closet on the left," Magda called after her.

His colleague returned with the suitcase. The crime lab would be able to prove that there really had been money in it. Pavel took a deep breath. It took him a moment to realize that the case had been solved.

Chapter Twenty-One

The sky was a fresh blue. The stiff breeze blowing the salt sea air over the land came from a good six miles away, causing a few clouds to float like feathers over the immaculate background. Pavel raised his face to the sun, and it warmed his forehead, where his hair was beginning to recede.

From the wood-clad tower of St. Florian, the last note of the church bell faded away. The weathercock—more like a weather swan here—seemed to bow to the wind. Shortly thereafter, the mourners emerged from the red brick church building. They began the procession around the church.

Pavel retreated to the shade of a linden tree. The power of the sun could not be underestimated, and besides, no one had officially invited him. On the one hand, they had found out who killed Toni. On the other hand, his parents were among those who suffered the most because of Toni's death. That was typical of crimes of passion.

Pavel heard pattering footsteps behind him. It was Enna Koopmann. He was glad she had made it. She paused beside him and leaned against the trunk of the linden tree, breathing heavily.

"They just finished the service," he said quietly. Enna was wearing shorts again today, black ones, but she had combined them with solid black socks, which gave her a surprisingly respectable appearance.

"There was no parking in front of the supermarket," she whispered. "It's a good thing you weren't there."

Pavel nodded. He had parked his bike just outside the entrance to the cemetery. It had been a nice ride from Fleetstedt, the perfect distance for Heino and him.

"Did you park right in front of the volunteer fire department?" he asked.

"Yeah, I figured my car wouldn't stand out because of the red paint." Enna grinned. "But no, I'm not that bold. I'm at the bus stop. Here in the country, the bus only comes twice a day anyway."

Pavel's neck muscles stiffened when he heard that. No, it wasn't his problem. He had to relax. The last few days had been a bit too much for him. He couldn't take spending too many days in a row with other people, no matter how much he liked them. Eventually it would end in a meltdown, something he had fortunately only experienced two or three times in his life.

The procession of mourners thinned out like a worm as it reached the cemetery, where it crawled along a sandy path. At the front, just behind the coffin with its six pallbearers, walked a lone woman.

"Oh, it's Ms. Munterer," Enna said.

She was right; it was Lisa, Toni's girlfriend. She was followed by Georg and Magda Sattelmacher, Toni's father, assisted by his wife. The eighty-two-year-old had been granted parole on account of his health. Their lawyer had been unable to negotiate bail for Magda. Right behind her walked two policewomen in uniform who would take her back later. They were followed by a crowd of people Pavel didn't know, perhaps acquaintances, certainly curious onlookers. Crime always attracted people. He wasn't surprised that the notary was nowhere to be seen. Heiner, Toni's half-brother, was also missing.

They were about to join the worm crawling past them when a man came running from the same direction Enna had arrived.

That must be Heiner. Pavel had never met him in person, but there was a certain resemblance to his half-brother. He paused next to them instead of joining the others.

"Hi, I'm sorry," he apologized. "I came by bus, but some idiot had blocked the bus stop. A wheelchair user wanted to get off, so a tow truck had to come first."

A nightmare. Pavel looked at Enna, but she remained outwardly calm.

"What?" she asked, a little upset. "There's nothing I can do now anyway. Why don't you go up front, Heiner?"

"What do you mean? With that woman? I don't even know her." Heiner grimaced.

"That's Toni's girlfriend. She's a nice woman. Believe me."

"All right, then. If you say so, Enna." Heiner put his hands in his pockets and walked past the procession. From behind, he looked very respectable in his black suit. He reached Lisa Munterer. They shook hands and Heiner quickly took his place at her side.

The bells rang for the fourth time as the congregation assembled at the grave. This way, the entire village could hear the funeral. The speeches were short. The wind picked up. Neither the Russian mafia—for whom Pavel had donned his bulletproof vest—nor Harry Krüger had shown up. All scores seemed to be settled. That was the way it should be when you solved a case.

It was strange that he always felt that way at the funerals that inevitably followed every solved murder. Would anyone ever feel that way at their own funeral? Pavel didn't wish for a violent death, but as a policeman, he definitely stood a higher chance.

"We solved our first case together," said his colleague. They were back in the shade of the linden tree. The smell of the sea had become stronger.

"Yeah, it was fun," Pavel said. "From what I can tell."

"It sure was, Pavel."

This was the moment when he was supposed to invite her to

use his first name. He was the elder and her superior, so it had to come from him.

A voice made him jump.

"You're here too?" Lisa Munterer walked toward them. Her makeup was smudged, just like last Saturday when they had visited her in Hamburg.

"Yes, it is routine," Pavel said.

"Are you coming to the reception?" she asked. "It's in the 'Klönsnack' over on the L10."

"I don't know... We're on duty."

"I'm inviting you. Anyway, I'm footing the bill for all this. The family has nothing left. But that's okay."

"You paid for the funeral?" Enna asked. "That's very kind of you."

"I had wonderful years with Toni. Crazy years." Lisa Munterer looked thoughtfully into the canopy of the linden tree. Individual sunspots moved across her face. She must have loved Toni very much. Pavel was happy for him, and at the same time angry that he had put her in the situation he had.

"I owe you an apology, Ms. Munterer. What I said in your apartment..."

"No problem. You were just doing your job. If you're ever in Hamburg, please drop by. The same goes for you, Inspector."

Munterer was really nice. Of course, such a visit would never happen.

"So, what about the reception? I hear the butter cake is delicious. I don't know anyone here, so I'd be delighted to have company."

Pavel shook his head. "To be honest, I've had too much company in the last few days. I'd rather ride my bike a bit more."

"And you, Ms. Koopmann?"

"That's very kind of you, but I want to make the most of the good weather."

"What are you going to do?" asked Pavel.

"Swim. The deep waters of the North Sea have a healing effect on me. But please say hello to Heiner for me. He's a good man. He always lived in Toni's shadow."

The office was wonderfully quiet. Berger had taken the day off and Enna was fighting the cold, rough sea. Brrr. It was a good thing she hadn't invited him along. Pavel stretched out on his swivel chair, pushed himself off, and did a few spins like a little boy, until he spotted the plastic tray he used as an inbox.

There was a letter wrapped in brown packing tape. He rolled forward and pulled it out. The sender was the crime lab in Leer. It must be the samples he had requested. The envelope did indeed contain a set of separately wrapped plastic tubes and a handwritten cover letter.

"Dear colleague! Please find enclosed the samples you requested for Dietrichsen. We don't expect to be able to extract any useful information from them but hope you can use them. Yours, Maria Doldinger."

Well, he wouldn't be able to use them, but his old friend Raphael could. At least Pavel hoped so, and he had already contacted him by e-mail. He put the samples in a fresh envelope and addressed it to Raphael's lab in Kiel. His friend sometimes worked as an independent expert for courts or the police. But above all, he was a lover of thorough research, just like Pavel. If there was something to be learned from a sample, he would find it. This could take weeks or months, because Raphael found it difficult to give up on a failed attempt. You had to choose carefully what you gave him. But Pavel had a good feeling about Dietrichsen, and a bad one—something was not quite as it seemed with the old man's death. It didn't necessarily have to do with a crime. But it usually did.

He would find out either way. Guaranteed.

The sixty-one-degree Fahrenheit North Sea splashed against Enna's bare legs. She was wearing her wetsuit, a short one, of course. What else would she be wearing?

She stood in the knee-high water for a moment, enjoying the sun and the wind on her face. She loved the contrasts. The warmth and the cold. The gentle and the rough. Koopmann and Neuhof. The question was who represented what...

The thought made her smile. They couldn't be any more different, but they made a good team. The way they had solved their first case, involving Toni Sattelmacher, made something inside her vibrate. She felt that things could work out well with Pavel. He would settle in and get used to her—and she to him. He was eccentric but lovable. And he didn't seem to be narrow-minded. Enna liked that in people. Few things annoyed her as much as narrow-mindedness.

The sand beneath her feet was washed away by the next wave. It tickled and the foam sparkled. A few bright shells became visible in the sand around her as the water receded.

Enna picked one up, looked at it for a moment, then threw it into the water so she could follow it. With determined steps, she waded out. The waves hit her hips first, then her stomach, and finally her breasts.

When she was deep enough, she untied the bright orange buoy she had tied to her back. It was attached to her suit by a thirty-two-foot-long rope and would drift behind her. Enna slipped her goggles over her eyes, checked that they were on correctly, and surged forward. She dived deep, drifted for a moment, and broke the surface again. Then she began to swim.

She soon found her usual rhythm. She swam a short distance out, and then parallel to the beach towards Fleetstedt Harbor. She thought of Toni Sattelmacher in his coat, how she had pulled him out of the deep waters of the North Sea. He had told them his last secrets, but he had kept one to himself: Why had he worn that old coat to meet his parents?

Would Pavel look into that?

Enna hoped not. There was no need to know everything in life. One had to let the dead rest in peace.

Just like the living.

Satisfied with the rushing silence of the tides around her, Police Inspector Enna Koopmann continued to swim in peace and quiet. Yes, here in Fleetstedt she was at home and in her element. This was her life—and now it included Pavel Neuhof.

Enna was curious about what surprises the coming weeks and months would bring, but the future was the future and the present was the present. Now she was swimming and she wasn't interested in anything else.

Enna was happy—in the deep waters of the North Sea.

A Cup of Tea

Dear reader,

I am very glad that we could get to know each other. You don't know much about me yet, although, like any writer, I have told you about my loved ones and myself in my novel. Naturally, it is never an exact likeness. You can imagine the characters a little like the paper dolls we used to play with: The head is Uncle Heiner's, the belly is Grandpa Paul's, the names are from our circle of friends, and the sassy mouth is our older daughter's.

Which she will deny, of course. What is indisputable is that Chief Inspector Pavel Neuhof is based on my husband. In chapter seven, Enna Koopmann suspects that her new colleague might be autistic. When I met my husband, the term 'neurodivergent' was known only in the medical world. I found him … unusual and pleasantly different from myself. Above all, he is the most relaxed person in the world, unless he has an appointment. He always has a fascinating view of reality from which I can learn, and vice versa. Of course, he read everything I wrote about Pavel Neuhof, corrected it where necessary, and approved the rest.

Nevertheless, it goes without saying that everyone is different and right in their own way. Pavel Neuhof is a fictional character, just like Enna Koopmann or Harry Krüger.

But you, dear readers, are real. I want to know who you are. Write to me at heide@heidehinrichs.de. If you like, I can include your name in one of my upcoming mysteries. If you would rather not be a victim, please let me know. Or if you absolutely want to be the secret star of every mystery (i.e. the victim).

If you want to read more about Enna and Pavel, please pre-order their second case here:

heidihinrichs.com/links/4314575

Do you think the two detectives deserve to have more fans? Then please write a review at heidihinrichs.com/links/4314496

Books without reviews are like herring sandwiches without fish – they don't sell as well as the original.

And one last invitation: If you don't want to miss any of Enna and Pavel's future adventures, please subscribe to my newsletter here:

heidihinrichs.com

As a special bonus, you will receive the two detectives' personal data sheets, which I obtained directly from their office computers.

Best regards,

Yours, Heide Hinrichs

Preview: Silent Cries

CHAPTER 1

"Go, Enna!"

Although almost everyone around her was shouting, she heard Lars's voice clearly. Enna gripped the board tightly. She felt the cold sand under her feet. It was soft for the first few steps, then became firm where the beach was washed by the waves, and then there was the water. She was struck on the upper arm as another board hit the water. Enna narrowed her eyes. The ladybird cap was her point of reference, and she couldn't lose sight of it. It was only eight or nine feet in front of her and had just disappeared behind the first wave.

"Now!" yelled Lars from the background.

Although the water didn't seem deep enough to her yet, Enna trusted his experience and threw her own board in. She jumped in after it and grabbed the edges. The jump gave her board a boost which she had to capitalize on. Up quickly! She dropped to her knees, leaned forward, and paddled with her arms as hard as she could.

Less than six hundred and fifty yards ahead of her. There was the ladybird again. The starter from Harsewinkel was considered one of the favorites. She was living up to expectations and was already sixteen feet ahead of the field. Enna controlled her breathing. Six hundred and fifty yards was a distance that could easily be underestimated. She only wanted to get out of her aerobic zone in the final sprint. Too bad her opponents seemed to have a similar strategy. None of them were attempting to chase the leader.

Out of the corner of her eye, she saw the next wave approaching. There had been a storm yesterday. The organizers had considered canceling the race, but the rules weren't affected by a few waves. In fact, Enna was pleased, since only a few of her opponents were able to train in the ocean on a regular basis. The wave came in at a slight angle. Here at the mouth of the Elbe River, the swell behaved unpredictably due to its funnel-like opening.

Enna tilted her board slightly. Lars had practiced the correct angle with her for hours. There it was! The water lifted Enna up and set her down gently as she started paddling hard again. Behind her, she heard a few disappointed cries, but she didn't have time to turn around. Suddenly there was only the ladybird in front of her. She was in second place!

But only for a moment. Another board was working its way up to her position. The woman steering it had her head almost on the board. She was wearing a cap with white triangles on a red background. It had to be the lifeguard from Halle – the second favorite. Enna had had a nice chat with her yesterday at the barbecue. She was a nurse by profession. What was her name?

Enna smiled at her briefly and Jeanette, that was her name, returned the smile, but at the same time increased her stroke frequency and passed her. She looked back at Enna, which was a mistake, because they had almost reached the buoy where they had to turn, and the Harsewinkel board was coming towards them.

"Ladybird!" yelled Enna. Jeanette jerked around and steered to the left, turning her board. The paddler with the ladybird cap was startled and swerved right, just as she was about to crash into her rival's board. At the last second, Jeanette managed to straighten her board.

"Yay!" she shouted and paddled on with all her might.

Enna had lost some momentum due to the near collision. She

rounded the buoy in third place but was overtaken shortly thereafter. The ladybird was flying towards a certain victory. Near her, on the beach, the rows of yellow beach chairs began. One hundred and sixty-four yards to go. It was now time to sprint. She quickened the pace of her paddling beyond her breathing rate. She no longer had to control her breathing. A board that had surged up to her position was left behind. The way was clear. The ladybird flew closer to the beach, to her destination.

Enna blocked out the world around her. She was no longer battling against the others. She was only battling against herself. Her body wanted to force her to slow down, but she refused to let it. Her lungs burned and her muscles threatened to cramp, but she knew no mercy. Her body would carry her forward, faster, faster – she could rest later!

A whistle brought her out of her trance. The first one was for the winner – she could ignore that. She paddled on. The second and third whistles were certainly not for her.

"Enna, fantastic!" yelled Lars.

She opened her eyes. Her hands paddled on until she noticed the buoy that marked her destination in the sea. She had passed it long ago. Exhausted, she stretched out on the board. Someone approached her from the shore. He was wearing an orange life jacket.

It was Lars. Enna took a deep breath and paddled towards him. She was drenched in sweat, so she let herself slide from the board into the water before Lars even reached her. She surfaced with a snort and looked at him. His forehead was deeply furrowed.

"Are you okay?" he asked.

"Yes, I'm fine. I was just a little hot."

Now she felt cool again. Her body must have run out of energy from all the effort.

"Oh, that's a relief," Lars said. "Congratulations!"

"I'm glad I made it too."

A few people waved at her from the beach. She recognized her teammates by their T-shirts.

"You made it?" Lars grabbed her shoulders and held her in

front of him. "You came in second! You even beat the nurse from Halle!"

The nurse? Enna felt sorry for her. She had talked a little about her demanding job. Enna didn't envy her.

"You're exhausted, aren't you?" asked Lars. "Come with me to the beach. Well done anyway!"

After changing her clothes and drinking half a pot of tea, Enna felt better. Her local group was participating in the German Life Saving Association competition for the first time. At first, it had been a Lars thing. Competing with others was not what motivated Enna to work as a lifeguard in her spare time. But it had been good for the small group – suddenly the training sessions were much better attended. Of course, they couldn't put in as much effort as the top teams, who usually trained every day. They all had day jobs.

Speaking of which... She had been given the day off today, Friday, and Neuhof had promised to cover for her, but for form's sake, she should check her cell phone at least once. She opened the beach basket assigned to her team and rummaged through her travel bag. There it was. Three new calls – all from her boss. Enna sighed.

"What is it?" asked Lars, who must have been watching her. "Remember the award ceremony."

"I just need to check my voicemail." Enna dialed the voicemail number and took a few steps across the beach. A huge container ship passed by, probably on its way to Hamburg. It was almost within reach. Such giants never docked in Fleetstedt.

"You have three new messages. First new message. Friday, ..."

Something scratched her upper arm. Enna changed the hand holding the cell phone to her ear and missed the first words.

"...promised not to bother you..." *then why didn't you keep your promise*, "but there's something I'd like your opinion on. It would be great if you could give me a quick call back."

"Second new message, Friday, eleven twenty-three."

"It's me again. There's a little problem. Kettler refuses to examine the victim just because it's a sheep."

A ... what? Neuhof was investigating the murder of a sheep? Were they even supposed to do that? Berger usually took care of such trivial matters.

"He said it was only property damage. I explained section seventeen of the Animal Welfare Act to him, but I'm afraid he took my well-thought-out arguments as a personal attack. Couldn't you ... Enna, you know. You've known Kettler for a long time."

Enna sighed. It was inevitable that the two men would end up bumping heads; it was bound to happen sooner or later. And she was supposed to clear up the situation now and maybe even beg Kettler, who would certainly take a long time to agree. Enna shook her head. She really didn't want to do that. She hit the delete button.

"Third new message, Friday, eleven forty-five."

"Enna, it's me. Please forget my earlier calls. I've found a way to get by without your help. Don't worry about it. Show the other lifeguards what the German Life Saving Association in Fleetstedt can do. I'll see you on Sunday."

Enna paused, then hung up. The sun had just come out from behind the clouds. The beach was golden. Up ahead, people were gathering. The German Life Saving Association was probably doing rescue demonstrations. The competitions were over for the day, especially since the tide had begun to go out.

I found a way. That didn't sound good. It meant Neuhof was getting creative. She could be at the office in two hours if she started driving back now.

"What is it? Trouble with your boss?" Enna was startled. It was Lars, who must have followed her.

She shook her head. "No trouble yet. But it could escalate. Maybe I should..."

"Enna, you can't do that to us. We're one of the sixteen best teams! That means we can participate in the rescue relay tomorrow!"

Enna sighed. It was the ultimate discipline: swimming,

running, rescue board, rescue kayak, with one competitor per team. Mike was a very good runner and had placed in the top ten in the beach sprint and flags. Lars himself had just missed the podium in the rescue kayak. Enna might not come in second on the board again – but her team certainly didn't need the longest overall time.

"A sheep seems to have died in Fleetstedt," said Enna.

"A sheep? Are you kidding me? That's none of your business."

"My boss thinks it is, and I believe him."

"But surely it can wait until Monday. We need you here tomorrow, well rested."

From his point of view, Lars was right. And the matter probably could wait. But sometimes cases had the nasty habit of escalating quickly, like a pimple turning into a boil. Then you regretted that you hadn't disinfected the harmless blemish with alcohol.

"For some reason, I have a bad feeling about this," Enna said. She couldn't put her finger on it, but it was probably because Pavel intended to handle it without her. She didn't like being left out.

"Please, Enna, think of the others. Was all that rigorous training for nothing?"

Was Lars really only thinking of the others? She was never sure with him. Pavel Neuhof was ... more predictable. He solved cases because they were important, not for his ego. But even if she could convince Nils to take a look at a dead animal, he wouldn't do it on a weekend. It would be fine if she took care of it on Sunday.

"All right," she said, "I'll stay here."

"Thank you." Lars put his hand on her shoulder. "I owe you one."

Enna smiled. Lars ran a butcher shop. How could he help her?

"I'm happy to," she said, "for the team."

"For the team."

"Come on, Heino!"

Pavel pedaled along. The average person would think that the whole coast was flat, but they were wrong. Even getting to the Deichkante was a challenge. Heino, the office bike, didn't have a newfangled electric motor. It didn't even have gears. Berger had suggested getting a better replacement weeks ago. The Fleetstedt city council collected abandoned bikes several times a year, which could be bought for the price of repairs. But Pavel was unable to part with something that had a name. He hadn't owned a car since the DMV had finally taken his Mercedes "Matti" out of service. But he didn't like to drive faster than nineteen miles per hour anyway.

"Heino, you can do it!" he shouted, surprising himself. Fortunately, no one was around to hear him. People thought it was strange to talk to yourself. That was illogical, since almost everyone talked to themselves from time to time. But for many people, logic was not the most important criterion for their actions.

Pavel began to sweat. At the Deichkante, he was only a few feet closer to the sun, but he felt like Icarus trying to reach the gods. Maybe he should have left his jacket behind on this beautiful late summer morning. Since no one would be waiting for him at the office today, he had decided to take a relaxing ride over the embankments.

Pavel stopped the bike, got off, and put Heino on its stand. How had the Fleetstedt folks come up with that name? To him, the unadorned and uncomfortable two-wheeler with the curved handlebars and the wide seat supported by squeaky springs was actually more like a Fiete or a Heiner. He would have to ask Enna.

But now it was time for some exercise. Stretching his legs with a view of the Wadden Sea at low tide was a luxury he had never enjoyed at the office in Kiel. But here it was normal to finish work at one o'clock on a Friday. Neither the people of Fleetstedt nor the tourists were particularly violent. There had only been three major break-ins, all very professionally done, and a few pickpocketings on the beach, which they had been able to trace back to a minor from Berlin. Berger took care of the minor stuff.

Pavel picked up speed, tensed his body, turned sideways, and jumped. His hands hit the grass. His feet flew through the air. He rose into a handstand, but couldn't stabilize himself, so he rolled, as he had learned in judo, and landed on his shoulder, facing the road. There, a Volkswagen Passat was just pulling off the highway into a meadow.

Probably a tourist taking a break. The meadow had not been mowed. If the farmer noticed the car tracks, he would be annoyed. And rightly so! The farmers needed the grass that was growing now to feed their animals in the winter. Pavel picked up Heino, got back on it, and cycled to the next ramp, which headed away from the dike.

The car had a Wittmund license plate. Tourists usually had HH, HB, or even LER. Pavel was about to turn around and continue on the country road when he noticed a doctor's sign behind the windshield. The driver had gotten out and walked further into the meadow, where he was bending over something.

Pavel dropped Heino into the tall grass and ran up to the man.

"What are you doing?" he asked.

The man spun around as if Pavel had caught him committing a crime. Then he reached into his pocket, but Pavel was quicker and pulled out his gun.

"Stop!" he shouted. "Don't do anything stupid!"

"I have nothing you can take," the man said. "Unless you want the car keys. They're in my pocket."

"I just want to know what you're doing here. Chief Inspector Pavel Neuhof."

The man visibly relaxed, although logically he had no reason to since Pavel hadn't shown him his ID and was still pointing his gun at him. He obviously didn't expect any threat from a policeman, which meant he was a harmless civilian and not a criminal. Unless he was he was putting on an act.

"So, who are you?"

"I am Doctor Sörensen. Didn't you see the doctor's sign on my car?"

Pavel shook his head. Anyone could buy a doctor's sign. But the name sounded familiar. From where?

"What are you doing here, Dr. Sörensen?"

"I was called to see a patient, so to speak."

Suddenly he remembered. Sörensen had been the doctor who confirmed the death of the old farmer Dietrichsen. Dietrichsen, suffering from advanced dementia, had committed suicide in the attic of his house a few months earlier.

"You investigated the death of the farmer Diepoldsen, didn't you?"

"Dietrichsen. You must mean Dietrichsen. In fact, I'm here now to see Dietrichsen."

It had been a test. Sörensen had passed.

"But he's dead," said Pavel.

"I'm talking about his daughter, Viola Dietrichsen, of course."

"It doesn't look like her lying there in front of you." Pavel came closer and craned his neck, but the grass was very tall, and Sörensen and his large medical bag obscured his view.

"She's not my patient, thank God." Doctor Sörensen stepped aside. Pavel saw a gray ball of wool, partially stained red. Only once the thick splotches disappeared from his mind's eye did he realize it was a sheep.

"What about the animal?" he asked. "That's blood, isn't it?"

"Looks like it. Not a pretty sight."

"Hunting accident?"

It sometimes happened that hunters mistook dogs or sheep for wild boar or deer at dusk. Pavel couldn't imagine how they could make a mistake like that, but the fact was that it happened from time to time.

"Come closer. Or have you already had breakfast?"

Pavel shook his head. He rarely ate in the morning. Strong, black coffee was enough for him. He took two steps forward while Dr. Sörensen crouched down, grabbed the sheep's head – and turned it over. There was a deep gash in its throat. He pushed the head back into its natural position and stood up.

Pavel had to swallow. This was no hunting accident. A cut like that would require a sharp weapon and plenty of strength. If it had been the murder of a human being, Pavel would have assumed that considerable rage was involved. But who would feel such rage towards a harmless animal? Cruelty to animals rarely involved emotion. It was a matter of careful planning and the need to see a living creature suffer.

"This is not the only injury," said Dr. Sörensen.

"They started somewhere else, didn't they?"

"How do you know this isn't the first?"

Pavel hadn't meant it that way. He assumed that the killer had rehearsed the cut on another part of the body.

"Did he make a test cut?" Pavel asked.

"One? Four." Sörensen pointed to the animal's limbs. "Shall I show you?"

"No, thank you, our specialists will have a look at it. I'll have to ask you to leave your fingerprints at our office."

"I already did so, after Dietrichsen's death."

"We deleted them a long time ago. You're a citizen of good repute, so we're not allowed to keep your personal data on file. So what is the other case about, and who sent you here?"

"Two weeks ago, Viola reported an injured sheep to me."

"You? You're a human doctor, right?"

"That's right. But we know each other well, and besides, I was just with her. Overnight, if you know what I mean."

Pavel understood. Viola Dietrichsen was divorced, and Sörensen was probably divorced, too. That was not illegal. But no one had told him about the relationship during the investigation into the old farmer's suicide. Her lover had apparently issued the death certificate that allowed the daughter to claim the inheritance.

But that doesn't matter, Enna would say now. *We didn't find any evidence of foul play in Dietrichsen's case, and Viola would have inherited the farm anyway.* He was already missing his voice of reason, and he didn't even know if they had a new case.

"When did it die?" Pavel asked.

"Judging by the state of the pools of blood, sometime

between midnight and early morning. Feel the fleece – it's wet with dew. But I'm not a forensic pathologist."

"It was a painful death, wasn't it?"

"I would assume so. From the amount of blood spilled, the agony was prolonged."

"Thank you." Then they had a case. Cruelty to animals was a crime under section seventeen of the Animal Welfare Act. "But why didn't you report the injuries to the other sheep? We might have caught the culprit by now."

"Viola didn't want to. The animal is fine now, she says. Besides, I had the one..." Sörensen broke off mid-sentence as if he had just said too much.

"What impression did you get?"

"None at all."

"Did Ms. Dietrichsen know who the animal abuser was and wanted to protect them?"

Sörensen shook his head. "Ask her. I'm an internist. None of this is my business."

"Whatever you say. But you should know that a significant proportion of animal abusers eventually change victims."

"You mean..."

"Yes, that's what I mean."

Sörensen looked at him sadly but said nothing more.

"You can go. Wait a minute. Viola asked you to come here? How did she know the victim would be here?" Pavel pointed to the meadow. It was not a sheep pasture. Either the animal had escaped, or its killer had brought it here. But why this particular spot, visible from the road?

"Viola described this meadow – between the dike and the small wood at the back, bordered by two drainage ditches. But she didn't tell me who told her about this place. To be honest, I thought I was going to meet her here. She sounded pretty upset on the phone. But now I really have to go. My patients are waiting."

"Would you have called the police this time?"

"Yes, here, see?" Sörensen showed him his cell phone. The number of the Fleetstedt police station appeared on the screen.

Sörensen had simply typed "Enna". The profile picture showed his colleague in a short-legged wetsuit.

"You didn't dial," Pavel said.

"I was just about to."

"What kind of photo is that?"

"It doesn't mean anything. I provide medical support for the local German Life Saving Association group. That's how I know your colleague."

Pavel nodded. He would have Sörensen checked out thoroughly. But for now, he had to make sure that someone would uncover all the secrets of the poor sheep's death.

"I need to ask you something, Mr. Kettler."

Pavel had thought long and hard about how to approach the forensic pathologist. He seemed to be a difficult person, even if Enna thought otherwise. In any case, he had not appreciated it when Pavel added his own ideas to what was said during their last meeting.

"Today is Friday. There's no way I'll be done by tomorrow," Kessler replied with a statement that only very loosely referred to Pavel's opening sentence.

"No, it would be okay if I could have the results by Monday."

"Oh, it would be okay? I'm happy to hear that."

Kettler's agreement pleased him, even if his reply was more of a courtesy. At some point, he would have to tell the man that he did not need such formalities.

"Yes, it would. I'll send you the coordinates. By the time you get here, the crime scene technician should already be at work."

"Are you saying I'm too slow?"

"No, it just means that the crime scene technician will probably arrive before you. I notified Ms. Doldinger before I called you."

Would he have to teach Kettler the basic concepts of propositional logic? Pavel was glad that he was at least competent in his profession. Not only Enna but also their previous cooperation had convinced him of that.

"Can you tell me anything about the victim?" asked Kettler.

He had dreaded this question. But he had prepared an answer. "I would prefer it if you could see for yourself."

"Jeez, Neuhof, do you have to do that? How do you expect me to come prepared?"

"I'm sorry, dear fellow, but this is part of my investigation strategy."

Pavel ended the call. He was betting that Kettler's curiosity would outweigh his annoyance with stupid Neuhof.

When the crime scene technician arrived, he got his first taste of Kettler's possible reaction. Maria Doldinger laughed briefly when she saw the dead animal.

But she immediately apologized. "I hope you catch the pig. I was just ... relieved not to have to examine human remains."

"I hope it stays that way," Pavel said. "Some animal abusers never get tired of this kind of behavior."

"I know," Doldinger said. "I can tell you right now that this is not the scene of the crime."

"Despite all the blood?"

Doldinger nodded. "That's from the cut throat. The wounds on its legs were inflicted before that."

So the killer had interrupted his ... work. Either he had been interrupted elsewhere – or he had wanted to prolong his pleasure. The latter was the least favorable option. Pavel stood up and looked around. The grass was trampled in several places. The crime scene technician's car was parked at the side of the road. From there, several tracks led to the site. Another led to where Sörensen had parked his Passat. And then there was a visible trail between the area where the body was found and the small wood on the other side of the meadow.

So as not to spoil any tracks, Pavel followed the trail on a parallel route a few feet away. The grove consisted mainly of deciduous trees and dense bushes. It was a colorful mixture of hazel, brush, and many other shrubs he didn't recognize. He had to fight his way through the undergrowth, but eventually, he came to an open space with a path leading out of it. It smelled pleasantly of moss. The grasses that sprouted in the clearing were crushed. A car must have passed through here recently. Pavel found a tire track that showed the pronounced tread typical of winter tires – unusual for late summer. It was still wet. Perhaps the owner of the car had been watching them from behind the trees and had just left.

Pavel ran back to where the dead sheep was found.

Once there, he asked Doldinger, "Is there anything more you can tell me?"

She shook her head. "I have to put it all together in my head, I'm sorry. We didn't find the murder weapon. What are we going to do with the animal?"

"Kettler will be here any minute. He'll pick it up. Can you keep an eye on it until then? I'm going to follow some car tracks I found in the woods. You might want to send a couple more guys out there."

"I'll do that."

"Thanks, Ms. Doldinger."

"You're welcome. And please say hello to Enna for me. I thought I'd see her here."

After about five hundred and fifty yards, the sandy road gave way to a gravel path, and then an asphalt side road that led past two farms. Pavel stopped at a single-story, two-winged brick building. A sign above the entrance read, "Vacation Apartment Available." He rang the doorbell, but no one answered. As half a basement level was visible above the foundations, the windows on the second floor were too high for Pavel to see inside.

He leaned Heino against the wall and climbed up onto the crossbar. Finally, he reached the windowsill and pulled himself up. The bike fell over, but at least he got a quick look inside, where brown sheets were spread over the furniture. The house didn't look like much of a rental.

As he fell and hit the ground, his left foot buckled. A sharp pain shot through his ankle. Damn it! That joint had given him trouble for years. Pavel forced himself not to limp as he crossed the street. Meanwhile, a window had opened and an old woman in a blue apron was looking out.

"What are you doing there?" She pulled her glasses down to the tip of her hooked nose.

"I was wondering if the house over there was for sale," he said.

"Why?"

"I represent some investors."

The old woman laughed out loud. "Investors, ha ha. And you're riding a bicycle?"

She pointed at Heino. Pavel felt he had to defend the office bike. After all, it was doing a good job. But the woman was right, of course – he should have come up with a more plausible cover story.

"I'm from the police," he said, holding up his badge.

The old woman took it and examined the document, looking at it from different angles. Then she handed it back. "So you're the new guy," the woman said.

"And you?"

"God knows I'm not new."

"I mean – what's your name?"

"Anna Winkelmann. Like it says on the doorbell."

The woman thought he was a bit slow, but that was okay. Pavel liked to be underestimated. It was probably because his face showed no sign of understanding when someone explained something to him, even if he understood it before the person who was trying to explain it did.

"Did you see a vehicle go into the woods this morning? Sometime between midnight and just after sunrise?"

"Yes. About three o'clock."

"What kind of vehicle?"

"It wasn't a tractor. Other than that, I only saw the lights shining through the cracks in my blind."

"You're sure of the time?"

"Yes. I was wondering who would be driving this way at that time of night. The road doesn't lead anywhere."

"Did the car come back?"

"I don't remember. I fell asleep again. But if it's no longer in the clearing, it must have come back."

What a surprise.

"Why is the road there, anyway?" he asked. "Plans for a new development?"

"Ha ha, you must've had a bowl of humor for breakfast this morning! There used to be a forester's cabin in the clearing. It burned down two years before the war ended."

"1943?"

"You can even do math, Inspector." The old woman grinned. She seemed to be enjoying the conversation, so he couldn't be angry with her.

"That house over there, is it for rent now?"

Even if the arrangement with his landlady, who washed and cooked for him, worked well, he would need a place of his own someday. Out here he would be far enough away from other people to be able to relax after being surrounded by them. It might be an option for him.

"It's a whole farm," the old woman said. "But it's been empty for ages."

"Why? We're not much more than three miles from the dike. It would be perfect for a farm vacation."

"The whole place is haunted," the woman explained, lowering her voice as if she were telling a ghost story.

"What happened?"

"Old Schepker is said to have sold his soul to the devil during a storm surge to save his family from the water. It didn't apply to him, but when the devil came for him, he went into hiding. In retaliation, the devil gradually took his family away from him. First his daughters, then his mother, and finally his wife."

"When was that? In the Middle Ages?"

The old woman furrowed her brow and crossed herself. "You shouldn't make jokes like that. Not about him." She crossed herself again. "The multiple deaths began over twenty years ago. Only Schepker was left. Two years ago he suddenly disappeared."

"Gone?"

"Gone."

"And they didn't look for him?"

"Well, he was alone and old. Nobody missed him."

Pavel thought about the sign over the doorway. "Who put up the vacation apartment sign?"

"A real estate agent from Fleetstedt." The old woman scratched her head. "Oh, her name is Meier. Jette."

Why wasn't he surprised? Henriette Meier had her fingers in many pies, even after having resigned from the chairmanship of the business association.

His cell phone vibrated in his pocket. It was Nils Kettler, the forensic pathologist.

"Neuhof here. Do you have something for me?"

"Mr. Neuhof, are you out of your mind? I'm standing here in a field and what does the crime scene technician show me? A damn sheep!"

"I thought..."

"Damn it, Neuhof! I'm not responsible for property damage! What did I tell you about my budget?"

"Animal welfare law, this is a punishable offense..."

"I'm not a damn vet, man!"

Kettler didn't let him get a word in edgewise. Pavel raised his eyebrows. Mrs. Winkelmann looked at him worriedly. He stepped out of her living room. There was a slight smell of mold in the hall. The floral wallpaper on the ceiling was peeling.

"I need to know how..." he tried again.

"I don't think you understand me. Find someone else!" His associate hung up.

Pavel couldn't believe it. He looked down at his cell phone for a moment, then went back into the living room.

"How about a Jägermeister?" Mrs. Winkelmann asked.

"No thanks, I'm on duty."

"Leave her. That sounded sooo mean. You deserve better."

The old woman seemed to have misunderstood. But Pavel

was too busy thinking to correct the mistake. There was a man on the loose in their neighborhood who had managed to torture and then kill a living creature in several deliberate steps. His only witness was a dead sheep. He had to question it, but it wouldn't give him any answers without a specialist.

Pavel bowed. "Thank you, Mrs. Winkelmann, for the story and the advice. I have to go to the office now."

The old woman smiled. "Drop by again if you want to know more about the history of Fleetstedt and the surrounding area. I know every family here."

That was good to know. As a newcomer, he still didn't know local history. What role did the Dietrichsens, the owners of the dead sheep, play? Had they become victims by chance? Pavel had a sinking feeling that there was a connection. He wasn't sure if he was happy about that, since it might lead him to the culprit, or if it was a sinister message, adding a dimension to the crime that made him fear the worst.

He arrived at the office shortly after eleven o'clock and was glad to be able to take off his jacket. The sun was still quite bright for a late summer day on the North Sea. Enna wasn't at her desk. She had been given official leave to take part in a German Life Saving Association competition.

The last few days had been quiet. A broken bike lock here, a few rowdy teenagers there. Nothing like that reached his desk. If he had known that an animal abuser would strike today of all days... No, he would still have approved Enna's leave.

But now he needed her. He really did. Unfortunately, he had promised her that he wouldn't disturb her.

Well, it couldn't hurt to at least inform her about the new case. What she did with it was up to her. Pavel dialed her number, but she didn't answer. He asked her to call him back – but when he hung up, he was annoyed with himself. Surely he should at least give her some information? The victim and Kettler's refusal were probably the most important points, so he left a second message.

Then he sat down at his desk. Pavel was edgy. He hated not seeing a clear path that would get him closer to solving his problem. And why was that? Because he was dependent on other people. Kettler, forensics, Enna... Wait a minute. He wasn't alone.

"Mr. Berger? May I ask you something?"

Sergeant Berger was sitting behind the counter at the entrance to the office as usual. He straightened his back and looked at Pavel with an open expression. Berger had a good grasp of things and was willing to think outside the box if given a little encouragement.

"Of course, Mr. Neuhof." How old was Berger? He had a round face and short hair, which made him look like a big kid. But Pavel had recently run into him at the market with his two sons, one of whom was a teenager, so he must be at least in his late thirties, mid-forties at most.

"Suppose you wanted to know exactly what a violent offender had done, but the forensic pathologist refused to help. How would you proceed?"

Berger scratched his temple. "You want something ... unconventional, don't you?"

"Well, the usual avenues are closed."

Berger nodded thoughtfully. "You should have let Enna talk to Kettler."

Pavel grimaced. He had realized that long ago. Enna had the forensic pathologist wrapped around her little finger. But that hadn't been an option.

"Where is the sheep right now?" Berger asked.

"At the crime lab in Leer, but they can't help me either. It's nice of them to hold it for us."

"It would help if we could have a look inside the body."

"Yes, Berger. Do you happen to have the qualifications to do an autopsy?"

Berger threw up his hands defensively. "Me? Ha ha, I can't even debone a fish."

"But you have an idea." Small wrinkles had formed around Berger's eyes, and he was tapping his foot. He was curious to see how Pavel would react to his idea. Pavel decided to welcome it, no matter how illogical it seemed to him. Hopefully, his face wouldn't betray him again.

"All right," Berger began, leaning over and pulling open the drawer of a small cabinet. He fumbled around for a moment, then pulled out an envelope and took out an X-ray. "Look, this is my right hip. I'm only thirty-eight, but the orthopedist thinks it's the hip of a sixty-year-old, and I need to be prepared for surgery."

Pavel tapped on the counter from below. That was bad luck for Berger, but the man was a civil servant and therefore had private health insurance. He would certainly get the best possible care.

"What I mean is – look at the picture. So detailed!"

Berger was right. The image clearly distinguished between bone and soft tissue, and Pavel could see where the hip joint appeared to be worn, even though he was a layman.

"Yes, the technique is fascinating," he said. But what did it have to do with the sheep?

Then it hit him. Of course! The wounds on its legs... If they could get an X-ray or, better yet, a CT scan of the sheep, they wouldn't need to cut it open.

"Berger, that's a great idea!" exclaimed Pavel. "Would you be so kind as to call the radiology department at the hospital? I'll get ready for the..." Wait a minute. Enna wasn't here. He would have to drive himself. Pavel shuddered at the thought. He'd rather ride his bike, even if it would take him an hour and a half. But what about Berger?

"Say, Ber..." he started, only to realize that Berger was already on the phone. Pavel ran to his office to get his jacket and leave an all-clear message for Enna on the answering machine. "...I found a way to get by without your help..." He wished her a successful competition and hung up.

"I'm afraid I can't reach anyone in Radiology," Berger said when Pavel came back to the counter.

"Let's go over there. Maybe we can still get results today."

Berger looked at his watch and sighed. "I really wanted to finish work on time today."

"I'm very sorry, Berger, but I need you. And if we leave right now, you'll be home with your family by two o'clock."

"I don't know – I had to wait two hours for my X-ray."

Pavel shook his head. "I'll give them a run for their money. Isn't that the saying? Trust me."

Berger picked up his cell phone and typed something. Then he reached for his uniform cap, flipped up the counter, and walked over to Pavel.

"Off to Leer, then."

Berger kept the siren on all the way. It was an annoying sound. Pavel didn't understand what other people saw in it. But at least it distracted him from Berger's driving. The man must feel magically protected by the sound, because he kept making daring overtaking maneuvers on the highway. The BMW painted in police colors seemed much more agile than Enna's red Polo.

"Maybe we should pick up the sheep at the crime lab first," Pavel suggested as they passed the Leer City sign.

"You think? What if we don't get an appointment?"

"That's not an option, Berger."

"Agreed. Could actually save us a few minutes."

The animal was stiff and cold. Berger lined the trunk with tin foil so they wouldn't leave stains. The sheep lay resting on the edge of the trunk, with Pavel holding it steady. Doldinger, the head of the crime lab, was not on duty when they arrived. That had probably saved them a long discussion. One of the workers had simply delivered the animal to them. The sheep was surprisingly heavy. Pavel estimated it to be about ninety pounds.

"Slowly," Berger said.

Pavel pushed the sheep forward. It tipped over the edge of the trunk with its legs sticking up. They wouldn't be able to close the trunk lid. Pavel pushed on the legs, but the joints were stiff and wouldn't move. Rigor mortis and cooling.

"We need to tilt it on its side," he said. Berger stood beside him. "On three. One, two, three." They pushed together, and the sheep obediently turned on its side. It could have been mistaken for sleeping if its legs weren't parallel to the ground. Pavel straightened up. Berger closed the trunk lid.

"Okay, let's get to the hospital," Pavel said.

The radiology department consisted of a hallway with patients waiting in uncomfortable chairs and doors that opened and closed erratically.

"Wait a minute, boss. I'll check things out."

Berger walked purposefully to a door with a window – albeit a closed one – and knocked. To Pavel's surprise, it opened and a woman dressed in white leaned out.

"Hello," she said, "what's up?"

"Hello. That one." Berger pointed at Pavel.

"Is he here from prison?" the nurse asked.

Berger was in uniform, so the assumption was plausible. Pavel straightened his jacket to make a good impression.

"A sex offender," Berger joked. "So it would be good if we could ... you get the idea."

"You're kidding, right? The man doesn't even have handcuffs on. Is he really? Please tell me you're joking."

Berger was on the right track. Pavel nodded in agreement. He was happy to play the sex offender if it meant they could get the X-ray faster. He grinned in agreement and licked his lips.

"This ... well, this is my boss. We need an X-ray. It would be great if it was..."

"Anything acute?" asked the nurse, who didn't seem to relax, but rather seemed annoyed.

"Acute?"

"Will he die if we don't treat him immediately?"

Pavel nodded.

"No," Berger said.

The nurse's eyes darted between them, and she shook her head. "Then sit down and wait. What's the name?"

"Neuhof."

"Good, I'll call you."

"How long do you think..." Berger started, but the door was already closed.

"But now you yourself are..." Pavel began.

"I know," Berger said. "But I couldn't lie to the nurse just to have our turn sooner. We serve the state. We have to be honest, don't we?"

"Or not," Pavel said. The people waiting didn't look like every minute counted for them either. But fine. He picked up his cell phone and started studying the anatomy of sheep.

After an hour, Berger was obviously getting restless, because he started pacing up and down the hospital corridor. If he had at least kept a steady pace, Pavel wouldn't have minded, but Berger kept halting. Sometimes he would look out of the front window, which opened onto a walled courtyard, sometimes he would talk to a patient, and sometimes he would just stand there. This made it impossible for Pavel to get the rhythm out of his head. Berger acted like a randomly dripping faucet, which was pure torture for Pavel.

"Are you stressed because of your wife?" he asked when Berger came to stand next to him.

"Not really."

"The family?"

"The sheep."

"You're worried about the sheep? There's no need. It's not even alive anymore."

"Have you looked out the window?" Berger pointed to the narrow opening through which the sun shone.

Pavel shook his head. Had the animal gotten out of the trunk and started insulting passers-by? Berger's face looked like it had. He got up and went to the window. The police car was three floors down. At first, Pavel didn't see anything to worry about.

"The doors are locked," he said.

Berger stood beside him and tapped the window with his index finger, leaving a thin smear of grease. "The sun has been shining on it the whole time."

The sun. It took Pavel a few seconds to follow Berger's meaning. Of course. You couldn't keep people or animals in a car in this heat. He had called the pound himself when he had noticed a dog locked in a car in the parking lot of a supermarket. Although the sheep was not in mortal danger in its current condition, the heat could cause its condition to take an unpleasant turn.

"Jeez, Berger, we should have thought of that sooner." He didn't exclude himself. Why hadn't he insisted on going into the underground garage? Because they had parked closer to the entrance so that they wouldn't have to haul the animal so far. He had thought of one thing, but not the right one.

"I'm sorry," Berger said.

"Me too." Pavel turned away from the window. If he was counting correctly, there were still four patients ahead of them. About an hour's wait. All four looked bored but quite alive.

He went to the window Berger had used and knocked hard. The same nurse opened it and jumped back with a shriek. Pavel had placed his badge on the narrow window frame. The woman covered her mouth.

"Excuse me. That policeman over there," she pointed at Berger, "introduced you as a sex offender."

"I heard. Yes, something like that is more likely to stick than just 'boss.' You have my full understanding."

"Thank you, Mr. Chief Inspector." She studied his badge.

"I'm sorry, but I have to ask for an immediate diagnosis. We need a CT scan of all the extremities."

The nurse stuck her head out of the window and examined him like a thoroughbred horse. "You look healthy, Inspector. Is this for preventive care? We have special hours for that. Why didn't your colleague say something? Then you wouldn't have had to wait."

"It's not for me."

"Is it your colleague?"

Pavel would not reveal the identity of the patient until he had the woman's consent. Very few people could go back on their word once given.

"No, the victim of a violent crime," he replied evasively. "Is that justification enough?"

"Why didn't you go to the emergency room? The person would have been treated by now!"

"Because the victim is already dead."

"Excuse me? You want us to examine a dead body? I don't think we're allowed to do that. You'd have to talk to the pathology department."

"I don't need an examination. Just the pictures. In the machine, out of the machine. It can't be that difficult, can it?"

The nurse sighed. "You wouldn't believe how complicated it is. The machine is expensive. Who is going to pay for it? Once a person dies, health insurance is no longer applicable. I will have to get a letter guaranteeing payment first."

Bureaucracy had struck again. He should add her to the list of suspects, since she obviously wanted to delay his investigation. But he would not allow it.

"I'll pay the costs," he said.

"As a private patient? I must remind you again that your health insurance will not cover this service."

"Yes, as a private patient." If necessary, he would pay the bill himself. He had a decent salary and hardly any living expenses.

The nurse sighed. "All right, I'll talk to the senior physician. Is there anything else I need to know?"

"What do you mean?"

"Did the deceased suffer from any infectious diseases, does their body need any special treatment? What about weight and height?"

Pavel stroked his chin. He hadn't shaved today. This was probably the moment to come clean.

"But you're willing to do the X-rays?"

"Yes, of course, but I don't make the final decision. That is the responsibility of the senior physician. What is it, is there something else?"

There it was, the *yes*. Only a conditional *yes*, because it needed to be reviewed, but that was the best he would get.

"The person we're talking about is not a person."

"Excuse me? Is it a child, or what are you trying to say?"

He had suspected he would cause some problems by telling the truth. They were like that, humans. They were supposed to love animals but then considered themselves better than them. "It's a sheep. But not just any sheep. It was cruelly killed, and I must find its killer before he strikes again."

Berger placed a hand on his shoulder. That was a typical reaction when someone wanted to reassure you. Pavel appreciated the gesture, even though there was no reason for it. After all, his arguments were valid.

But not to the nurse. "'Inspector, I'm sorry, but we're not veterinarians! Next thing you know, dog and cat owners will be coming to us! For hygienic reasons alone, we can't help you."

Pavel lost his voice and, for a moment, his breath. The bureaucracy suddenly had this woman's face and wore a white coat. He would put her behind bars. At the very least.

"Thanks anyway," Berger said on his behalf, slowly pushing him away from the window.

"Thank you for understanding," the nurse said.

Pavel didn't understand at all, but his face probably didn't show it. Was that an advantage or a disadvantage? He willingly let Berger lead him to the car like a sex offender.

A strange smell came from the trunk. The legs of the sheep were now bent as if they were relaxing in the heat.

"Let's get back to the crime lab quickly," Pavel said.

"Yes, that would probably be best." They reached the institute shortly after four o'clock. Pavel rang the bell, but no one answered. Damn it! This day did not look like it would end well. When he had cycled over the dike this morning, everything had seemed so idyllic. But the people here were no better or worse than in Schleswig-Holstein or Bavaria. There were murderers and saints here, too.

"We could put the sheep in the basement of the office," Berger suggested.

"But it's heated," said Pavel. He knew that for sure; there were old files down there that he had consulted once or twice.

"Our fridge is too small," said Berger.

"You can't do that to your wife, Berger. I don't want to be responsible for your divorce."

But Berger's idea was essentially a good one. All they had to do was bridge the gap until Monday when someone at the crime lab would open up for them. Who had a freezer big enough to temporarily house a sheep?

"An undertaker," Pavel said.

"That's right, an undertaker should have a walk-in cooler. So should a butcher."

"Or a restaurant. But they won't let us in for hygienic reasons. Just like butchers."

"Food regulations."

"That's right, Berger. Businesses that have to comply with food regulations can't help us."

This also excluded the Fleetstedt brewery, which produced an excellent pilsner. Too bad – he would have liked to visit the beer cellar.

"So an undertaker," Berger said. "We have two."

Pavel entered the service as a keyword on his cell phone and got two contacts. He dialed the first.

"Sorry, you're calling outside business hours. Please..."

Crap. He dialed number two. Again, only an answering machine answered.

"No one's there," he explained.

"There's an emergency number on the website in case someone dies over the weekend," Berger said. "Should I try that?"

"Hm, they won't be interested in a dead sheep." But he had a better idea. There was a huge freezer in his landlady's pantry. Miss Winters had once boasted that it could hold half a deer.

"Half a deer, that's about the same size as a sheep, isn't it?" asked Pavel.

For some reason, Berger laughed briefly. "You could say that. The deer is probably longer, the sheep wider."

Pavel had seen whole ducks in the chest, two of them side by side. The sheep wasn't much bigger than that.

"I know where we can store it," he said.

"Leonie Winters" was written on the doorbell. Pavel pressed the button. The window next to the entrance opened.

"Oh, it's you, Mr. Neuhof. Did you forget your key?"

"No. I need to talk to you for a moment, Miss Winters." His landlady was in her seventies and insisted on being called Miss Winters. She had probably been a teacher at the local girls' school when it still existed.

"I'd like that very much!" His landlady left the window. A moment later, the lock buzzed and he pushed the door open.

"Please wait by the car, Berger." Pavel stepped inside. Miss Winters was waiting for him at the front door. She had divided the townhouse into two floors. The top floor was his.

"What can I do for you?" she asked.

"I'm on the trail of a terrible crime." Miss Winters was very interested in his work. But he usually didn't tell her anything, which made her all the more curious.

"Oh, how exciting."

"It's about an animal abuser who killed an innocent sheep."

Miss Winters put her hand over her mouth. "What an evil person!"

"That's what I say. But you can't tell anyone about it, okay?"

Miss Winters shook her head. Of course she would tell her friends, but news of the animal abuser was probably already making the rounds.

"Well, I'll find the person. I have to. But I need your help. Can I count on you?"

"If it's not dangerous? Yes, absolutely."

"It's totally harmless."

"Then I'm in."

Very good. The problem was as good as solved. "Good, the poor sheep will thank you. I need your freezer."

"My ... freezer?" Miss Winters turned pale.

"Yes. Don't worry. I'll cover any losses. We just need to make some space in there."

He deliberately didn't say what they needed the space for. Miss Winters already knew. If no one said it, she could imagine it was for something else entirely.

"Yes, if it has to be..."

"It has to be. You're helping to find a cruel person before he strikes again."

"If you say so."

"I'll take care of everything, with Berger's help. It's great that you're so cooperative. I don't know what I'd do without you."

Leonie Winters blushed. Pavel smiled gratefully, turned, and ran outside to Berger.

"And drop it!"

Pavel slowly let the foil-wrapped dead sheep slip through his fingers.

"Fits perfectly," said Berger.

They had laid the sheep on its back. That way it would fit into the tub-shaped recess they had made in the freezer. A few packages of frozen vegetables had to be moved to Pavel's refrigerator, and there was room for a few more pre-cooked frozen meals in the freezer compartment of the refrigerator in the kitchen. Pavel had given Berger a whole duck. He would reimburse Miss Winters.

Pavel closed the chest, which was in the basement among stacks of canned goods and bottles of wine.

"If an asteroid hits Earth, I'll bring the whole family with me to stay here," Berger said.

"Or if you need to temporarily store a corpse again," Pavel tried to joke.

Berger put his index finger to his mouth. There were footsteps on the basement stairs.

"We're just about done," Pavel called.

"May I offer you gentlemen a beer now?"

Pavel looked at his watch. It was after six, and he was home. "Yes, I'd love one," he said.

"And your colleague?"

Berger was probably expected by his family. "No, thank you," Pavel answered for him.

"Yes, please!" Berger shouted much louder. He said to Pavel: "I'm going to be late getting home anyway. I'll need some courage."

Courage? What was going on? They should talk about it sometime. It was important to Pavel that his employees were happy in their personal lives, since it might affect their work. But for now, he looked forward to having a drink with Berger and Miss Winters.

Pre-order the second case here:
heidihinrichs.com/links/4314575

Printed in Great Britain
by Amazon